BEST GAY EROTICA 2 0 0 0

BEST GAY EROTICA 2000

Richard Labonté,
Series Editor

**Selected and
Introduced by**

D. Travers Scott

CLEIS
PRESS

Published in the United States
Cleis Press Inc., P.O. Box 14684, San Francisco, California 94114.
Printed in the United States.
Cover design: Scott Idleman
Text design: Karen Huff
Cleis logo art: Juana Alicia
First Edition.
10 9 8 7 6 5 4 3 2 1

To Asa Dean Liles & Percy the dog, always.

For my friend Justin Chin, romantic.

Contents

Foreword

Richard Labonté

This year's judge, D. Travers Scott, makes the point in the introduction that one of his pleasures in picking this fifth volume's table of contents is that he wasn't bound to any particular theme. *Best Gay Erotica 2000* is not a collection of the best teach/coach/brother/neighbor/gym buddy/straight friend/best friend fantasies or the best Daddy stories or leather stories or fetish stories; it's not all kink or all vanilla, it's both rough and romantic, traditional and experimental, fiction and memoir...the best of the best.

I read near to one thousand manuscripts this year, both on-line and on paper, though I'd say more than three-quarters of them were rejected quickly. A couple of hundred were read to the end, about fifty were set aside, about forty were sent to Trav, and what he liked is what you get.

I'll discuss this year's winners in a bit, but what of the non-winners? Bad writing, of course, ruled out most stories (but not all; there were a couple of entries this year, as there have been every year of the four I've edited the series, where a fine story shone through ragged writing, work from a writer willing to be edited); other nixes were the result of ineptitude in the visualization of the act of sex itself (there are some contortions practice could never perfect); but, most of all, the nonwinners lacked any connection between sex and character, between sex and passion, between sex and humor, between sex and soul, between sex and emotion. That is to say, the sex was mechanic, an act without consequence, perfunctory performance with no art about it. Those are stories someone somewhere might jack off to, sure, but the pleasure in the reading would be merely in the release, and good erotica, good porn—good storytelling— pleasures the mind and the heart as much as the cock.

There's much to be pleasured by this year. This hustler suite of stories reprises one theme of recent years: what once was illicit except in fiction has been legitimized by a spate of tell-alls, including the books *Assuming the Position* by Rick Whitaker; *Hustlers, Escorts & Porn Stars* by Matt Adams; *The Consumer's Guide to Male Hustling* by Joseph Itiel; and *Suburban Hustler: Stories of a Hi-Tech Callboy* by Aaron Lawrence. Lawrence's story in our collection, "In the Third Person," presents a look past the sex itself and into the mind of the hired erection; the line between fiction and fact often blurs, but this account of his encounter with a creepy client rings with an unadorned, unabashed authenticity.

Getting inside the mind as well as the butt of the client is the shared theme of two other stories this year: Don Shewey's compassionate "The Nether Eye Opens" and Ishmael Houston-Jones' considerate "Kim: Beloved Friend of All the World." In the former, a masseur must suss out what his client really, really wants, and in the latter a man with the clock ticking needs to figure out what it is he wants from the man he's paid to be in his bed. Are the two tales pure fiction, embroidered fact, or a hybrid? Only the authors know.

With "Shooting Stars" by Luis Miguel Fuentes comes from the collection *Diary of a Dirty Boy* and is one of several escapade essays presented as penned by a teenage hustler from the early to the mid-'90s, and printed in the *NAMBLA Bulletin.*. Whether written by a fifteen-year-old or not, there's a definite well-defined voice at work, telling a story about how there is a sweetness to life, and a sexual reality, at any age. Life's not sweet in Francisco Ibanez-Carrasco's sad-edged "Strictly Professional," an ode to peculiar but not misplaced obsession on the part of an AIDS patient towards his not-even-gay doctor; the unlikely ardor it professes has an undeniable power.

Douglas A. Martin's "201 E. 12th St" takes place almost entirely in the mind; it's a tight tale about what through yonder window breaks, about sex without touching, lust without words, the power of the imagination to arouse. On the other hand, there's nothing left to the imagination in Ian Philips' imaginative gender-skewing "Walt," about the sexiness of touch and the power of poetry, a vivid, daring celebration of the triumph of attraction over expectation.

Romantics will savor several stories this year, among them Dimitri Apessos' wistful "Thomas, South Carolina," a gracious, yearning memory piece telling of first love, and Andy Quan's cute, hot shaggy-dog story "At First Sight," about finding unexpected love while posing as a loner. (You all do know what a shaggy-dog story is, don't you? Oh. Well, it's a story with a cute ending, in this case a shaggy-boyfriend.)

There's romance, too, in M. J. F. Williams' "Finding," excerpted from a novel-in-progress; its spare, Haiku-inspired text introduces two generic teens, the kid at the end of the block who skateboards to class, and the lad who works in the library after school, finding each other. Finding each other is also an element of Matt Sycamore Bernstein's nervy, witty "Thugs," a wry take on gay class and style written with flair.

And for anti-romance, there is Shaun Levin's bleak but immediate "The Whole Bloody Story of My Life from

Beginning to End," a fast first-person account of a raw and angry pickup without sentiment.

Written porn, or if you like, erotica, is actually the little brother of video porn. I've been surprised at the paucity in past years of submissions dealing with the older sibling. Video porn seems to offer such an obvious framework for porn stories. That's why I'm pleased that two such stories are included this year, C. Bard Cole's "World's Horniest Slackers Caught on Tape" and Tom Woolley's "White Bitch Faggot, in each of which the camera is the eye, the narrator is the voice, and the reader is the ear of the action on the tape. In Cole's loopy reenactment of a porn shoot, the focus is on what happens during the shoot; in Wooley's more profound account, the impact of a video on the viewer is primary.

There are four stories this year which I would group loosely into the category of good, old-fashioned fantasy sex fables. Dominic Santi's joyous "Pansy Juice" and Simon Sheppard's evocative "Sightseer" are the most porn-mag traditional in their telling: Santineau dresses her cum-charged characters in a San Francisco park, late at night, on the set of a staging of *A Midsummer Night's Dream,* and Sheppard transports his wrestler/frat boy to the Sistine Chapel for a night of implausible but wonderfully imagined fucking under the gaze of God.

M. Christian's "Spike" is implausible, but charmingly, cleverly so; it's about the brothers Spike and Spike, about their hunger for each other, and about a sudden shift in the equality of sexual favors they share. Karl von Uhl's "A Beating" is the most serious of the traditional stories, dealing as it does with internalized homophobia, the meting out of justice, and, of course, a steamy sexual initiation.

Two nontraditional stories this year (in voice, in style, in surface detail, in explicitness) are "Bonehead" by Lawrence Ytzhak Braithwaite and "About Rapture" by Ferd Eggan, both of which use language, alertly and adroitly, to confront the elliptical urgency of need and desire, of passion and—what a sexy, soulful word—rapture.

Rounding out the collection are two excerpts from novels I'd encourage any reader to seek out in full. Michael Jensen's *Frontiers* and Henry Flesh's *Massage* are both much greater books than the electric, erotic parts I excised for *Best Gay Erotica 1999*. *Frontiers* is a well-researched historical love story set on the late eighteenth century frontier, with a central character who matures into the legendary Johnny Appleseed, and *Massage* is a sturdily-crafted, almost Dickensian take on the edgy East Village hustler/drug/AIDS milieu of the 1980s, with a central character who comes late to maturity and self-acceptance.

Incidentally, more than half of the contributors to *Best Gay Erotica 2000* (the fifth edition in the series, my fourth) — Apessos, Cole, Flesh, Fuentes, Houston-Jones, Ibanez-Carrasco, Jenson, Lawrence, Levin, Martin, Santi, von Uhl, Williams, Woolley — are new to the series: that speaks well to the breadth of quality erotica. The "best" is the best, of course, but I'm pleased that *Best Gay Erotica* and its judges manage every year to add newer and/or younger writers, and previously-unpublished veterans, to the mix.

Some thanks, again, for the fourth time, to Ken White, Caroline Boyden, and Tommi Avicolli Mecca at A Different Light Bookstore in San Francisco, who continue to try to teach a stupid person computer tricks, then sigh and do them for me; and, this year, to Kirk Read at home, for the same patient cosseting. Thanks, too, to Lawrence Schimel, whose apartment in New York I used during his year in Spain and in which I read hundreds of early submissions while working at A Different Light Bookstore in New York over a hot hot (meteorologically speaking) summer. And thanks to D. Travers Scott, who took on the task of judging with alacrity, met every deadline, and made several smart editing suggestions along the way.

October 1999
San Francisco

Let Me Inside You: Introduction

D. Travers Scott

All good writing is erotica (which is certainly not to say that all erotic writing is good). A good piece of writing—on any subject, in any genre—stimulates, excites, and arouses. An erotic charge sparks not only from Sam Steward and Carol Queen but also Denton Welch and Anne Brontë.

In introducing the 1999 volume of this series, Felice Picano praised the sensuality of books—the tactile pleasures of the cover, the scent of the pages. While I fully appreciate these pleasures (rapidly fading in our e-text age), I must champion the opposite. Writing is erotic because of its lack of concrete sensuality, its absence of sensory stimuli. Writing is possibly the most abstract art form, and therein lies its uniquely erotic charge. The pleasures Mr. Picano cites are fetishes—pleasures invested due to the absence of something else.

Writing is about absence; that is the source of its frisson.

Unlike the visual or performing arts, in writing there are no sensory aspects to enhance the exchange between artist and audience. Some paintings make me feel bittersweet nostalgia because the sepia tones look like old photographs.

Some movie's fast editing excites my retinas. Rothko's colors provoke my contemplation with their shimmering beauty. The sweat on Keith Hennesey's body as he moves across the stage makes my dick grow. Writing, however, has to accomplish all of its impact using nothing more than squiggles. An author takes something deeply personal and processes it through multiple layers of abstraction: visible squiggles which represent sounds, which combine to represent words, which combine into language to represent and attempt to communicate direct experience. If successful, the author manages to strike a chord similarly deep inside the reader: "How did he know that about me?!"

Writing is about getting into someone's head, penetrating his or her mind—a much more vulnerable and protected space than any sphincter. Reading is about opening up, letting the author in.

As Christopher Bram pointed out in his introduction to *Best Gay Erotica 1998,* what the reader brings to the stories completes much of their erotic experience. The stories do not live as independent objects; they come alive through collaboration with the reader's consciousness, experience, and memory. I majored in writing in college, but at a visual arts academy rather than a traditional university. This greatly influenced my approach to writing and editing. The process Bram described is the same championed by Marcel Duchamp, an early twentieth-century French artist whose work exerted a pervasive influence on modern art. By putting ready-made bottle racks and urinals inside a gallery and calling them art, Duchamp pointed out that art does not exist independently in its own space. Art is not what hangs on a gallery wall, art is what occurs in the viewer's head upon encountering that object on a gallery wall; likewise, writing is not the squiggles on a page, writing is what happens inside the reader's head upon deciphering those squiggles. A total stranger's subjectivity, deep inside, intimately touches your own.

It is much like sex.

Despite our displaced, fetishistic emphasis on the physical body, sex is not about bodies. The miracle of sex—good sex, I should clarify—is that the body is merely a means to an end. Physical stimulation catalyzes and facilitates a spiritual, emotional, and mental experience. In sex, intimate recesses of heart, soul, and psyche reveal themselves to others. In sex, I can communicate dreams, fears, and parts of myself that I cannot fully express any other way. Sex is the closest experience we have to sharing consciousness, becoming united, and experiencing the essence of someone else. Much like writing.

This past summer Edward Rothstein wrote an article on erotica for the New York Times. "Erotica as a Portrait of the Age" addressed the politicization of erotica in anthologies. "Erotic writing is no longer merely a matter of sexual arousal," Rothstein writes, "it has become a declaration of identity."

The publishing of those stories is more complex than Rothstein acknowledges. In some cases target marketing seems to be a greater impetus than politics. Judging from the slipshod quality of some anthologies, many publishers' prime reason for publishing erotica appears to be simply because it sells. Queer erotica has boomed because some publishers have steadily learned how to milk queer markets, and sex sells best of all. While there's nothing wrong with staying in business or supporting less commercial titles through porn's income, what is troubling is when the porn is not held to as exacting a standard as a publisher's other titles.

Rothstein bemoans the crossover of erotica from private, coded rituals into public media and commodity. "Coded behavior and signals, the secret language of sexual subcultures, are now common parlance. And little is considered forbidden or outrageous." A particularly urban view: Rural teenagers may see smut on the internet or pass around battered copies of Madonna's *Sex,* but they cannot form a queer youth group at their high school. A pair of public high school teachers in Fort Lauderdale are currently facing possible suspension for visiting a swinger club on their private time (and they did not mention it at school, either). The dance of the libertine may be over in Manhattan, but not in the rest of the United States.

Public purchase of erotica is not the same as public experiencing of it. Even if you boldly purchase *Bitches with Whips* at your popular (and independent!) bookstore without a hint of shame, that does not make your erotic reading of it later a public act. As I explained earlier, reading, especially erotic reading, is an extremely intimate and private act. Finally, as a writer and editor who has for years championed and participated in public and group sex, I feel the need to reassure Rothstein that transporting sex into public realms does not lessen its power at all.

Rothstein does not find much erotica very arousing and places the blame on the fact that it has lost the thrill of the forbidden. "Because of the political edge given to it by ethnic and social movements, erotica doesn't just embrace the public, it dismisses the private. Erotica tastes become political declarations.... For many readers, this approach is stimulating unusual demand, but for one left unseduced, much recent erotica is painfully dull and anxiously insistent."

Yet, who previously was in on the forbidden secret? Should the erotic lives and pleasures of queers, women, the disabled, people of color, and others, all be sacrificed in order to preserve the dominant minority's insider thrill of possessing a dirty little secret? It smacks of angry white males whining about their losses. As a white male, I have witnessed my loss of cultural dominance over the last thirty years, but I try to think of it not as loss but as sharing.

In some ways, I agree with Rothstein. Much recent erotica is "painfully dull and anxiously insistent." It is not, however, due to the greater availability of porn, it is because much erotica published is simply poor writing. An anthology may have some story in it, say, a lesbian albino fisting story, that absolutely sucks but is in there because it is a lesbian albino fisting story.

Some editors do this out of political leanings, striving for diversity in their collections. Others do it for an edge on the market. Hey, in a field as crowded as smut, ya gotta have an angle, hence the proliferation of ever-more-specific theme anthologies *(Bite the Big Apple Empanada: Stories of Gay Latinos Having Sex on Their Lunch Hour in Manhattan)*. There is also the novelty factor of genre stories *(Stiffies: Stories of Zombie Sex)* and bandwagoning onto other popular media *(Heather and the Blair Witch: The Untold Story)*. Much like in developing TV shows, high concept wins out over high quality. Editors, publishers, and publicists know a customer will buy a book to check out an outrageous idea; it does not matter if the book leaves the reader limp.

As a guest judge, and not a publisher or editor whose reputation rests on this book's success, I had the luxury of resisting these tendencies. I was not looking for token Daddy, LTR, leather, or FTM stories. I was not aiming to highlight an under-represented area of gay literature or to espouse a political agenda. For this book, I was not an activist editor. Neither did I worry about whether stories were erotica or porn, and I am not going to waste much ink on that tedious debate here. I find the whole discussion a lesser version of the gay-writing-versus-just-plain-writing debate: elitist navel gazing that is ultimately counterproductive. How many writers manage to get published, erotic or otherwise? Precious few. Of those, how many are in a position to make demands about whether they are published by an erotic, porn, literary, gay, or straight imprint? Isn't the reality simply that most writers are desperate to be published at all and will often go with whomever takes them? The debates on these issues strike me as specious whining by writers who don't want to be considered gay or pornographers and are coveting that Holy Grail of mainstream crossover. My personal philosophy is simply to write what has to come out of me and not worry about upon which bookstore shelf it will reside.

As a reader, I simply read and do not worry about whether I am reading a novel, a gay novel, or an erotic novel. In looking for the best in gay erotic writing, I simply looked for good writing. I looked for the most exciting (in all senses of the word) writing from all that was submitted. I did not look for stories whose kinks clicked with mine nor avoided those whose authors' tastes left me cold. I picked the stories I wanted to have sex with (not literally to live out the experiences described, though sometimes that would have been okay, but to share in the headspace of the story's creator), writing that celebrated and exemplified an exchange of intimacies, writers that got inside my head.

I wish to express gratitude to Matthew Stadler and Jay Porter.

August 1999
Seattle

Thomas, South Carolina

Dimitri Apessos

Thy neck is as a tower of ivory; thine eyes like the fishpools in Heshbon, by the gate of Bathrabbim; thy nose is as the tower of Lebanon which looketh toward Damascus. SONG OF SOL. 7:4

Right on the northern tip of South Carolina we stop in a town called Thomas, mostly as a joke, as that is my ex-boyfriend's name. "You've got issues," Geof quips as we park outside the biggest building in town: a Masonic temple. Right away, it's clear that something is wrong with the town of Thomas.

There are only two things I hate about being on the road. One is that my eyebrow ring often becomes inflamed when I go too long without showering. The other is the trucks. I have nothing against truck drivers and have often considered trucking as a future profession that would allow me to drive and smoke simultaneously. But I have never managed to get over the story of how Thomas lost his virginity, as he told it to me once in Barracuda in New York, on a humid afternoon in July.

1

Turns out that Lexington, Kentucky, where Thomas grew up, had a bar which, although not gay per se, had drag shows and hence attracted a mixed crowd. Unable to get in anywhere else, Thomas would go with a friend who claimed to be bisexual but who had never tested his hypothesis of sexual fluidity.

When he was a senior in high school, Thomas met a big, muscular truck driver there who took an interest in him and bought him a couple of drinks. Cheered on by his eunuch friend, Thomas went back to the man's truck and gave him the most valuable thing a closeted seventeen-year-old boy in the South has to give.

The back of a truck, Thomas?

"He had it made up really nice, back there. He had this carpet and lights. It was nicer than most houses."

A truck driver, Thomas?

"He was buff. He was hot. He was really built."

Perhaps. Still, I cannot see a truck without conjuring a vision of the young Thomas, not then knowing that the gay metropolis lay in his future, frightened, silent, following this man to the far end of the parking lot. Parting his immature legs, facing the truck's inner wall, his arms lifted in painful ecstasy, a large, unkempt man of the road behind him, thrusting and pushing into a boy the frustration of life on the highway, further excited by the disbelieving relief of having found a boy for the night. In how many towns was he this lucky? One out of three? One out of six?

Biting his lip, Thomas tried not to cry. In the back of this majestic sixteen-wheeler something was starting—a life of clubs and bathrooms and missed connections, casual sex and failed relationships, trying to return to that spot, trying to get back to that place that hurts so sweetly and feels so good, because it allowed a seventeen-year-old boy to be held by someone so much larger, so much stronger than himself, that he couldn't help thinking it may just be okay after all. Not a single person is walking in the streets of Thomas, South Carolina, and the only shops are of a religious bent. People are staring at us from behind dirty store windows and dusty windshields. The population appears to be predominantly black and exclusively Methodist. Maybe a freed slave colony?

A pair of young black men roll down their car window and, without slowing down, throw an exaggeratedly queeny catcall in our direction.

"Hey boys!"

Are they really gay? Do they think we are? We decide to get the hell out of Thomas, South Carolina, without finding out. My fondest memory of Thomas is not of the Sex Scandals through History Halloween party we went to dressed as Socrates and Plato. Nor is it of the Valentine's Day weekend we spent at my schoolmate Valerie's in Vermont, back when I was still in the closet and we pretended to be just friends, frightened that she would figure us out and overjoyed when she told us the only space to sleep was her roommate's double bed. No, the fondest memory I have of Thomas has no specific date attached to it. It is of a random sunny midsummer morning in my frat house in New York.

I don't know if it was a weekend, or if I just had woken up with enough time to waste before we both had to go to work. What I remember is sensing the luxury of time, with the early morning sun searing in through my window and the faint humming sounds of the city's construction workers and garbage trucks providing a permeable screen to reality.

Thomas was always a heavy sleeper, and this morning was no exception. The smell of him in my bedroom, excitingly alien yet comfortably at home, and the sight of his lean, boyish body on my mattress, sparked a flashback of all the affection and tenderness I had ever felt towards him. Usually he was the forward one and I was the one who let it happen;

3

he was the aggressive initiator of intimacy while I went along for the ride. But not this morning. Waking up next to him, seeing him lying there on my bed half naked, gave me a devoted urge I had never thought I would experience. I wanted to serve and service him, please him while receiving no pleasure other than that of knowing I had pleased him. I wanted him to lie back, half-asleep, and to be reeled slowly into the reality of the day by my lips and my fingers.

Running my fingers along his naked torso, smoothing his skin, caressing his form, sliding my hand down to his waist, then lower, reaching the daily morning anchor between the sleep and the body, I was turned on as never before. Energized, I sat on his legs, placing one hip on either side of him, and started kissing his neck. Taking in the smell of his body—a blend of sleep and sweat and morning dust—I worked my way down, kissing his bony collar, his lean chest, his hollow stomach.

At his waist, I paused to honor his strong morning hardness. I licked the bulge in his briefs, still taking in every smell as he slept. His cock twitched, moving purely because of the friction between my tongue and his skin, like a flower turns to the sun without the earth's awareness.

Excited beyond the point of control, I pulled down his underwear and leaned back to admire the full hard size of his thick and long morning glory. I kissed the tip with tenderness, as if I were meeting his lips or exciting his ear, and then parted my lips to go down on it as far as I could. His sleepy moan startled me; I had been viewing him as a painting or a photograph. I had objectified the picture of him glowing under the sunlight on my bed, knowing already that the image would stay with me—a memory fueling nights of longing and nostalgia long after he and I went our separate ways.

Loving his half-asleep, half-awake excitement, I took his erect cock deeper into my mouth, faster, faster again, with confident rhythm—a circular motion from the neck, as he had taught me. When he put his semiconscious hand on the back of my head, I lost it. Moaning now with each circling of my neck, as his hand guided me, I stayed on him for what seemed like hours; in reality it was probably forty-five minutes. (Thomas always took a long time—especially in the morning—but this particular day I did not mind.)

When his own moans intensified and his neck arched, pushing his head back as he propelled his pelvis upward, I knew what I had to do. For the first time ever, I swallowed his morning juice, completing the connection, directly from his insides to my insides, through his cock and down my throat.

When it was over, I couldn't bring myself to move off him, so strong was my affection for the form of his body. I stretched out my legs and lay my head on his chest, falling back into sleep with him, the sunlight illuminating the dust as it descended on us and around us, filling my bed and the room with particles of the morning, of New York City, of the Upper West Side, on a lazy summer day.

Before leaving Thomas, South Carolina, we get a double cheeseburger with fries at Hardee's and buy a Jerry's Kids muscular dystrophy shamrock. I sign it *George Rupp* and the lady behind the counter puts it up on the wall next to the cash register using messy Scotch tape.

Walking back to our parking spot, we see a woman in her fifties leaving her car, without locking the door, and walking towards a gloomy shop offering "What Would Jesus Do?" paraphernalia. It appears that in South Carolina the law requires only one valid license plate, because her car's front is adorned with an impostor. It says "I" followed by a heart and ending with an empty, complex circular shape. I love clouds? I love smog? I love the sound of one hand clapping?

Geof asks her.

"Cotton," she answers, without a hint of humor.

Just the other night, Thomas slept over again. We broke up almost a year ago, and in the meantime we have traveled many times back and forth on the road between civility and talking shit behind each other's back. But college was only a couple of weeks from being over, and I wasn't even sure where he would go or what he would do. I had been thinking about him but had too much pride to call and talk to him.

Tony and I had been downtown, hitting the bars, and I didn't get back to the neighborhood until three in the morning. I needed one more beer before going to sleep, but I was completely broke. Maybe my friend Sheila would be bartending at Saints and maybe she would treat me. It was worth a try.

Of course, when I walked into Saints, Sheila wasn't there. But Thomas was, sitting at the bar with two of his fraternity brothers, drunk off their asses while he was sober. I sat with him, and we talked until the bar closed. He told me about the job he would soon be starting, the studio in Brooklyn he was moving into, what he had been up to, and he promised to call me when he had his new number. Almost an hour later, mutually shocked at what seemed like an indication that he and I could be friends after all, he walked me home.

On my stoop, we hugged. I took in his smell—and all the old memories flooded back. We stood hugging on the corner of 113th Street for fifteen minutes, maybe more, as I breathed him in and relived the greatest moments of the most romantic year of my life.

On his neck I smelled all the overly long lunch breaks we had taken from our summer jobs together at the Manhattan Mall; how sexy he had looked crying on the night I told him I needed to be alone; how good it felt to be held by him when I broke down in his arms after I came out to my parents. Most of all, however, I smelled on his neck that summer morning in my bedroom, and at that moment we both knew what had to happen, even if it was just once for old times' sake.

We kissed. I asked him to come upstairs. He asked if we were crazy. I didn't answer. That night I relived the full year I spent with him, the year that I discovered the male body, the looks you get when you walk down the street holding a guy's hand, the innocence and relief that is only associated with coming out with a loving, experienced, totally devoted boyfriend. The knowledge was in there—in the bed with us all night—that this could not be a return to what we had once shared. Too much time had passed, and we had hurt each other too much. But for one night it felt great to pretend that we were still together. that nothing bad had happened, and that I was still with my first boyfriend, thinking that what we had may just last forever and unsure of what I would do if it didn't.

The lady outside the WWJDshop points at my Che Guevara T-shirt and asks me if that is a picture of John the Baptist. I tell her that it is, then Geof and I climb into our car. Driving off, we pass by what seems to be the only theater in town. It's playing *Arsenic and Old Lace*—an extremely old movie about two nice elderly ladies who kill their dinner guests. I recall Peter Lorre being in it.

"At least now we can both say we've been in Thomas," I joke as we rejoin I-95 North.

Geof groans. After a week in New Orleans, a night in Savannah, and that gay bar in Mobile, I think he's getting sick of my faggot shit. (I appease him by promising to take him to lesbian night at Life when we get back to New York.)

201 E. 12th St.

Douglas A. Martin

I was poor, and when I first moved here I was forced to stay in Manhattan with friends in a building across from one full of square windows, university students sitting behind them. The city was lonely. Car horns would come from the street with couples inside being driven.

In that apartment I was staying in, I was waiting for some match that would light up the dark. The halls were mostly empty, and when there did happen to be one or two tenants checking mail or entering as I was the building, they didn't look up.

In the city, windows give a view of a number of other windows, a field of bodies and faces across, up, and down. You can almost feel them if you see them so often. In the apartment I stay in, each room gives a slightly different view of a bank of bodies across the loud street, slots of activity.

I would stand in front of the window and count to one hundred. If by then nothing had happening, I went to bed.

One night I see a man.

He is on a couch in gray-green shorts. The couch compliments. His hand goes down his pants, slightly. He's lying on his back on the couch, so I have a clear view of him and his body. Every once in a while, he will look up at where I could be, out his window.

Where I am, looking down almost on top of him, into his living room across the way, a flight lower than my floor, still close enough to see. If I went over and tried to get in, would he let me? Come down for me.

What if I were to see him in passing on the street? It's likely. He is so much like men I've seen, I've wanted, was interested in. He could be any one of them.

He drinks from a carton he gets out of the fridge. He stands there with it in his living room. Then he goes and puts it back, gets something to eat, takes that back to the couch where he unwraps it. Some kind of dip, something else to dip into the dip.

He is eating to fill something, feel something. Time, it ticks. He chews chips, crackers. His hands, thumb, fingers, meeting. He holds something in them, some object, looks so right, closely. He holds the bowl, tin, or bottle, between his legs. He holds something, feels better having something rest there, against it.

His shorts so loose and full of legs that look tan from way over here, the shorts eventually tent, I see that. He screws a cap lid back on. Just sitting there now holding it, in his hands, watching TV, looking like he's about to try and nod off or start something.

In a minute, he gets up and puts the food back, gets a pitcher out of the refrigerator, swigs.

Maybe he is looking across the night for something like me. I watch his light go on, off. On. He starts to turn himself on.

His head tilts to the side of the couch. Turns it back and forth, between me and the open window, to the side, where his arm is up near. Up, lower. His mouth meets his arm, starts kissing, an open mouth working on it.

Then something catches his attention, the way he turns his head abruptly to the side. Then he looks back over at me, up where I am, starts flicking on himself. Lightly at first, pressing himself through those shorts.

He mouths words to himself. Or for me. Nobody else in the room. His head goes back into lots of cushions, pillows. I watch how fast he touches himself, his speed jerking, and I join along, adjusting myself to him. He alternates hands, knowing how to use both to cause pleasure. He gets up from the couch, holding his dick in his hand, going off into another room for some reason or another. I remove my shirt, wait for him to come back and when he does he'll see we're both naked at the top now.

He has such beautiful hair I want to touch. When he comes back to his couch, gets on it, he is slowing down, slower than when he first started. Then he lets it build up, again.

Another night one of the people I'm living with talks on the phone in the living room where I can see him best. I watch his window across from the wooden table I'm sitting at pretending to read. I'm pressed tight under the tabletop in my shorts. My foot beats lightly in time to his up and down strokes, tapping on the floor, his pace mine, pretending like I'm just looking out the window at air.

He gets up off the couch, moves farther into places where I can't make him out, rooms I don't have a view of. Maybe he's stopped for tonight, calling it an evening. I hope not. At least his lights are still on.

I will remain there now the person I'm staying with has gone to bed, hoping to see more of him, get a better and better look. Able to scrutinize more closely, without having to hide what I'm doing. Across the street I see clearly his lit window is empty now. He isn't on his couch.

He comes back from the recesses of his apartment to put back on the shirt he'd taken off like he does so many nights. This is the second time already tonight.

He has gone up onto the roof so he can look down at me. That's where he first startles me, gazing out and down, when I see him above me now, looking over for him. He is on top of his building for fresh air. He can see I'm trying to find him. He gazes steady, intent. I open a window a little farther, to see how he'll react.

Then I move over to my couch as he looks down on me. I give him a clear view, let him see me doing, start doing, what he's been doing off and on all night.

Then look down at the street, pretend he isn't.

I sit at the table, watching him laid back on the couch having at himself, how he can last all evening long.

I've got my shirt off. The people I live with might wonder why I'm half-naked every time they come in, nipples hard. No shoes or socks on, either. I'm looking across at him.

I'll pretend I was just getting some water, when I saw him.

It's five, the morning rising over the pink, pale city. Light makes lite blue, relieving imprint of metal towers, a spire. I jerk off in front of the window, dawn now.

I go up to bed while he drifts off on his couch.

I sink into the sheets, under gauze, the canopy of a bridal net that drapes down from the ceiling, in a bed with someone I'm not interested in.

First I let him see me turn off all the lights with my pants down, hanging myself out for his admiration, before going up.

As early as seven the next evening, I wait for dark to fall so I can see inside his window and what he has planned.

I see him enter from work, his day. Thought I saw him twice on the street today. Within a walk through the room he is already naked ready for me.

By now his body is a golden familiar, his specimen luminescent in blue flickerings of TV lights he rewinds some nights, remote control in hand, one, knees bent legs up and thrown over the arm and back of the couch, extending. His other hand goes down his pants, periodically grabs ahold until it gets so worked up he pulls his shorts down again for me. Gladly, I see. He is large, so that when he gets going good and relaxed, coaxed thinking there is audience enough in me, hard attention I'm paying routinely, it's no problem to catch him going up and down the length of shaft, from all the way across. He must know I'm looking. Must. How couldn't I? How couldn't he?

I wanted to pleasure myself cautiously, but I am drawn to him more and more.

Does he maybe want to go down and meet me in front of our buildings?

Or does he feel more relaxed, brazen and seductive keeping it across the street, behind windows and glass, curtains he ties back for me, his arm flexing strain to entertain us both.

Just watching him, I come twice in one night, almost every night I'm there. He sees me. We move in sync, both hands down our separate pants. Then go ahead and open them to each other, show each other.

Our eyes lock on. Doors closed, but windows we stand in front of open.

Watch this. As we do it for each other.

Walt

Ian Philips

San Francisco. Saturday night. Almost midnight.

I was at The Hole in the Wall. Alone.

I know, I know—I'm making it sound like a bad thing. And it wasn't. No way. I'm just trying to picture it in my mind so you can in yours.

Okay, Saturday night. So I wasn't bummed, really. Or scared. It's just I'd never been there before without my room-mates—the guys.

Okay, so maybe I was a little nervous.

Cuz I'm shy.

I mean it's not like I'm ugly or anything. Brown hair. Brown eyes. I keep my goatee trimmed real close. I've got a big mouth. Honest. And a big nose. I don't like it. But this hot guy told me it was "classical." He said I have a Roman nose. Makes sense. I'm Italian. Okay, my mom's dad and my dad's grandparents are Italian. So I try to remember what he said and how sexy he said it when I get self-conscious. Like Saturday night.

I know, I know—BFD. What's my problem? Especially when most guys just want you to have meat on your boner.

No sweat, then. I don't mean to be bragging, but I gotta big, fat dick. What can I say, it came with the body. And when I used to fuck around with most guys, I scored all the time. But what gets me hard, you know, dick-pointing-to-the-sky rock hard, is men with meat on *all* of their bones.

So? Shit. I forgot to tell you I'm real skinny too. So, I'm always thinking, since I am so skinny, those guys won't want me. They'll throw me back in the water just like my dad does with any fish he thinks is—his words, not mine—"a runt." Okay, it probably doesn't help that that's his nickname for me too. And I'm not that small. It's just my dad's 6'1", and I'm 5'8". And, I guess, if you put only 130 pounds on 5'8" worth of bones, you gotta runt.

Whatever. By the way, none of what I just told you was to throw me a pity party. I swear. It's so you'll know why I didn't tell Walt to go fuck himself when he came onto me. Even if he did seem a little crazy. Hell, he *is* crazy.

Great. Now I want my men big and crazy.

Well, right now, I just want Walt.

No, he isn't one of the Naked Guys or that guy that barks. Though they were all there last Saturday night. But maybe you've never been. Sorry. I keep forgetting. I'm supposed to see it so you can see it. Okay. The Hole in the Wall. It's like that bar—you know, the one in *Star Wars*. Honest. Except this time everyone's a fag and horny. They call it a biker bar. I guess it is. There's always a bunch of guys there who look like they're Hell's Angels.

But, to say it's a biker bar, you gotta include mountain bikes with the Harleys.

Okay. Right. Saturday. It was packed. Two deep along the bar and three around the pool table. In the back—you know, where that mural is of the great daddy bear riding a Harley and his boy into heaven, the one right beneath the sign that says "Booty Juice Rules"—back there, it was so thick with bikers and bears and boys it didn't take much to guess what was going on.

I looked across to the bar. Then looked up front again to see if my guys had decided to show up after all. Nothing. Then I looked straight ahead again. And two blue eyes were staring back. Staring right through me. This blond bear—bear cub—was cruising me. Heavy cruising. No looking away. No blinking. But there was something odd about him. He had the cruise down, but, even though his thick lips never moved, I could tell he was grinning at me. With his eyes. You know. Like that cat in *Alice in Wonderland.* The one that had the shit on everyone and just smiled, driving them crazy cuz they all feared just how much he knew. Yeah, his face was a lot like that cat's. Then the eyes, the smile, the face, him—they all moved toward me.

His belly pushed guy after guy out of the way. Kinda like those big rocks in streams that water has to split itself in half to get around. Except the stream was men heading for the bar or the john. And the rock kept moving towards me. God, my eyes musta been bugging. I almost had to bite my tongue to keep from grinning back. I wasn't nervous anymore. Okay, maybe still a little. But, mainly, I was stoked to be singled out by such a hot man. All I could think was: *Please, sir, don't stop.*

I braced my butt against the ledge that runs along the wall. I didn't want to start shaking. But I was getting so excited. *Omigod. He's getting so close. Is he gonna kiss me? Yes, c'mon, daddy bear. Closer. C'mon.* And he kept coming. Till his thick gut was pressing hard against my belly-flopping stomach. He was only a few inches from my face. He leaned in. *He's gonna kiss me.* I closed my eyes. I dunno why. *You're such a girl,* I screamed to myself. But I didn't care. I waited for his bristles to poke my lips.

Then I felt them. On my ear! He was snorting in my ear. Okay, breathing. But he was a heavy breather. Like a crank caller. Like a bull.

My ear prickled and burned till my whole face musta been red. Then, his body gently crushed mine, and he whispered, *"I sing the body electric."* And I felt it. The current coming from his fingers as he grabbed my shoulder blades. *"The armies of those I love engirth me and I engirth them."* His hands dropped slowly along my spine. I thought—I hoped— he was gonna shove them down my pants, but they kept going till he'd pushed my butt from the ledge and held a cheek in each hand. *"They will not let me off till I go with them, respond to them."* Then he pulled one hand from my ass and dragged it around my hip. If he was going for my dick, it wouldn't be hard to find now. It was making as much of a pup tent as it could in 501s one size too small. I breathed in. Closed my eyes tight. He found it. I had a raging boner by the time he crushed his palm into my crotch and said, *"And discorrupt them, and charge them full with the charge of the soul."*

After one hard, slow squeeze, he pulled his hand from my dick and up along my stomach—totally belly cartwheeling now—and over my chest till he held my chin. I felt his breath before I heard it. My lips grew warm. *Please, kiss me.* I waited. He waited. I opened my eyes.

"It's Walt."

"Hey, Walt. I'm Joe."

He laughed. A burst that softened as it fell down the register. *God, he's cute.*

"No, Walt Whitman. That was from a poem by Whitman."

I think I've seen just one picture of Walt Whitman. He was a really old dude. Probably sixty or seventy years old. Maybe not. Back then, life was rougher. He mighta been forty. But that Walt didn't look like this Walt. That Walt—Walt Whitman—he looked like Grizzly Addams' friend. You know—the old guy, not the bear. What was his name? You know. Well, it was the same guy that played Uncle Jesse on *The Dukes of Hazzard*. This Walt didn't look like either of them. Okay, maybe he looked like Grizzly Addams. But a few inches smaller with a shorter beard.

Now all that thinking I just did really happened in a second. Well, as long as it took to get one good look at his face. Okay, I'm not sure. It could'a been longer. I'd been drinking. Good thing or I never would'a had the balls to do what I did next.

I leaned up to his ear and grabbed his dick. *It's hard too.* Then I said it. "Wanna go to my place and fuck?" I felt his whole body shake. He laughed till I thought it was the laughter lifting me in a bear hug.

We held hands the whole cab ride to my house. I didn't let go of his paw till we got to my room and I had to plug in the strings of pink flamingo lights on the wall above my futon. It was just them and the lava lamp across the room. Enough light to tell where the buttons in our jeans were.

I looked up from the outlet, and there was Walt. He was grinning for real now. He'd propped all my pillows up against the wall. Then scooted his whole bulk into his new chair, pulling most of the blanket up under his ass. He was patting his thigh. His thick fingers thudded against his thicker leg. It was a drum beat I couldn't ignore.

I bent down and tore at the laces of my boots. Yeah, it was light enough to see a silver button, but there was no way in hell I was gonna untie a little black knot fast. I think I said one of those strings of "Shits" out loud. Finally, I got both boots off. I marched up and onto my bed, straddling Walt's legs. I tried to kneel down slowly but he grabbed my hips and tugged. My ass fell hard onto his lap but I didn't even knock the wind out of him. Nope. He wasn't even fazed. Just pulled me in closer and kissed me.

His lips were heavy and wet. Mine slipped around on them, scratching against the edge of his beard if I rolled too far, till he had my mouth and me anchored to his tongue. He tasted so good. Honest. Like really dark beer.

He slipped his hands up under my shirt. It wasn't difficult. It'd come untucked, and it was a velour pullover anyway. A real deep purple. They were warm—his hands. He fanned them across my chest. " 'The curious sympathy one feels...' " He slipped them under my arms. I jumped back. I couldn't help it. It tickled. But he kept talking, " '...when feeling with the hand the naked meat of the body.' " He lifted my arms, then his, and, with it, my shirt up and over my head. *One cool move.*

"Was that Walt, too?"

He smiled. *God, he must know every poem Whitman ever wrote!* He didn't say anything, just placed a palm right on top of each nipple. Then he arched his hands so only his fingers and my skin were touching. I watched them and waited. They looked like they were gonna play the piano. He dragged them real slow down to my stomach. I was shaking. A big quivering shudder ran up and up then down my spine. He was getting closer to the rim of my jeans, to the buttons. And my dick was getting closer to rock hard. It was show time.

Leaving one hand waiting at my waistband, he took the other and started fumbling with my top button. I sat up on my knees, sticking my butt up like a cat. *Pop.* One free. His hand slid under the denim. *Pop.* It was at the tip of my crack. My dickhead jumped out. *Pop. Pop. Pop.* His fingers slid into my butt crack, digging for my hole, while my dick sprung up to my stomach like one of those flowers in time lapse that comes up outta the earth in full bloom.

Before my cock could cool in the open air, Walt had it in his grip. His hands were fucking huge. This one held almost three-quarters of my dick. He squeezed. I groaned. He squeezed even harder. His thumb stroked my sticky hole again and again. Quickly, it was sliding back and forth. He breathed more words in my ear. "*Without shame,*" his thumb kept counting out the beat, "*the man I like,*" back and forth, "*knows and avows*" back and forth, "*the deliciousness of his sex.*"

I was "unnhing" by now. Which isn't bad. It sounds hot. It feels hot. It's just if he kept thumbing and I kept "unnhing" I was gonna shoot way too soon. So I grabbed for his dick. It was long and hard against his thigh. I tried to squeeze it real rough like. *Shit, this fucker's thick.* He barely noticed. So I pulled on it. I couldn't tell if he was moaning or laughing.

I gripped it harder and yanked it. He got quiet. He stopped thumbing me but didn't let go of my dick. My other hand was still holding onto his ledge of a shoulder. I let go and made a grab for the back of his head. I pulled him in till his open mouth was on mine.

There's no better way to say it: we were sucking face. No shit. I thought he was gonna swallow my head like a Tootsie Pop.

Somehow I was able to keep up the tongue-wrestling match we had going while I unbuttoned the top three buttons of his flannel shirt. *Plop.* I broke the vacuum seal. I gulped down a breath and then dropped my face into the brush of his beard. His hairs pricked my lips and tongue again and again as I dragged them down his face to his neck. Walt's hand had long let go of my dick and joined its twin on my ass. He held each cheek tight while thumbing my butt crack. As I pushed my mouth down his neck, I inched my hole towards his thumbs. I was sitting on them by the time I got to his chest. His skin was smooth with sweat and sweet smelling. Then, finally, I found it, that patch of dark blond hair. I matted it some more with my face. I was getting real close to his meaty tits.

Okay. I know the minute I said "meaty" you were thinking I meant the usual two sirloin steaks circuit-queens either grow or have glued onto their chests. Nope. In fact, "meaty" is kinda lame since I'm a vegetarian. I just mean those big, thick ones you can totally suck on. Like the monster-man tits in *Bulk Male.* You know, they look like two huge mud slides on Pacific Coast Highway 1.

And Walt had them. We're talking El Niño mud slides. With the biggest, pinkest nipples I'd ever seen on a guy. I sighed in awe, and that got Walt's thumbs to wriggling at the edge of my hole. My ass sent a quick message up my spine to my brain. If I wanted any nippage, I was gonna have to totally scrunch down on his thumbs. Two holes filled in one move— yeah, it was a sacrifice I was willing to make.

I stuck out only the end of my tongue and moved in. I flicked it against his fat nipple. A butterfly kiss. Walt shook. The futon creaked. My asshole danced over his thumbs as they took turns jabbing it and each other to get in. I quickly locked my lips around the tip of his tit and the Waltquake stopped.

His thick knot stiffened between my lips. He growled, and I sucked. Then I pulled away till I held the tip of his tit in my teeth. I bit down, real gentle like at first, then not-so-gentle like.

Walt belched out something that sounded like "Ah, shit!" My asshole was pulling around empty air. His thumbs were gone. He tugged at the back of my head with both his hands and pried me loose like I was some kinda tick.

I slipped free, dragging my tongue down through the trail of hair to the edge of his jeans. I kept expecting his belly to shake like that bowlful of jelly under the weight of my tongue. But it was one solid block of fat and muscle. I was leaking some serious precum now.

I reached for his belt buckle. My hands fumbled like I was a kid, up since 4 A.M., tearing into his first Christmas present, finally, at 9 A.M. *Got it!* Now for the button fly. Top button down. Then another. My whole body was shaking. I wanted his dick. Now. To let him know just how bad, I gripped it hard and squeezed.

Suddenly my face was swallowed in the palm of his hand. He tilted my chin up from his crotch till our eyes met. "*Whoever you are holding me now in hand, without one thing all will be useless,*" he said as he smiled just like that cat again. "*I give you fair warning before you attempt me further, I am not what you supposed, but far different.*"

I guess if I was listening to what the words meant, I might have stopped then and asked him just what the fuck he was talking about. But he used so many words. Some pretty. Some weird. Some really vague. They all sounded like what a genie in a fairy tale says or a fortune cookie. I didn't really care. I just wanted to see his cock and suck it. Talk later.

I shoved my fingers under the tight waistband of his black underwear. It was leather. A leather jockstrap. *Kinky.* I had to see his dick bad now. *Please, let him have a Prince Albert.* My asshole twitched. *Amen, sister.*

I kept pushing down. At some point I knew my hand would find that odd spot in the damp, wiry hair and soft fat of his mound where a hard, thick stick grew. But I kept pushing down. *Where was it?* It's supposed to be just south of the belly button. Then my fingers slid over another curve of fat and into this warm, wet crease. I panicked.

"Where's your dick?"

"You pushed it out of the way for my cunt."

"Your cunt?"

I yanked my hand out of his pants as fast as I could.

"How can a man have a cunt?"

"I just do."

My face was swallowed again by his hand. For a sec, I got scared he was gonna crush my head like a walnut. But, instead, he held it real tender, like I was this little baby bird that'd fallen out of its nest.

Then he let go and grabbed my hand. I started to wig when he tried to push it back down under his jockstrap. He just held tight and shoved my fingers into his sweaty and steamy bush. *"Have you ever loved the body of a woman?"* I watched him pull my wet hand up his stomach and onto his stiffening nipple. *"Have you ever loved the body of a man?"* My fingers were almost cold, and he pulled them up and into his mouth. He sucked till they were warm, then dragged them out over his soft, wide lower lip. *"Do you not see that these are exactly the same to all in all nations and times all over the earth?"*

"Is that another poem?"

He smiled again.

"Could you just fucking stop with the poetry crap."

My dick was shrinking like a dying balloon, and I was cold.

"Stop and listen to their words. Feel them. They're so beautiful—like you."

I forgot what I was gonna say. Then I blurted out, "You tricked me."

"You tricked yourself."

Okay. Reality check. Yeah, I thought right then about telling Walt to get the fuck outta my house. For a sec. Or two. Maybe a minute. I was kinda shocked. All right, I was pissed. But before I could say anything, my dick had to go and put in his two cents. Well, more like his eight-and-a-half inches.

Walt, my dick and I agreed, was—even with a pussy under his dick—one of the hottest guys we'd ever seen. Honest. I wasn't that drunk. And, my dick reminded me, the last time *we* got laid was two weeks *before* finals, and my last final was almost two weeks ago. Hell, that's a month.

I snapped outta my head just in time to see Walt groping around in his pants for his dick.

"Here." He pulled it loose and it flapped up between us. "I'll keep it on the whole time. Okay? You just get it wet, and I'll fuck you with it. All right?" I stared at it. It was pretty realistic, for a dildo. You know. You could tell the head from the shaft. It had veins. Even smelled like skin from being in Walt's pants. But I knew it'd taste like silicone.

"He's hot," my dick shouted. *"A month. Thirty fuckin' days, and no one's touched me but you!"*

Walt pushed me off and stood. Snapped his fingers and pointed to his feet. I scurried over and tried to make a go of it.

His dick was about 8" long and 6" around. It was hard. And Walt knew how to face fuck like it really was his. In a few minutes, he was shoving it down the back of my throat. He was a rough, mean fucker and didn't care if I was choking and sobbing. I shoulda been happy. Real happy. It felt good. Honest. But something was missing.

I know you thought I was gonna say "a real dick." Wrong. It's just the more I sucked, the more I thought. And the more I thought, the more I knew that no matter what he did with that dick, he couldn't feel me and I couldn't feel him. I mean I'm pretty good with my tongue. But it was wasted on his dick. I wanted Walt to feel how excited I was by him. And I wanted to feel, from the surge of his skin and blood, that he was excited by me.

You have to understand this. You just do. It's real important. Really. So you'll get why I did what I did.

Okay. First, I raised my hands off his cock and onto his belly, pushing it, pushing him, to lie back on the futon. I started to get up off my knees while keeping the dick in my mouth. Of course, now I can see it wouldn'ta withered in the cold air if I'd popped it out of my mouth. So, maybe it was outta habit. Or respect. Whatever. There I was crouching with his dick in my mouth and hoping he'd figure out what I wanted him to do next.

Maybe it was the luck of the first date, but he did. He laid back. All this time, I was still casually blowing him and waiting. He hadn't been on his back long before he was tweaking a nipple real hard and sliding his other hand down his heaving belly towards my head and his dick and his cunt. He stopped for one rough tug on my head to remind me to keep up the pace. And then, it was under the band of the dildo harness. You know, the leather jockstrap.

He grunted. Low. He moaned. Lower. He snorted. He sighed. Still, he was a long way from orgasm. But he musta been getting hard under there. Or flushed. Whatever he called it. I didn't care. I just knew each loud breath was a good sign. So I started "unnhing" again. I wasn't hard or anything. Walt wasn't even touching me. I was doing it cuz I thought if we're both making noises he won't hear me popping his harness open.

Snap. One down. I wasn't sucking his cock anymore. Just pushing on it so he'd think I was. *Snap*. Two down. I needed to get the dick out of the way now. I thought of pulling the harness up and over it. But I woulda had to yank the back side of it down and out through his butt crack first.

Not too subtle.

So I crawled up onto the futon alongside Walt. Then I tilted the dildo at an angle and pulled real gentle. You know like in the *Grinch Who Stole Christmas* when he takes the candy canes from the sleeping babies. And Walt didn't notice either. And me, all I was thinking was that I had to see his cunt. I had to touch it. With my hands. Hell, with my face. I don't know why, except, like I said before, I had to feel him getting it up for me.

I pulled back the leather triangle. And there it was. The first cunt I'd ever seen. Honest. Its lips were big, fat, wet, and pink—real pink. The pink of bubble gum. Not that hard, dry pink of Bazooka Joe, but the soft, squishy pink of Bubbalicious—before you bite into it.

I watched his fingers to find the clit. And there it was, under this thing that looked like the awning on some fancy apartment building. A little dickhead with wings, no bigger than a thumb or a Vienna sausage, you know, a cocktail weinie. Honest. I'm not trying to be mean. That's just what I thought at first. I didn't think it looked gross. Just kinda weird, kinda different, kinda cute.

"Well, boy, whaddya think? Too small fer ya?"

For a sec, I thought it was my dad talking to me about some fish. Or me. *Why is size such a big fuckin' deal?*

"Well, boy." A hand yanked hard on my hair. I snapped outta my head. This wasn't my dad. He never touched me.

"Hey," the hand let go and slapped my head, "you asleep?"

"No, sir. It's no runt, sir."

"That ain't no pig yer talkin' about. That's my dick, boy."" The hand rubbed the top of my head, mussing with my hair. "Be more respectful."

"Yes, sir."

"Well, go on now. You kin touch it, boy."

You'd think touching a dick that was a clit woulda been weird to me. But it wasn't. I wasn't even thinking that. What I didn't get was why Walt was talking now like Festus on *Gunsmoke.* You know, some old prospector or something. I guess cuz it made his voice sound deep. Like Darth Vader's. It was odd but hot.

Whatever, I sighed to myself. He'd grabbed hold of my dick. "Ah, fuck," I said out loud. The thumb had found that magic spot right were the dick meets the dickhead.

Then he let go so I could scooch down. I put my face in, and it felt like his cunt was giving me a big, slobbery kiss. My cheeks were sticky, but I kept going. I puckered and aimed my lips for where I thought I'd seen it last. I was gonna try and get it all in my mouth with one suck. *Won't Walt be impressed with his pussy-eating virgin.*

"Fuck!" He grabbed me by the back of the head and yanked me out.

"Listen, boy. I may call it a dick, and you may think it's a dick. But it ain't just like *your* dick. So don't be getting all riled up to tug at it like it's your teenage peter in a circle jerk."

"I'm sorry," I mumbled.

Good thing it was dark. I was blushing. I felt so dumb.

"First rule: tonight, no fingers. We'll work up to those." I suddenly got excited. He was already talking about a second date.

"Next rule, use your tongue. But think of my clit as a thousand times more sensitive than either of your nipples." He gave both a hard twist, and I jumped. "Okay?"

"Okay."

"And five hundred times more sensitive than your cock." He stroked the underside of my dickhead lightly, and I shook. "That's more like it."

I sighed and gave him this real goofy grin. *God, I'm such a 'tard.*

"Now, kiss me." I did. I went all out. *What the hell,* I figured. Might as well let him know that when I kiss I like to get my face wet and my lips sore. Minutes, maybe hours, later, he pulled out for air

"You're a fuckin' good kisser," he gasped. "Now, do it again." I leaned in and bumped my lips against his finger. "But this time, my tongue is my clit."

I know my eyes bugged this time. Walt just laughed. "Geez, that sounded way too much like a paper I wrote in school."

I think *he* was blushing.

"Okay, I want you to *pretend* my tongue is my clit. And I want you to use your tongue to get it off."

I almost had "but" outta my mouth.

"Don't worry," he said. "I'll do a little old-fashioned operant conditioning to let you know when you're doing it just right. Trust me. Now, close your eyes."

I couldn't even blink.

"Trust me. Close your eyes and feel the force, Luke."

I laughed. "Feel it."

Walt rubbed his thumb beneath my dickhead. I closed my eyes. "Kiss me." I barely had a chance to mush lips or even get them wet when he goes and shoves his tongue into my mouth. *So much for fuckin' foreplay.*

I wasn't ready. I just poked his tongue with mine. Then his thumb pushed down from my piss slit. I poked it again. The pressure grew less. So I touched it lightly. The thumb was gone. *Fine.* I jabbed it from underneath. He left my dick waving in the air—alone. *Oh-kay.*

I was getting pissed, and I panicked. *Whaddaido?* Then an idea.

I pulled my lips back from his tongue until I sucked only the tip. Walt stroked my dick. I kept sucking. Stroke. I prodded his tongue with as much careful force as he was using to rub my cockhead. Stroke. Then I got creative. I lapped at its underbelly as it curled away from me. I kept at it. And Walt repaid me by rubbing his thumb in circles below. I was going "unnh." His tongue pulled away.

"Good. Now git down there and suck my clit, boy." A final flick of his thumb, as if he hoped to get a spark from my dick.

I knelt into his cunt. "Close your eyes."

I looked up.

"Close 'em."

I did.

"Follow your instincts. Follow the heat."

I inched closer.

"Remember what I've taught you, Luke, and someday you may just become half the Jedi pussy-eater your sister Leia is."

I opened my eyes and gave him a look that said, "You are *so* weird." Of course, the longer I stared the more it said, "You are so weird, but *so* hot."

Walt was grinning back. He gave my hair a yank. "Okay. Close 'em."

I leaned in towards the heat. The smell. Somewhere between micro-brewed beer and musk deodorant in a really sweaty armpit.

"Now lick my lips. Go on." A few mouthfuls of hair, and then I touched skin. "Now, suck my clit, boy."

I kept expecting to taste salt. You know how precum a lot of times tastes like when you're drinking a plain margarita and the rim's all crusty and you take a sip and all you get is that sting of salt with a little tequila.

That didn't happen.

And I thought the first kiss from his cunt was wet! He drooled on the bridge of my nose, then all over my cheeks as I pushed my face in. I stuck my tongue out slowly into the hot, sticky-sweet darkness. Walt's clit didn't leap out to greet me like it had in his other mouth. I was gonna have to dig deeper. So I stretched my tongue till it bumped up against a hard, hot rock of flesh that wouldn't budge. But it sure did shiver. Then Walt's whole body,

wrapped around my head, did the same. I thought he was trying to twist my head off with his thighs. *Captain, I believe we've just made first contact.*

I brought my tongue back to his clit. I pushed against what had to be the clithead. A steady pressure. Then pulled away. Then back, but longer. Walt shuddered. *Now,* I thought, *time for the fancy stuff.* I did an underbelly lap. Then again. Then a sideswipe. I knew I was doing something right, cuz I couldn't hear a thing, his legs were crushing into both sides of my head that hard.

I got into a real pussy-eating rhythm after a while. Some slow and steady tonguing followed by spurts of tongue acrobatics. Not that different from cock sucking. And I didn't hate it or anything. It's just after a while I got bored. My tongue can only feel so much. It was time to send in my hypersensitive probe. Just one thing—Walt had originally thought he was gonna fuck me. Now I had to let him know, real nice, that there'd been a *temporary* change in plans.

I dragged the tip of my tongue across his clit. I lifted my head and said, "Fuck."

"Fuck," Walt groaned.

"I wanna fuck you." I dragged my tongue back over the clit. It was getting so hard I was afraid it might pop.

"Fuck."

"I wanna fuck you." I wriggled my tongue against the head.

"Fuck," he grunted. I kept on flicking my tongue. "Fuck me." *Man, I've seen guys with sensitive dickheads,* but…if Walt had balls, they'da been blue by now.

I pulled up leaving his cute, little dick pointing into the cold, cold air. Then I really startled him.

"I said I wanna fuck *you.*" I bent down and gave it a few laps of my tongue like a cat. "Right now. *Here.*" I lapped one more time, hoping. "I've never done it before."

He pushed my head away and sat up. "Fucked a man?" He sounded nervous, hurt.

I shook my head.

"Oh, a pussy."

"Yeah. A real man pussy."

"A what?!"

"You know. Like in the personals. A man pussy."

"Asshole," he said, real serious.

"Huh?" I said back, real casual, but I was so scared I'd pissed him off.

"They mean asshole."

"I'll fuck you there if you want. But I'd really like to fuck you in your man pussy. Then you can fuck me anywhere." He laughed, then grew quiet as I put his hand beneath the super-swollen head of my cock. He gripped it hard till a bubble of precum popped outta my pisshole. My dickhead was red, bright red.

"Okay, but to get my cunt really wet, I need a lot of tit torture."

"Sure," I said. I couldn't wait to chew more on his soft, thick, hairy tits. I leaned forward. My chest bumped up against the palm of his hand.

"Oh, no, boy. Not mine. Yours."

He shoved both his hands into my armpits and heaved. In one move, he dragged my body up along his legs, held me in midair like a baby, and plopped me down so I was riding his lap.

"Much, much better," he said. *Yeah, for you,* I thought. I was totally naked with my balls dangling in the wind.

It wasn't that cold, for a San Francisco night, but I was shivering anyway. Suddenly, I felt the warm, wet weight of his palms pressing into each of my asscheeks. He pulled me towards his mouth.

Okay, my nipples are nowhere near as big as Walt's. But they ain't the size of dimes either. Or innies. But it still took him a few tries to get one snug between his teeth.

He bit, then licked the sting away. Another longer, sharper bite. Again. I sucked in my breath. He snorted back. I think he was laughing. He moved over to slurp on the other nipple. And hard. So hard I started to freak he was gonna draw milk or blood outta it.

Then the heat was gone. The pressure was gone. Walt was reaching for his pants. He swung for something glinting in the shadows. A chain. *Probably to his wallet,* I thought. *What's he want with that? Condoms? I've got plenty of those.* He tugged, and it slithered out of its nest in the jean's pocket. It crashed hard on the floor. It wasn't a wallet. It looked more like two high-tech clothespins held together by a bicycle chain. I flinched from the back of my scalp to the balls of my toes. Tit clamps! They rattled as he dragged them across the floor. The heat rolled back towards me.

"I am the poet of the Body and I am the poet of the Soul." *His broad* tongue squashed one nipple then another. *"The pleasures of heaven are with me...."* He sucked in what I thought was my whole right pec, holding it between his lips while his tongue poked my aching nipple. I was wriggling. Then he did it all over again to my left tit. I was totally squirming and sighing now. He pulled away and his spit grew cold and my nipples harder. Like goosebumps. *"(A)nd the pains of hell are with me,"* he hissed. Then I did. Something thick, heavy, bit into my nipples. Both of them. Not like a pinch. Not like teeth. Heavier. And it didn't let go. *"The first I graft and increase upon myself, the latter I translate into a new tongue."* He got his tongue up under one nipple, wetting it. It was one hot ache. I thought there'd be steam. Then he dragged his stinging beard over my tightening, shaking skin to the other.

At some point, he musta stopped again to talk. "Boy, you're getting yer Uncle Walt real wet." He yanked the chain. My chest burned. "Now it's yer turn."

He wrapped his fingers slowly around the chain and pulled it towards him. The pressure built, I threw myself ahead of it and landed on his face. Our tongues were pushing, then slipping in sync with the moving of his fingers between my legs. He pushed my dickhead into the tight hat of a condom. My skin was hot and dry while it was cool and wet. He tugged and rolled it down my boner. In my head, I kept jumping back from my tongue to my dick.

Somewhere I heard what sounded like a baby with the runs. He was getting the bottle by my bed to cough up some lube. I kept kissing as he greased up my dick. I felt that odd, solid cold of the lube where the condom ran out and my skin started.

He guided me between his legs. I sank in. Slowly. The lips of his cunt—warmer and softer and wetter than any mouth that had ever blown my dick—were rising up on both sides to pull me deeper. He slapped my butt and pushed me in all the way. I pulled out, and the warmth fell away. I pushed back, and it thickened against my cock.

I wanted to start out slow. Go so far, so fast. Let my hips keep time. Really get into feeling my butt tighten then relax. Rock on my hips. Each thrust I'd dig a little deeper. I wanted to work up to slamming his cunt with the full length of my cock. You know, do his man pussy just like I like having mine done.

And it did start out that way. But Walt was up to something. He didn't sigh or groan or snort. He just smiled that cat smile. And it got wider and wider as I began to get a rhythm.

I was thrusting and thrusting and thrusting. The sweat was welling up at my hairline. Then the first trickle down my back, then my forehead. I was getting a pretty good fuck going, I thought. But Walt just smiled and looked so fucking content, so calm. Like he was coming onto X or something.

I was startled, but relieved, when he spoke.

"*Ebb stung by the flow…*" I closed my eyes. I was trying to feel the fuck, shut out the words. "*And flow stung by the ebb, love-flesh swelling…*" Then, outta nowhere, Walt arched his back, his belly, up, and I thrust down—bam—to the bone under my bush. I gasped, but Walt kept on talking. "*And deliciously aching…*" I heard his back hit the futon. At least the bed was groaning. "*Limitless…*" his fingers dug into my ass, "*limpid jets of love…*" and pushed me and my dick as far into him as we could go together. "*Hot and enormous…,*" he squeezed my hips with his palms, "*quivering jelly of love…,*" and almost popped me back out, "*white-blow…,*" only to push me down again and pull me out again. "*And delirious juice…,*" he blurted as he slapped my ass down into him.

Now I was pumping. Really pumping. It sounds stupid, but, at that moment, I am my dick. And I think I'm banging the hell out of Walt's cunt when he goes and really does it.

"What's that grimace fer, boy." He was panting. "Ain'tcha having fun?"

I grunted this deep wild moan. And bared my teeth. I was trying to smile. I think.

"C'mon, boy. Whoop it up." He reached towards me, my chest, and ripped the tit clamps off with one jerk.

I was stung. The air was cold. It felt like a sharp slap. The jab of a needle. Then stinging hot. Like a sleeping foot waking up in one second. Burning. Breaking out in a cold sweat. I was choking. Couldn't swallow. I'd forgot how to breathe. I couldn't get air in or my scream out. Then Walt smacked my butt, and I coughed it up. And somehow, I was able to holler and fuck at the same time. I was mad. Raging. I was gonna bang him till he broke in half.

Well, that's what I was shouting. Walt was getting pretty red faced himself. And gushing sweat. Looked like he was gonna have a baby or something.

I almost jumped out of him when he reached down toward his cunt. I thought he was gonna grab my dick and get me to fuck him even harder. But, without looking, he stopped at his clit. He must have felt the heat. Hell, I could feel its heat. And it was as red as the end of a cigarette.

I was still huffing and puffing. Squinting all my tits' pain into the pounding of my dick. And I was gonna make sure he felt every inch of it. But I was also on autofuck. Kinda. Watching his hands, hearing his voice.

"Bridegroom night of love..." He was almost barking the words out. *"Working surely and softly..."* He pressed his finger down onto his clit and rubbed a circle around the head. *"Into the prostrate dawn..."* He never let the finger up. He was groaning now. *"Undulating into the willing..."* He dragged

his finger up the underbelly. *"And yielding day..."* He pushed his finger back down. His fingernail was white. *"Lost in the cleave of the clasping..."* He ground his finger around and around and mashed it up and down. If that had been my dickhead I woulda come by now and hard. Hit the ceiling even. But Walt kept panting out more words. *"And sweet-flesh'd day."*

Under the flickering of his lids, I could tell his eyes were rolling. Like a mad dog. And all this show was getting my slip-'n-sliding dick so stiff I knew if I didn't come soon it was gonna snap.

"Ah, fuck." Another Waltquake had begun. This was gonna be The Big One. "Ah, fuck." The bed was rocking and creaking. He was thrusting his hips as high as he could and lifting me with him. "Sweet-fucking-day!"

And then, I think I'm still pumping. But I'm not. It's Walt. His pussy's yanking on my dick. I don't mean squeezing like some virgin butthole. I mean like a hand. A big man's hand. That does it. I shoot. And shoot and shoot. And his cunt keeps on squeezing all the cum out of my dick. Like so much so that any part of me that isn't coming is freaking the condom's gonna explode. Next my arms are wobbling like some newborn colt's legs. Then they finally give way and I fall onto Walt's chest, into Walt'sarms.

"We two boys together clinging," Walt said over my panting as he gripped my butt. *"We two boys together clinging, one the other never leaving...."*

I kept my eyes closed and let my hands slide under and down his tree trunk of a back till I could dig my hands into his ass. I pulled us together as tight as I could. Walt chuckled and kept murmuring, kept kneading my butt. And I kept repeating to myself, *"We two boys together clinging, one the other never leaving...."*

At First Sight

Andy Quan

Love is a four-letter word. We curse it, we use it to draw attention to ourselves, to be cool. We wrap our lips around it to feel its power. I've never felt much use for it, since I don't see the point in cursing or drawing attention to myself.

Plus all the jabber-jabber I hear from my friends. I mean, look at Gary, perfectly presentable, nice guy, good job, no spectacular childhood traumas or kooky family history; you'd think he'd have his head screwed on right. But no, he walks around with this big gaping hole in the side of his body that says, "want, want." Flops around like a fish on dry land.

He's waiting for Romeo, or Julio, or someone, but won't go out looking for him, gets himself caught up in work, too scared to be set up on dates, spends time with the same old friends or takes care of his nephews on weekends. Too often, I think. All the time wanting this house to land as if from the tornado in *The Wizard of Oz*. Plop. Crashes down upon him. The house of love.

But active searching hasn't helped my other friend, Albert. Not actually a friend, I guess, but he hangs around Matthew, my ex-boyfriend, so much, we end up drinking at the same bar. Albert has joined about every organization in the city, making himself available. Almost drowned trying out for the gay water polo team. Sung through five seasons of the gay men's chorus. Faked his way into the gay professional's group by borrowing Matthew's Hugo Boss suits. Dinner clubs, Queer Nation, that new-age meditation group—he's tried it all. I think it's the neon sign above his head that scares people off.

Why can't people learn to be single, I've always thought. Learn to live with yourself, sleep on whatever side of the bed you want, jack off when you want. Come and go as you please. I know they bitch about me behind my back, whether from love or jealousy: "He never seems to be interested in finding someone. Spends too much time at sex clubs and saunas."

It's a bank holiday weekend, bless the god of four-day weeks. All the queens in town are deciding what to do, which big party to go to. I'm opting for Famous Five: huge space, tons of boys down to London for the weekend, five different DJs and dance clubs, that's where it gets its name. I've never been, and I hear that it's going downhill. They better come up with a new gimmick before they crash and burn, yesterday's news. The cops didn't help the ambience one time, either; one friend was caught with five tabs of E and hauled off to the station. His boyfriend, already high, spent the next five hours decorating the dance floor with tears, the light show in each room beamed onto his wet shiny face. They're probably not going tonight, but I will.

Stroke of midnight, I arrive just after. I only have one lager and a quick shuffle on the dance floor to "Everybody's Free." When are they going to stop playing that song? They start playing the dance remix to that *Titanic* theme song; I run into another section, and they start playing it there, too.

So here I am in the darkroom in the bottommost club. Like a homing pigeon, I just zeroed in closer and closer, saw pre- and postcoital facial expressions, sweat and flesh, and clusters of men in that stance they do against the wall outside of darkrooms.

I jump in right away. I never hesitated before diving into swimming pools, either. It's like one big swim team, dozens of men, some huddled into each other as if listening to the coach's rallying speech before the race begins. Competitors and teammates, tall and short, some stretching down on the floor, others bent over like at the starting block, a few stretching up and to the side, others casual, pacing.

Stepping over this cluster, I recognize this guy I'd seen downstairs, a model type, straight out of the pages of a fitness magazine. He's blowing this broad-shouldered Asian guy, a bit chunky around the midsection, who's tongue kissing this skinny redhead who looks about sixteen. The equality of flesh and desire. Unexpected pairings.

I strip off my shirt in the glowing darkness: a single exit sign in the corner that throws a red blanket over everyone. I can feel the pockets of energy forming, whipping into frenzies in different corners. I easily glide towards the warmth, through the packed crowd. Faced away, I feel smooth wide backs against my chest and stomach; faced towards me, round pectorals, nipples, front corners of biceps, meaty forearms. I free my hands from their cages, let them roam through the space in front of me, feel the outline of torsos and their warm sweat, cup and squeeze balls, this one a plum, that one a large avocado. I lift, grab, stroke, pull cocks, short and fat, long and thin, long and fat.

Yin and yang in the corner, these couple of guys, one black and tall, gleaming white teeth, muscular but in a way you can sink into, fingers press and bounce into that athleticism. His cock like a flagpole out of tight curly pubic hair. It's thick and fleshy, like the rotating round of meat in Lebanese shawarma restaurants.

Whitey is shorter and pale, thin lips, you can't see his teeth, his mouth is closed but smiling. He's taut and lean, maybe one of those guys who dances each weekend straight through on ecstasy, twenty-four hours, thirty-six, drinking only water, the calories fly off, the fat disappears. Strip the shirt off like bandages from a plastic surgery patient. It's a topological map, rivers and valleys, blue veins, beautiful beautiful lines, higher elevations that you want to explore. His cock is thinner, longer, hard, and tight like his skin; it's like a pen you want to grab to write that novel you've always thought you had inside you.

They look at me, I return the look, this triangle of desire closes and suddenly we're kissing, all three of us at the same time, heads in close, our tongues in and out, a three-note chord sounding over our heads, percussive moans and rhythms.

It's at this very moment, the corner of my eye, I see him next to us, with another guy. Not even see him, really, but just a flash of dark eyes, a glimmer of darkness inside of his mouth before his lips connect with flesh and travel down a body and out of sight.

Now our trio is moving in rhythm, we're back-up singers swinging in perfect time, it's doo-wap-a-shoo-bop, one down, two up, two down, one up, my face in an armpit, the crevice of a chest, between two legs, between four legs, surrounded in dark warmth between two bodies, a pulsing womb.

I rise up as if out of water, and I'm filled with love, my heart is ticker-taping messages to the crowd. The guy I spotted earlier and his partner have moved closer, my couple notices as well, and then we're five, a surging ball of energy, perspiration, and limbs, a flock of orifices, a herd of phallii. The tongues are hard and soft and quick and slow, and in between hot black breaths, and not being able to think at all, lost in ecstasy, I notice him, onyx eyes and shaved head, noticing me.

I like the way he gives pleasure to the others, the mischievous smile of it all, playful but tough. His generosity, too, taking a ripe cock between his lips, and then offering it to me; we start to kiss as we reach to lick the same nipple. Notice our simultaneous, similar desire.

As if a whole ocean has drained out of our bodies, the tide going out, we come into consciousness, an awareness of people around us. We stand facing each other, the others have left, and I faintly recall murmured farewells from them. Goodbye. Thanks. Ta. Ciao.

He takes my hand, leads me out the door. Love at first sight, forever.

Pansy Juice
Dominic Santi

Whoever thought of having "Shakespeare in the Park" in
Mission Dolores Park must have been out of his fucking mind.
Yeah, there were a lot of us fairies flitting about at night in
that part of San Francisco, but it wasn't exactly courtly love
central.

Some rich jerk up on Nob Hill had decided to give his
Shakespearean-actress bride a wedding present of a "realistic,
modern reenactment" of A Midsummer Night's Dream; however, there was way more love than logic in Mr. Moneybag's
romantically demented gesture. Even the costumes we were
wearing looked like they'd been lifted out of a straight porn
flick. I was annoyed. Our illustrious patron had obviously
never tried walking on wet grass in four-inch stiletto heels. I
was lucky I hadn't broken my fucking neck.

I knew I'd have to carry the damn shoes if I were ever going
to make it up 18th Street to Castro. Shit. I trudged wearily over
to lean against a tree. This had been one long fucking night.
Dress rehearsal. We opened tomorrow, May Day, and the play
ran through Midsummer's Night on June 23. While I liked

twelve weeks of a steady paycheck—they were even paying us for rehearsals—this dressing like a cheap het whore was driving me crazy.

It's not that I didn't like the clothes—which I got to keep, by the way. Black leather miniskirt that fit like it was painted on me. Seamed stockings and garters that led the eye right to my firmly curvaceous butt. See-through silk blouse with a bustier to emphasize the huge nipples on my fake tits—they were fine.

It was the fucking patent leather spikes that were pissing me off. I would have accessorized the outfit differently, given it a classier look. Taken the wet grass into consideration, for crissakes.

I reached under my skirt to resituate myself. Thank God, I'd brought my own underwear, red satin panties that were tight enough to hold all seven inches of my shaved nonfemininity out of the way. I rubbed myself a couple of times, smiling as my cock twitched appreciatively. In spite of my balance problems, I knew I looked good, in a brassy, slutty sort of way.

I also looked like a chick.

Straight-acting is not a term I've ever used to describe myself. Shit, if I'd tried, anybody looking at me would have choked to death on his drink or my sequins, depending on where his face was buried at the time. But I've always been able to "pass." Sometimes even when I'm not trying, if you know what I mean.

These days, I was passing as Francis Flute, the effeminate bellows maker—a.k.a. Thisby, the doomed heroine in the screwed-up performance put on by Flute and his fellow loyal artisans for their king's wedding feast. Well, I suppose, who better for the part than a drag queen named Frank. Or Francine, depending on my attire.

I certainly looked the part, if I do say so myself. Diminutive—5'7", a slender 125. Soft, wavy blond hair that I was letting grow longer than it had been since junior high. My voice didn't hurt, either. It's what I call extremely tenor, though I've learned to make it husky when I need to. And no, for the record, I don't have a fucking beard—or at least much of one. I'm only twenty-six—I'm a late bloomer! Besides, my smooth complexion helped get me the part of the infamous baby-skinned Thisby, in spite of my lack of acting credits. Let's just say, I've always been dainty.

Unlike my lover, Nick. He's playing my erstwhile thespian paramour, Bottom, in the play. Nick fits the part perfectly— loud, funny, extravagant, as well as arrogant, bossy, self-centered, and good looking enough to make any audience gasp. Short dark hair. Startling green eyes. A sleek pelt of thick, black chest hair. The muscled body of a big man who spends long hours in a gym. He's got "Top" written all over him.

And let me tell you, that Bottom's ass is mine. This here demurely petite queen wields a mean fucking whip. Yeah, I'll let Nick raise my skirts in public and spank my cute, sexy little butt until it glows rosy. But when he decides to show off like that, the night's not over until my Bottom finds himself chained to the wall in our basement dungeon while I work his ass and back with a nasty little leather quirt until he's begging for mercy. Then I fuck him senseless.

Nick and I signed on with the theater group because I was pissed at him for lying about screwing one of my cattiest friends. Like the guy wasn't going to tell me. In our favorite watering hole, in front of everybody we know. I felt like a total ass. So, I figured a few weeks of wearing a donkey's head in public would be good for old Nick. I didn't expect the director, Peter, to fall ass over heels in love with my partner. And then to put me in these stupid heels—on wet grass—so that I looked like a total jerk wobbling around, trying to keep my balance.

By the time the dress rehearsal was over, I was exhausted, and I'd been downing coffees to keep awake. When I ducked into the bushes to take a quick piss, El Director told Nick I'd caught a ride with somebody else and offered to give my gullible partner a lift home. At least that's what the night watchman told me as I was rearranging my skirt when I stepped back into the staging area.

Damn, I was pissed. Knowing Nick's powers of resistance, I had no doubt that by now Peter had Nick bent ass-up over our bed, no doubt with my pillow shoved up under him. Fucking him silly. And here I was stranded in the park, dressed like a sleazy het whore, wearing fuck-me heels I could hardly walk in, and the full moon was rising. A lot of fairies were coming out in that park, and the looks they were giving me were not warm and receptive. There are times when being believable in drag is not an asset.

To make matters worse, my slinky feminine undergarments were giving me an almost constant hard-on—at least as hard as I could get with my dick tucked firmly behind the satin panties. Nick had noticed it before he left. No matter how often I'd hissed in his ear, threatening mayhem when we got home, he was into his public butch routine. Ignoring the cat-calls, he'd pressed me up against a tree and kissed me while he stuck his hand up my skirt and fondled me. He'd rubbed my dick until my satin panties were damp with precum, right where my cock's tip was tucked down and under—and then he'd boasted to onlookers about how realistic my drag was. So I was pissed even before I discovered he'd gone. And, damn, I was horny, too.

Of course, my wallet and street clothes were in Nick's gym bag. So this here lady of the evening was going to have to walk home. Shit, shit, shit!

"You look like you could use some coffee, ma'am."

I glared into the twinkling eyes of the night watchman. He was holding a steaming cup out to me and grinning from ear to ear.

My first reaction was to knock the coffee out of his fucking hand. But as I saw the steam rising from the dark surface, I realized that I was freezing. The wind had come up as the fog started rolling into the park.

"Thanks," I said, forcing myself to be polite and trying not to shiver as I took the cup from his hand and gratefully lifted the coffee to my lips.

"Careful," he said, laughing. "It's hot and it's spiked."

I nodded, sipping slowly and carefully, this time shivering with pleasure as I felt the burn of the heat as well as the brandy. My short skirt and light silk blouse were no real protection against the cold, and the night chill was settling in fast.

"I see Pete made off with your costar." He grinned. I couldn't stay angry in the face of his winsome smile. The guy was cute, in a gawky, late-adolescent way. He looked barely old enough to qualify for the adult-only graveyard shift.

"Yeah," I smiled back, ruefully. "All my stuff is in Nick's bag. So I'm stranded. No cash, no lover, and I'm so fucking horny my dick hurts. How's your evening going?"

He laughed, choking on his coffee and yelping as the hot liquid sloshed out and scalded his hand.

"Better now," he said, wiping his hand gingerly on his pants as he winked at me. "That is, if you're up for a tryst with a fairy in the park. By the way, my name's Rob."

He stuck out his hand. When I took it, he held on a lot longer than he needed to. Then he let go and started rubbing the front of his uniform pants. The pronounced bulge there was growing considerably. As my own dick filled again, I knew I had to do something, or I was going to end up with balls the color of our quickly disappearing starlit sky.

There was a good-sized portable shed the company had erected by the stage to serve as a combination dressing room and storage locker. Rob nodded towards it, and I followed him. He lifted his keys—on the right hip, I noticed—and unlocked the door. I hoped the keys on the right were in keeping with tradition. I'll let somebody up my ass if I have to, but I don't get off fucking unless I'm buried up to my balls in a hot, willing asshole.

Rob kept his flashlight pointed towards the ground so as not to draw attention from the other guys prowling the park. The swishing of gym shoes and boots on the sidewalks, the rustling of bushes, and the low murmur of hurried conversations were the only sounds nearby. The occasional distant roar of a passing car made the streets seem as distant as another planet.

The moonlight shone in the open door as Rob's flashlight moved over the careful jumble of costumes and props: the asshead mask, the king's throne, curled boots and wings for the various fairies. Close by the door was a low table with a thermos and lunch cooler on it.

We stopped next to the table, by the pieces of the fairy queen's bower bed. I reached around Rob and grabbed his solid tits through his shirt. "This is far enough, moonbeam," I said. "Turn off your light, and let's get down to some woodland magic."

He laughed, then stiffened as I bumped my groin against his ass, grinding myself against firm welcoming mounds, all the while pulling and twisting his nips.

"Guess what, Rob," I said, biting softly on his ear. "This here courtly lady is all top. You got a problem with that?"

"Ah, no, sir, I mean, ma'am."

He groaned, arching back against me as I sucked his earlobe. I kept my mouth soft and wet and very insistent. "Damn, that feels good."

"Turn around," I growled. The husky voice. When he did, I shoved my tongue into his open mouth—halfway down his throat. He tasted like coffee and peppermint candy. And he knew how to kiss. I hate it when a trick can't kiss.

"That's a talented mouth you have, boy," I breathed against his lips. "How's about putting it where it'll do some good."

"Yes, sir," he whispered. He kissed his way down me; I stopped him when he got to my boobs.

"They're fake, moonbeam. Find something real to play with."

He nodded. I shivered as he dropped to his knees and ran his hands up my silk stockings. Over the smooth expanse of skin where my thighs peeked out above the garters. Up to my panties. He worked the tight skirt halfway up my ass, running his fingers over my satin-clad cheeks. I groaned as his tongue traced the outline of my cock and balls through the tight, softly confining material. The friction was warm. It got hotter as he wet the fabric with his spit. I heard the zip of his uniform pants, then the steady beat of flesh on flesh as he jerked himself off while he licked me.

His slurping was a helluva turn-on. It wasn't long before my dick really couldn't take being bent any more.

"Take it out, fucker," I said. Real husky. "Pull down my panties and swallow that dick."

He didn't argue. He grabbed the elastic of my skin-tight designer undies and yanked, sucked me down in one swallow. I shuddered against him in relief. God, there's nothing like the first touch of tongue on bare dick. I was gasping when he reached towards the table. He went down on me again, and my cock was bathed in warm coffee. It seeped under the foreskin of my blissfully-stretched-out dick. I shouted, shuddered, erupted, pushing him away as I spurted.

He grinned, coffee and cum dribbling off his chin as I sank down onto the floor—onto the dismantled pieces of the queen's bower bed.

"C'mere, bud," I said breathlessly, motioning him towards me as I tried to keep my voice low. "Show me how much you appreciated swinging on my dick."

"Yes, sir!" He walked over on his knees.

I gifted his rock-hard, cut head with one kiss. Then I leaned back and snapped, "Now get to it!"

He stroked a few times, then looked at me and smiled shyly, one of those helplessly smitten young boy looks. "Um, sir, if I may ask, sir, my asshole's really hungry."

I looked down between my legs. Good looking as this boy was, Mr. Happy wasn't going to be helping us out here.

I motioned him towards me and stuck my fingers in his mouth. "Get them real wet boy. You know where they're going."

"Yes, sir!" He went to town on my fingers. Let me tell you, that boy had one talented tongue. Pretty soon even I was feeling a stirring between my legs. I pulled my fingers free.

"Spread. Wide!"

His pants had fallen to his knees. He moved his legs as far apart as the material allowed, arching towards me as I lifted his balls with one hand and touched the dripping wet fingers of my other hand to the hot moon deep in his crack. He was so loose and ready my finger slipped right in, then another, then a third. He groaned and arched further towards me, his cock straining up in his hand.

Then I purred low in my throat, "Show me your appreciation, boy."

"Oh, yes, sir!" he gasped, jerking hard and fast. I worked my fingers deep inside, twisting and pressing and sliding in and out. I was enjoying watching his face shift and grimace in the moonlight as I worked his hot, compliant asshole.

"Oh, please, sir...," he moaned. Even in the shadows, I could see his dick had turned a dark burgundy. He took a deep breath, holding it involuntarily. "Oh, please...."

I pressed hard against the nut of flesh inside his rectum. "Now!" I barked.

His asshole clamped down around my fingers and with a long, low groan he shot all over my face. I mean, he anointed my face with his cock juice. The sweet, musky smell was like ambrosia, like nectar from a blooming night flower—orange blossom maybe, or honeysuckle. Or pansy juice, I chuckled to myself. After all, that was the magical essence of Shakespeare's fairies.

I pulled my fingers out of his ass and wiped them clean on his underwear. Then I pulled my panties up and laid back on my bower bed. "Mistress Thisby is tired, moonbeam. Wake me around midnight so I can go home and deal with my shit-head lover."

I woke up a couple of hours later to the sound of a car stereo blaring in the distance. It took me a second to get my bearings. As the sound faded, I remembered where I was and relaxed into my makeshift bed. My head was resting on the fake lion's mask, and someone—Rob, no doubt—had covered me with a robe, so I was warm enough. The night fog had settled in, and the park was quieter, though I could still hear the soft background rustle of fairies cruising their way through the bushes.

I could also sense the presence of someone in the shed.

"Rob?" I asked, straining my eyes in the soft glow of the moonlight. I could see to the door, except where a costume, a wall with a chink in it, was blocking my view. Then I saw the silhouette of a man rise from behind the costume. Well, the body was a man. The head was the ass mask. He stood quietly, leaning toward the wall, waist high to the chink—the hole that was just too small for Thisby and her paramour to kiss through. Then the man-ass bumped imperiously against the wall, and I understood. I slid over and reached towards the hole. Sure enough, a hard, swollen cock bobbed through—about eight inches. Cut. Thick. Delicious.

I knelt, rubbed the tip over my face, inhaled the musk of velvety skin, and a whiff of latex and lube—like his dick had been inside a rubber. Like he'd already fucked somebody that night. Greedily, I opened my mouth and was rewarded with the taste of dried cum. I licked him clean, every inch of his hot shaft and around the curves of his balls. My own cock was nestled comfortably, sliding against the satin this time as my dickhead stretched out and up into my panties. The man-ass said nothing, just lurched towards my lips.

"You like that?" I worked my tongue into his piss slit.

He gasped, and the ass head nodded.

"Let me show you how Francis Flute the Bellows maker takes care of hot pipes."

If he was confused by my offer, he didn't show it. He thrust again into the wall, gasping and spasming when I took his dick down my throat, all the way on the first gulp. I have a reputation for making a man's dick sing. His twitched and quivered, stiffened even more.

"Gonna come!"

I drew back as his sperm shot onto my face. Thick, hot, creamy man juice. There's nothing like it.

And it smelled just like Nick's. Not that I'm an expert at identifying people by the scent of their semen, but Nick and I had been together for almost five years. Suddenly, even through a glory hole, I knew that dick.

I stood up and slapped the mask.

"You son of a bitch. Leaving me here in this fucking park in these fucking heels while you dragged your slutty ass off with our asshole director—what the fuck were you doing?"

"Aw, wait man. C'mon. It wasn't like that."

It was Nick's voice all right. He danced back, his cock flopping outside of his jeans while he struggled to lift off the mask.

"Damn, it's hot in there."

"Well, it's been fucking cold out here," I snarled, advancing on him with a petitely lethal stiletto-heeled shoe in my hand.

"Wait, Frank," he said, backing away. "I didn't know you were still here. Really." He stopped when he bumped into the wall. "Peter said you'd gone."

"So you took him home and fucked him while I was freezing my ass off here in the park." I didn't keep the sarcasm out of my voice, although I lowered the shoe.

"No, man!"

I glared at him, and he stammered, "I mean, yeah, I fucked him. I'm not lying to you, Frank. Really. But I didn't know you were still here. Peter told me you'd gone out with the rest of the guys. He thought it was all some fucking joke. When he saw I was worried about you, he confessed."

Nick moved his hand gingerly towards me, not sure I wouldn't bite. When I didn't move, he gently touched the drying cum on my cheek, wiped it off my nose, smoothed it over my eyelids. "I fell asleep. I was dreaming about you, ya' know? My pillow smelled like your cum, from when you jacked off on my face this morning. I kept waking up and thinking about how you always call if you're out cruising in your hooker drag, so I won't worry that you've been bashed." He shrugged and smiled sheepishly, his thumbs grooming my eyebrows. "I came back as soon as I figured out what was going on. And I brought the bike, so you wouldn't have to walk."

I couldn't stay mad at him. He looked so sweet in the moonlight. And so cute.

"I'm still horny," I growled, stifling a smile.

He shoved his jeans and Jockeys down to his knees and bent forward over the wall. He stuck out his ass and wiggled it enticingly. "Rubbers and lube in my back pocket. My ass is all hot and hungry for you, untouched this magical evening."

"Oh?" I said, digging the requisite supplies out of his pants. "You fucked El Director?"

"Right up his pinched little asshole. Ahhhh...," he gasped as I shoved two slicked fingers up his ass. His asslips kissed my knuckles. "Damn, Frank. That feels good."

"Who's Bottom are you now, boy?" I rasped, stretching him firmly from side to side as I worked in a third finger.

"Yours, man," he moaned, arching back towards me. "Oh, yeah." He squirmed on my fingers, then he looked over his shoulder with a shit-eating grin. "I'll even proclaim my devotion to you all night, as eloquently as you want, anywhere you want, for as long as you want, if you'll stick your cock up my ass. Now, please? Sir?"

I laughed and pulled my fingers out, then guided my latex-sheathed sword in, slowly for a few seconds, then hard and fast, relishing his sharp gasp, his groan of pleasure, the sensation as his ass closed around my dick like a warm, velvet ring.

"Start talking, boy!"

I fucked him long and hard, my cock throbbing and my balls tightening as he recited every butchered snippet of Shakespearean sex verse he could remember. I was as lovely as every virile maiden, as fair as any lusty youth, hung like the proverbial lion. Nick clenched and shook, gasping through his orgasm, as he declaimed me the most wondrous of all the fairy queens. And when he'd almost caught his breath, when he was panting that I was better than any wet dream, when my dick was as stiff and swollen and ready to burst as the ripest seedpod on any fucking magical flower, I shot my load right up his ass. I came so hard, I thought my heart stopped.

Nothing like true love to make a boy happy, I thought as I collapsed, hugging Nick tightly to me. I admit it, I'm smitten with my Bottom.

When we left, Rob was sweeping around the stage, making sure the trash from the evening's festivities was cleared away for opening night. I held Nick's hand, and he carried my heels as we walked to the bike. Okay, so maybe the guy who wanted Shakespeare in the park wasn't completely crazy. Maybe just a little nutty. Good things happen when you turn fairies loose in a park.

Sightseer

Simon Sheppard

Everything was dark. Dark and still.

He was walking, being led, rather, down echoing corridors, corridors he couldn't see. It's where his sense of adventure had gotten him. His sense of adventure and his hard dick.

It had started, as so many Roman stories must have started, on the Spanish Steps. It had started, as so many Roman stories must have started, with a glance from dark brown eyes.

"How are you?" the man said in a deep Italian voice. Jason knew what it meant. Jason was young, but he was neither stupid nor innocent. Nor was he enamored of his dorm room at the shabby hostel, ten college-age backpackers bedded down side by side in a stuffy room of what must have been a nobleman's villa or something a long time ago. A long, *long* time ago.

Jason, still kind of stoned, had been absently staring at a fountain that was shaped like a sinking ship. Now he looked up, into dark brown eyes. The man was old, mid-thirties maybe. And not particularly good looking. Not really homely, just ordinary. But well dressed. And therefore rich. Not that Jason was out for money, not exactly. But he'd parlayed his good looks and wrestler's body into some nice meals and a bit of spending cash while he was at Dartmouth, careful not to let his frat brothers know. And there'd been that guy around his age in Paris; he'd stayed with him almost a week in his flat on the Place des Vosges. He never went out of his way for any of this; it just came to him.

"Fine," said Jason, smiling as he got ready to rise to his feet.

"Would you like some dinner?" It was only late afternoon, but the guy didn't believe, apparently, in fucking around.

Jason smiled. Pay dirt.

The sports car was a Lamborghini Diablo, not that Jason would have recognized it; he found out from the name plate. And the restaurant was a good one, near the racetrack-shaped Piazza Navona.

So far so good, thought Jason, as he bit into butter-soft veal. An expensive dinner in a place where the headwaiter knew the name of Jason's "friend"—Signore DeAngelis, Paolo—and where the excellent wine and tender baby calf were being paid for out of someone else's pocket. Jason found himself wondering if this Italian guy had done this sort of thing often, if he was just one of an endless parade of horny young backpackers from Perth and Prague and New York, boys that Paolo had tried to pick up and fuck.

The conversation was polite, friendly, slightly awkward on Jason's part, though DeAngelis never stumbled. Since the subject of *lire* never came up, Jason figured money wasn't going to change hands, which was fine with him. He was glad to spend the evening in someplace besides that lousy hostel full of clueless, clumsy straight boys. The gate to the hostel was locked at ten o'clock, but he should have no problem talking this guy—Paolo—into letting him stay the night, unless he....

"Huh?" Jason said. He'd missed whatever Paolo had asked.

"I said, are you ready to leave?"

Paolo paid the bill without flinching. Jason didn't even offer to chip in. They left the still-half-empty restaurant, the valet brought the Lamborghini 'round, and they set off into the Roman evening. Jason didn't ask where.

They were driving toward the Ponte Sant'Angelo, the bulk of the ancient Castel hulking on the opposite shore of the Tiber, when Paolo asked, "Do you like surprises?" Baroque statues of angels gestured toward the Lamborghini, heavenly simpers frozen on their faces.

"Sure, I like surprises," said Jason. He did.

"Then put this on." Paolo handed him a blindfold, the kind they give you on first-class airplane flights. It was a weird request, but Jason had heard weirder, and some of them he had obeyed.

"Do you understand Italian?" asked Paolo.

"The only words I know are 'pizza' and 'ciao.' "

"Fine," Paolo said. Jason heard the beeps of an outgoing cell-phone call, then Paolo's half of a conversation. His voice was firm and quiet; the only word Jason caught for sure was "ciao."

"You trust me?" DeAngelis asked Jason.

"Yes," Jason said. *No,* he thought, or *not sure.* But he figured he could take care of himself pretty well, and besides, he liked an adventure. A bit of excitement, danger even. And besides *that,* Paolo's hand was between Jason's legs, kneading his inner thigh, just inches from the American's dick, which was hard.

The car made its way through the soft Italian night for a little while, then pulled to a sudden stop.

"We're here," said Paolo DeAngelis. "If I guide you, can you walk with the blindfold on?"

"No problem," Jason said.

The Italian got out of the car, walked around to Jason's door, opened it, and guided the young man to his feet.

"Wait here," Paolo commanded. Jason did, dick still half hard. Paolo walked off, had a brief, hushed conversation with someone, then came back and grabbed him by the elbow. "This way."

Jason heard a heavy door swing open on its hinges, then slam shut behind them after they'd passed a few paces on. Very little light leaked in beneath the blindfold; wherever they were, it was dimly lit. After being led through corridors, down ramps, and up a flight of stairs, he was beginning to wonder just what the hell this surprise was. He was beginning to worry. He was starting to think he should have just suggested screwing in a suite at the Hotel Excelsior.

"We're here," Paolo said. "Stand still." The Italian's hand left his elbow. From beneath his blindfold, he saw that lights had been turned on. And now Paolo was back. "Strip," he commanded Jason.

Jason did as he was told, awkwardly, since he was standing unsupported, and he couldn't see. Naked, he shivered. There was cold stone beneath his feet. Paolo pushed him backwards, up against a chilly metal grille.

"Put your hands above your head."

Jason, half playing along, half in earnest, asked, "And if I don't?"

In answer, he felt a cold metal blade against his throat.

"I'll kill you," Paolo said.

Jason raised his hands. Paolo wrapped rope around the American's wrists, binding them together, tying them to an upright bar of the grille. Jason might have fought back, torn the blindfold off, tried to overpower Paolo, grab the knife, run. He didn't. Instead, he just hung there, naked. Like Saint Sebastian. Like Saint Sebastian with a hard-on.

He heard Paolo spit, felt one, warm, wet hand wrap itself around his cock while the blade, in the other hand, returned to his throat. The guy was crazy, Jason knew, fucking crazy. But it *was* an adventure. And adventure was better than nothing.

Anyway, the rich Roman sure knew about masturbation. His hand had a direct line to Jason's pleasure centers. Even in his fear and uncertainty, Jason felt close to coming. It was as though his dick was disconnected from his mind; it was a feeling he'd had several, no, many times before.

Paolo said something. Something in Latin. "Sorry," Jason said. "I'm lapsed. My Latin's a bit rusty."

The edge of the knife bit into his throat. The Italian leaned close and whispered in his ear.

Jason figured he'd misheard. "What?" he asked.

DeAngelis repeated, "You are the Light of the World."

The knife pulled away from his throat, dropped with an echoing clatter on the stone floor. A large room, then. Where *was* he?

"Where am I?" he asked.

Paolo's hand left his dick. *Put it back!,* part of him wanted to beg.

The blindfold came off.

Jesus, risen in triumph, raised his arm above his head in a muscular gesture that condemned the damned to hell. Saints and martyrs swirled about him. The dead rose from their graves. The damned, dark in sin, were ferried down the River Styx.

Jason blinked. It was Michelangelo's titanic painting of the Last Judgment.

They were in the Sistine Chapel. Jason was tied, naked, to the choir screen of the Sistine Chapel.

"*What...how?*"

"It helps to have money. Rome may not be totally corrupt, but everything can be bought. Everything. And an archbishop who wants his secrets kept is never ungrateful."

"But, Jesus...*the Sistine Chapel?*" For a sudden, giddy moment, Jason almost laughed at the thought of Charlton Heston in a false beard, supine on a scaffold, painting the Sistine ceiling while white gobs of something—paint?— dripped onto his face.

DeAngelis, still fully dressed, sank to his knees, looked up prayerfully at Jason's face, and took the young man's dick into his mouth. As good as Paolo's hand jobs were, his blow jobs were even better.

Take, eat, this is my body, thought Jason, and he felt like giggling again. And he felt like coming. "Wait, wait, wait. Back off," he said. Across the room, some near-naked martyr glared at him.

Paolo's mouth slipped from his dick and moved to his balls. The kneeling Roman nuzzled between Jason's thighs, his tongue moving back toward the young man's hole. Jason spread his feet farther apart, thrust his thighs forward. Paolo shifted around so his tongue could lick Jason's hole. The tip thrust inside him. It felt great, just great.

"Fuck me," said Jason. Across the chapel, Jesus sent the unrepentant to perdition. The fires of hell.

Paolo rose to his feet. He had the knife in one hand again and his dick, sticking through the fly of his expensive trousers, in the other. Sliding the blue steel blade between Jason's tender wrists, he sliced through the rope. Jason's arms were free.

DeAngelis removed his sport coat and laid it on the cold stone floor. Jason noticed the label: Armani. Paolo gestured downward with the knife. Jason lay on his back, mostly on the sport coat, his legs spread, his knees in the air.

Slowly, carefully, Paolo undressed, folding his clothes, piling them neatly next to his supple Italian loafers. When he was naked, big uncut cock sticking stiffly before him, he stared down at the boy lying there, a weird sort of joy on his dark Italian face. He said something else in Latin. This time,

Jason didn't ask for a translation. Paolo dropped to his knees, kneeling between Jason's thighs. Paolo was hairy, which Jason liked, and had a thick, well-muscled body. The kind of body that could do harm.

At last, Jason allowed himself to look at the ceiling. He'd been meaning to see the Sistine Chapel ever since arriving in Rome a week ago. But he'd always found something else to do. Like hanging out on the Spanish Steps. Like going to dinner with a filthy-rich man with a Lamborghini.

And now he lay there naked, the fresco looming above him. Prophets. Angels. Women who looked like men; Michelangelo was a fag, Jason seemed to remember. The coldness of the hard floor seeped through the sport coat. Jason shivered again.

Paolo's hands grabbed Jason's ankles, forcing his legs back and up, up into the air, toward the ceiling, toward heaven.

Remembered scenes, stories from Jason's childhood. The flood, Noah's flood, animals two-by-two. Noah, later, drunk; after saving the world, a guy's entitled to party. David and Goliath, over in the corner, the boy's sword upraised, off with the giant's head. And everywhere prophets, grim and forbidding.

Lying there, looking up, Jason felt Paolo's dick against his hole and idly wondered if the man had a condom on. He stared again at David, the blade's expected thrust.

Paolo spit into his palm, smeared it into Jason.

The serpent, strong and swelling, curled around Eden's tree, Evil with a human face, offering up the fatal fruit.

Paolo's dick pressed into him. Not enough lube, a moment of stabbing pain, then Jason relaxing, taking in the man's flesh. Paolo pulled out, stroked in again, pumping, pumping at him.

The Angel of God, telling Adam to get lost.

The stroking inside him. *It hurts,* he wanted to say. He didn't.

Adam hides his face from the Angel of the Lord.

It hurts.

Paolo slaps Jason's cheek.

Jason thinks of Father D'Onofrio. Back when he was just ten years old, Father D'Onofrio...

It hurts.

The priest's hands...

"Cursed is the ground for your sake..."

Paolo slaps Jason again.

"...and darkness was on the face of the deep."

God stretched his hand out.

Jason thinks of the man in Verona, a middle-aged business-man.

"Fuck me," says Jason.

As the man slept, Jason stole the businessman's wallet and started to creep out of the room.

Adam stretches his hand out.

Paolo grunts into his thrusts. Jason, gaze shifting from the ceiling to the man's face, sees...what?

The man woke up. Jason punched him.

God stretches his hand out.

The man cried.

Jason flails his arms, hands, feels Paolo's knife lying on the floor. Cold steel.

Paolo shoots into Jason's ass.

Hot as flame.

"Take me,"" says Jason.

Their fingers touch.

Their fingers touch.

And in the morning, the museum guard found the American boy on the floor of the Sistine Chapel, tears dried on his cheeks, curled up in a fetal position, lying naked on an Armani jacket, the Hand of God stretched out above his head.

World's Horniest Slackers Caught on Tape

C. Bard Cole

Blue screen: FBI warning-don't duplicate; for home viewing only; for adult audiences who request sexually explicit information for education, entertainment, blah blah blah. Next screen says, All models 18 or older Records on file at 2321 Washington Avenue, New Paltz, NY 12560.

Black screen appears with the words, Generation SeX Productions Presents. Next screen says, World's Horniest Slackers. Cliche sound effect of an anvil being struck adds the words, Caught on Tape, in a bright red diagonal across the screen. One of those rubber-stamp looking fonts. All powerpoint slideshow computer design shit.

Next screen says, Directed by (line break, big letters) The Generation SeX Guy. Next screen says, Starring Petey "Boogs" DiGrasso, Seymour Booty, Dodie Wiles, and introducing Razor.

Video opens with boy sitting on couch. Boy, nineteen to twenty-three, straight brown hair past his chin, plastic armybrat horn-rims, Cramps T-shirt, brown high-water khakis, sockless blue Converse high tops, turned up nose and damp pink lips, features small for his wide-browed face. Couch: your typical poverty-furniture-store brown nubby plaid. Cinder block wall behind it is painted yellow, two posters— one a BMX bike thing, the other Marilyn Manson.

"Is it rolling?" the boy says, looking into the camera and dorkily pushing a clump of hair behind his ears. He rolls his lips inward to moisten them, drops his hands loosely between his knees.

"Okay, what name did you come up with?" says a deeper but still youthful voice behind the camera.

Some smoke-related hacking.

"My first pet, okay, was this cat Petey. My mom's maiden name is DiGrasso. So it's Petey DiGrasso, right?"

"I thought that was the formula for the drag name," says another voice off screen.

"It doesn't make a drag name, though." His eyes dart around the room, and he sits back in the couch, giggling and coughing. His skin looks pasty on video.

"I want to call you Booger. How about that?"

The boy shakes his head. "Man that's gross," he says. "You're gross."

"Okay. Booger."

He fumbles in his pocket for a pack of cigarettes, pulls it out, places one in his mouth. "There's no formula for drag names. They're like Indian names, you have to earn one by your deeds." He produces a lighter from his other pocket.

"Whatcha got there, Boogs?"

The boy holds up the lighter, a miniature oval tank, sports-gear yellow, with a serious looking black handle. "Shit, did I show you this before? It's my crack lighter."

"You're smoking crack now?"

"No man. I got it at this drug store; I thought it was a windproof lighter, but look at the flame." He flicks it, igniting a pointy ice-blue flame. "See, it's for a crack pipe."

Another off screen voice calls out, "Lemme see....Kevin, man, throw that here."

"It's Petey, asshole," the boy says. "Don't say my real name." The camera pans across the room to where three boys are sitting, smoking cigarettes. One of them is on a wooden folding chair drinking a beer, a Red Stripe in its stout little brown bottle. He's cute, a skater type, kind of built, dressed in a black T and baggy denim shorts. The other two are sitting close together on the floor. One's skinny with sandy blond hair cut short on the side but hanging down over his eyebrows in front. Dressed in a red Phillies Blunt shirt, he holds his cigarette like Bette Davis or something. The other boy's got short brown hair, buzz cut, thick set; he's wearing baggy jeans and a black sweatshirt. Maybe he's Latin. He's got a barely discernible goatee thing going on. "Kevin!" the sandy-haired boy repeats insistently.

"It's Booger," the camera guy says. Sandy-haired boy catches the crack lighter. "Now who'd you decide to fuck?" He swings the camera back to Kevin who looks somehow stunned to be caught again.

"Oh shit," he says. "I guess Mike."

A bemused and semi-enthusiastic cry from the other side of the room. The beer-drinking boy hops over the coffee table and into camera range. Close-up of his face. He's got short, bristly hair of indeterminate color, a nose ring, several eyebrow piercings. The camera pulls back and focuses on the black patterns of tribal tattoos showing on both calves below the hem of his jeans shorts.

"Mike, did you pick your porn name?"

He falls to the couch and with a broad smile says "Seymour Booty." He's missing one of his incisors, flicks his red tongue out and laughs. Kevin pats him on the arm, looks across the room, and cracks up.

A derisive snort from the other boys. "Whatever," one of them says. "Hey Kev, take your lighter." The crack lighter sails towards Kevin, bounces off his outstretched hand, and falls into Mike's lap. They reach for it simultaneously, and their hands tangle.

"Wait, man," says Mike, lifting up his leg and grabbing the lighter off the cushion. He sets it on the table next to his beer and the ashtray.

"Tell me why you picked Mike," says the camera guy.

"I don't know," says Kevin. "He's cool and all." Mike shrugs with a trace of pride.

"Do you think he's cute?" the camera guy asks.

"Kinda." He and Mike make eye contact but Kevin looks away quickly. "I like his tattoos," he says finally.

"How many tattoos do you have, Mike?"

Mike looks at Kevin and then at the camera. "Well, you see the ones on my legs," he says, holding his legs up awkwardly, feet in the air. "And I got an armband on this one," he says, pulling up his right sleeve, flexing his arm. "And this one." Lifting his left sleeve he reveals a gothic-lettered tattoo on his deltoid which reads: BETSY.

"Is Betsy your girlfriend?"

"Betsy's my dog, man. I don't have a girlfriend, I'm a fag, remember?"

"Boogs, have you seen Mike's dick yet?" Kevin shakes his head. "Mike, show him your dick."

Mike snorts, leans back, and unzips. He pulls out his limp dick, holding it by a fold of skin. Kevin pointedly looks at it, miming astonishment and shock. Then they look at each other and giggle.

"What do you want him to do to you, Mike?"

Mike shifts position and his limp penis slips back inside his open fly. "I don't know, Rob, it's your fucking movie."

The two off-screen boys start chanting, "Fuck'im, fuck 'im." Mike sticks out his tongue and mimes some pelvic thrusts.

"That's enough from the peanut gallery," says the camera guy.

The off-screen boys boo. "I wanna see somebody get fucked," says the more girly voice.

"You're next, Dodie," says the camera guy, "so I'll keep that in mind. Kevin, why don't you take your clothes off?" Kevin starts untying his sneakers. Mike starts to strip out of his T-shirt. "Not you, Mike. Just Kevin. Stand up, too."

Kevin tilts his head. "Lemme take my shoes off." After he removes his sneakers he stands up, undoes his pants, and lets them drop to the floor, revealing skinny, hairy legs and a cheap pair of boxer shorts, white with a pale blue diamond pattern and kind of see through. "We're really letting the whole porn name bit go to shit today, aren't we?" Kevin says to the camera. He pulls his T-shirt over his head, revealing a bony chest with a kind of indent at his breastbone, two red red nipples with sprouts of dark hair around them. His glasses are now askew on his head.

"Take your shorts off, okay?"

Kevin turns his back to the camera and steps out of his shorts. He has a little ass, hairy in the crack but relatively smooth and pale, except for a prominent zit. When he straightens up again, his boner's flying at half-mast. With a modest gesture he shields it by wrapping his hand around it, holding it against his stomach.

"Don't hold your dick." Kevin lets his hand fall to his side, leaving his boner bobbing out in front of him. "What do you think, Mike?"

Mike lets his mouth hang open in a noiseless laugh. He shrugs. "Nice," Mike says indifferently.

"I want you to pick up his shorts and smell them." After a short hesitation, Mike leans forward and picks Kevin's boxers up off the floor. He holds them up to his nose. "Can you smell his ass on them?"

Mike fumbles with the shorts, trying to find the waistband. He slips them over his head, turns them around some. "Yeah, okay," he says.

"Show me where it smells most like ass. Kevin, don't sit down."

Kevin straightens up again, watching Mike with a doofus grin. Mike makes some exaggerated sniffing noises. "Right here," he says, pointing to a place on the back panel near the middle seam.

"Cool," says the camera guy. "Throw them over here."

Mike pulls the shorts off his head and tosses them off screen. He and Kevin both look at the camera.

"Okay, Mike, now I want you to kneel on the couch—No, the other way, so you can rest your elbows on the arm. Okay." Resting on his knees, Mike hunches forward over the arm of the couch. "Now just undo your belt, push your shorts down. I want you to bare your ass."

Mike lets his shorts down until his white butt comes into view, then leans forward slightly.

"Nice, Mike," yells the more butch of the off-screen boys.

"Fuck you," Mike says.

"Michael, you get fucked a lot?" camera guy asks. Mike nods. "You like it?"

"It depends," he says. "It's okay. Sometimes it hurts."

Kevin's boner is sticking up at a steep angle now.

"Kevin, you get fucked a lot?"

He shakes his head. "Not really."

"Good, because you're a piece of shit," the camera guy says with a surprising sharpness. Kevin's brow folds in bemusement. He takes off his glasses and sets them on the coffee table. "I want you to lay on the couch, on your back— not that way, the other way." Kevin nervously sits down and lays back, his head near Mike's exposed butt. "Okay, Mike, I want you to sit back on his face."

Mike gently lowers himself until his butt's resting over Kevin's head.

The camera zooms in on this, blurring for a moment before refocusing.

"Kevin, I want you to put your tongue in his asshole."

Kevin cranes his neck up, tilting his head back; his chin and pink bottom lip come into view nestled between Mike's buttcheeks. He makes a muffled grunting noise, reaches a hand up to push against Mike's thigh. The camera suddenly points down at the gray shag carpet, the toe of a worn Doc Marten boot in one corner. With a jumpy lunge, it records the edge of the coffee table. "Dodie, can you put this against the wall?" the camera guy says. Rotated horizontally, the camera catches the sandy-haired boy's red shoulder as he slides the coffee table away. The other boy, the sweatshirt boy, is sitting cross-legged on the floor, taking a hit off an orange plastic bong. Bolting upright again, the camera guy's settled behind the other arm of the couch. Naked Kevin's stretched out in front of him, pink tongue squirming around Mike's ass. A pretty clear close-up shows it actually penetrating the sphincter. Mike's bouncing a little bit.

"Is he up there good?"

Mike looks back over his shoulder. "Yeah," he says. "Yeah, it feels nice."

"You can jerk off if you want, Kev."

Kevin takes his right hand off of Mike's left thigh and brings it down to his own dick. He starts pumping it. The camera jerks forward slightly, shooting from a higher angle. The camera guy's left hand suddenly appears on Kevin's leg.

"Why don't you finger your asshole, Kev?" Kevin obediently takes his hand off his dick and, pushing his balls to one side, starts feeling around behind them. "Spread your legs a little bit, let me in there." The camera lurches again, now closer to Mike's butt level. The camera guy's bare knee is now in the picture, at the bottom left corner of the screen between Kevin's feet. "Mike, you can take off your shorts all the way. I want you to sit facing me now."

Mike stands up, his shorts falling from his knees. He looks at the far side of the room, flashing his eyebrows at the other boys. He has a fairly thick dick that curves to the left, and a thick brown bush of pubic hair. He puts one bare knee on the far side of Kevin's head and tries to get back in position.

"Hey, wait," Kevin says, taking both hands to guide him. Mike's balls are resting on Kevin's chin. The tip of his dick brushes against the hem of his T-shirt, leaving a glistening snail trail.

"Yeah, give that to me," the camera guy says in a quiet voice. A flesh-colored dildo, semirealistic, rolls between Kevin's thighs at the bottom of the screen.

Kevin slides out from underneath Mike and sits up. This puts him very close to the camera, his face fills the screen. His mouth looks puffy, his upper lip has reddened. "Kev, do you usually kiss boys when you have sex with them?"

Kevin nods. "Yeah." His eyes dart around waiting for an instruction logically connected to that question. It doesn't come.

"Get on your hands and knees."

Kevin's ass is now pointing back at Mike. Mike catches the dildo as it's tossed to him. The camera's mostly showing Kevin's back, his head's now off screen. Mike puts the head of the dildo in his mouth, chomping down on it with his teeth showing.

"Don't fucking put puncture marks on that thing," the camera guy says crossly. "Besides, you don't know where it's been. Hand him the KY," he adds in a whisper. The sweatshirt-wearing boy appears briefly to hand Mike a tube of lubricant.

Mike uncaps the tube of lube and squeezes some onto the head of the dildo. "Shit," he says, as some drops on the couch.

He puts down the tube and scoops up the errant blob, wiping it in Kevin's crack.

His head still out of frame, Kevin bumps the camera with his shoulder, making a lip-smacking sound, and says, "That's cold!"

"You keep sucking that," says the camera guy with a quiet urgency.

Mike looks to a place slightly below the camera, pauses, and then rubs around Kevin's ass with his thumb. He looks down intently as he slides his thumb in and out of Kevin's asshole. This isn't actually showing, but you can tell what he's doing. He's holding the dildo in his left hand, against Kevin's hip.

"How many guys have fucked you, Mike?" the camera guy asks.

Mike looks up. "Mmm," he says. "Three or four."

"How many guys have you fucked?"

"Me?" Mike says, pointing to himself.

"Why don't you take off your T-shirt?"

Mike puts the dildo down between Kevin's legs and pulls his shirt over his head. His torso is skinny but his pecs are bigger than Kevin's, with brownish nipples and a scant streak of hair at the center that matches the sparser patch on his stomach.

"I guess I've fucked, like...two."

"You used to fuck Dodie, right?"

Mike nods, sticking his finger in Kevin's asshole. "Yeah, we both did. I mean, sometimes I fucked him and sometimes he fucked me." Kevin's shoulder bumps the camera again, and the camera guy gasps. The camera tilts down awkwardly—camera guy's got his dick out, and Kevin's nursing on it. Quickly the camera points back at Mike.

"So you and Dodie don't fuck any more?" Mike shakes his head dismissively. He squeezes some more lube out onto the dildo and, squinting, pushes the head into Kevin's ass crack. Kevin lets out a wet-mouthed gasp; his shoulders tense.

"Why don't you and Dodie fuck any more?"

Mike is seriously studying his dildo insertion. "Um," he says. "It was a while ago, we were a lot younger. He's my friend. We don't like to do it anymore."

The dildo finds its mark. Mike slides a small length of it in and out. Kevin's shoulders are hunched up. "That's not hurting you, is it?" the camera guy says quietly.

"Mike gave me crabs," says the boy off screen. Mike turns to give him a dirty look.

"Shut up, you fag," he says. He bites his lip as he works the dildo around in Kevin's ass. "Dodie thinks he's bi, but he's really a faggot."

"You're the faggot, faggot," the sandy-haired boy says in an unfortunate whiny tone of voice. The shot's interrupted by a bad edit with a millisecond flash of black, a garbled comment from one of the boys. The sandy-haired boy and the sweatshirt boy are sitting against the wall, fully dressed, with their dicks out. Only the sandy-haired boy's dick is hard. He absent-mindedly tugs on it while saying, "And she was letting us crash with her for a couple days. I knew she wanted to have sex with me but I didn't want to. And Mike and I would kiss and shit, you know, and we ended up on her couch in my sleeping bag fooling around and shit. She was all like, you guys are so hot, it totally gets me all wet thinking about you making out and shit."

Close up: the sandy-haired boy has kind of a big nose, freckles, chapped-looking lips. His bottom lip splits prettily in the middle. His eyes are green and slightly bloodshot. He's got a zit by his right nostril.

Sweatshirt boy laughs, shaking his head.

"You think that's funny," camera guy says.

"She wouldn't have been that bad to fuck," sweatshirt boy says.

"Bullshit," says the sandy-haired boy. "She was a total fucking skank."

"So you're our token straight boy today?"

Sweatshirt boy rubs his chin with his hand. Close up: sweatshirt boy is indistinctly something, Latin or middle-eastern or maybe just a Jewish boy with a good tan. He's got a broad, squarish jaw and heavy eyebrows. Long, long eyelashes over brown eyes. His goatee almost passes as teenage chin fuzz, but you can tell it's carefully clipped that way.

"I've sucked your dick, man," says the sandy-haired boy off screen.

"You really wanted to," says sweatshirt boy, looking straight into the camera.

The camera pulls back. "You came and shit," says the sandy-haired boy. He stops tugging on his dick, licks his fingers. "You can't see his dick without wanting to suck it, man. Frank's got this total donkey dick."

"Dodie, shut up." Sweatshirt boy shifts uneasily. "Bitch-ass queen."

"I mean when it's hard," the sandy-haired boy says.

"Then get it hard already," camera guy says. Now the camera's facing the couch dead on. Mike's fucking Kevin missionary style, Kevin's legs wrapped around his back. They're sucking face really hard. A couple times Kevin turns his head and sighs loudly, pants sharpening into little cries. "Oh, fuck," he says. "Oh fuck, oh fuck." Mike slurps along his neck or licks at his ear. The sound of their moist skin slapping together gets increasingly loud. Mike's breathing heavy; his thighs are taut and his clenching buttocks look fleshy and round. He leans back on his haunches, leaving Kevin sprawled across his lap. He spits in his hand to jerk Kevin off. Kevin's pretty close to coming, obviously, squeezing Mike between his thighs. As his vocalizations become linguistically incoherent, Kevin seizes one of his nipples between his fingers and grimaces.

The camera guy enthusiastically yelps, "Oh yeah!" as Mike strokes Kevin's dick to a series of frothy spurts, two long ones that splatter Kevin's chest and three or four shorter ones that drip down Mike's knuckles and cling to Kevin's pubic hair. "Oh, that's really nice," he says.

As Mike lays down on top of Kevin again and starts to hump some more, the camera guy wanders around to get a good shot of Mike's butt. Kevin hooks his ankles together, and he and Mike French kiss sloppily, their tongues wildly lapping in the general vicinity of their mouths. Their semen-covered bellies smack together with a fartlike slurping sound.

"This is all about your ass, Mike," the camera guy says. "You have a fucking awesome ass."

Mike turns his head for a second. "Thanks a lot, Rob."

"Don't stop because of me."

The camera zooms in to the penetration shot. Seen between Mike's legs, Kevin's butt looks flat and featureless, his tailbone showing, asshole stretched around Mike's rubber-clad cock. Mike's asshole, a tiny puckered slot masked by a down of light-catching hairs, is at the center of the screen. "Shit," says the camera guy.

Kevin lets out an "Ow" or two.

"Hold on," Mike whispers to him. "Hold on, I'm gonna come soon."

"Don't pull out, Mike. Go ahead, come in his ass."

Mike grimaces and lets out a predictable series of breathy moans, climaxing in some sinusy high-pitched chirps.

Camera swings around the room. Sweatshirt boy's down to his undershirt and boxers, sandy-haired Dodie's laying across his lap, sucking his dick. Dodie's bare assed. "Let's see," camera guy says. Dodie raises his head to show off Sweatshirt boy's big dick. He licks at its head. Sweatshirt boy's smoking a cigarette like it doesn't matter to him at all.

"That's nice, right?" Dodie asks, playing with Sweatshirt boy's hard-on. He gulps it down, gags when he tries to deep throat it. He raises his head again, wipes his lips. "Shit."

A couple seconds of black. Camera shows Kevin sitting cross-legged on the couch, Mike sitting on one leg, dangling the other off the edge. Kevin watches expectantly as Mike carefully slides the condom off his softening dick. When he gets it off, the semen-filled tip dangling like an underfilled water balloon, Mike waves it towards the camera like a trophy. He brings it to his lips like he's going to slurp it down, looking into the camera and smiling self-consciously. Then he pushes Kevin backwards and empties the condom down Kevin's chest, rubbing it around. Mike brings his finger to his mouth and licks, making a disgusted face. "Tastes like fucking latex," he says, laughing.

"Did you like that?" the camera guy says. Mike nods. "Kevin, how'd you like getting your ass reamed?"

Kevin sighs, looking at the ceiling. "I could get into it."

"Kevin, are you a whore?"

Kevin rolls his eyes and shoots the camera guy the finger.

Another glitchy edit. On the couch, Sweatshirt boy and Dodie and Kevin are naked in a three way. Sweatshirt boy's nailing Kevin in the ass, doggie style. Kevin's sucking Dodie's dick. Dodie's holding Kevin's hair at the nape of his neck, keeping his face clear for the camera. Sweatshirt boy's knuckles are white, he's leaving red fingerprints on Kevin's hips. You can't really see how big his dick is, but Kevin looks pained, keeps letting Dodie's dick pop out of his mouth. Dodie's guiding it back in with his hand, muttering, "Come on, come on." He's looking rather intently, slack jawed, at Kevin's ass getting fucked.

"Kevin, come on," says camera guy. Dodie looks towards the camera. Kevin starts to stand awkwardly, leaning forward and gasping when Sweatshirt boy's dick pops out his asshole. Kevin stumbles off screen. Dodie takes his place, getting down on his hands and knees, reaching between his legs to grab hold of Sweatshirt boy's dick. Sweatshirt boy stares at the camera. Dodie backs himself onto Sweatshirt boy's dick.

"Ew," says Mike, off camera. "Change the fucking rubber, dude."

Sweatshirt boy's already pumping away, though, eyes closed. He slides his hands up to Dodie's shoulders, pressing down and throwing his weight on top of the smaller boy. Dodie's making a lot of noise, Dodie's saying "Ow," and "Shit" and "Fuck yeah" and "Come on, Frank."

Sweatshirt boy keeps his eyes closed or looks straight down at his dick with Dodie writhing on it.

"Reach around," camera guy says. "Reach around!"

Kevin's voice, off screen, barely audible: "Mike, are my smokes over there?" Pause. "No, I put them on the table." Pause. "Well, give it to me."

Sweatshirt boy clasps Dodie across the chest, wildly humping, his eyes tranquilly shut. His arms pinned to his side, Dodie gropes for his own dick. He wriggles his left arm free, grabs one of Sweatshirt boy's hands and guides it to his cock. He's basically jerking himself off, holding Sweatshirt boy's hand in place.

Bad edit. Dodie sitting on couch, masturbating with his eyes closed. Sweatshirt boy sitting next to him, his big hard-on draped across his stomach. Dodie says, "Here it comes," and a thick clot of semen starts dribbling out his cock and down his clenched fist.

Bad edit. Sweatshirt boy's dick popping out of Dodie's mouth, spurting. Spooge hits Dodie on the cheek and ear, gets in his bangs. Dodie does this combination yawn-smile thing, gingerly wipes his face, wipes some of the semen onto Sweatshirt boy's stomach.

"Nice," says camera guy as Dodie rolls over, pushes Sweatshirt boy's leg away. "Maybe next time you'll get fucked." Sweatshirt boy smiles and shakes his head. "You won't get fucked for me?" camera guy asks. "Aw, come on." Sweatshirt boy keeps shaking his head no. Dodie stands up, his cock bobbing around, lets out a wide-mouthed sigh, and walks bowlegged past the camera. His blurry hip blocks one side of the screen.

"Fuck," he's saying, rubbing his butt and holding it out funny. "Aaugh!" he cries in exaggerated anguish. "My aaaass. Jesus fuck, Frank." He flops back toward the couch. Sweatshirt boy covers his dick with his hand, pushes Dodie away, smiling.

A neater fade-to-black edit precedes the next scene. Mike's voice saying, "This button here?" Kevin's put his glasses back on, and his boxer shorts too, part of his cock visible through the gaping fly. Kevin's arm's draped around the shoulder of a guy with Gothy black hair and blue eyes, reasonably cute despite the reddish acne scars in the hollow of his cheeks. The guy is wearing gray-fleece shorts and a brown T-shirt that says "Fuck," script in an oval just like the Ford logo.

"Yeah, the green one," the guy says. He's the camera guy. Rob. Same voice we've been hearing. "Yeah, you got it, the light's on."

"Alright, um...." Mike says. "Did you come?"

Kevin smirks. Camera guy says, "No." Kevin shoves him. "No, I mean I got pretty wet. Look." He arches his back and pulls a section of his shorts taut, showing off a quarter-size dark spot wet with precum. "I'm wearing underwear and everything. That's what's soaked through."

Mike goes "Hmmm."

Kevin picks a pack of cigarettes off the floor. "Where's my lighter?" he says, putting a cigarette in his mouth. He digs in the couch cushions and finds a pack of matches. "Go ahead, ask him," he says to Mike, somewhat impatiently. He lights his cigarette.

"Why do you make movies of other guys fucking your boyfriend?"

Camera guy picks up Kevin's hand and moves it to his lap. Kevin blows out a plume of smoke. "Because he's a pervert," Kevin says, taking his hand back.

"Because I think he's beautiful," Rob says, "and I like to watch it."

Mike lets out a blank stoner's laugh. "I fucked your boyfriend, man."

Rob nods. "Yeah. I remember. I remember seeing that somewhere."

Mike turns the camera to the far wall. Dodie and Sweatshirt boy, back in their underpants, are looking back and forth from the camera to the monitor. The monitor is showing Dodie and Sweatshirt boy looking back and forth from the camera to their own images on a tinier monitor. They nod and smile, the tinier boys nod and smile, to infinity.

Fade to black. Screen says, The End.

Screen says, Copyright 1997 Generation SeX Productions.

Screen says, Also from Generation SeX.

Sugarloaf Snowboard Sex.

Twenty seconds of two boys with tattoos fucking a skinny girl with tattoos in a motel room. One boy ejaculates on the girl's stomach while the other boy's fucking her.

Daytona Horn Dogs.

Another motel room. A boy with long blond hair fucks the same skinny tattooed girl while she blows a stocky frat-boy type. Close-up of him fucking her ass. Next shot two naked white boys with gutterpunk dreads struggling to stick their dicks in frat-boy's mouth.

Mardi Gras Dick Bandit.

A series of quick, poorly exposed takes of drunk boys flashing their dicks for the camera in the French Quarter. Kevin sucking some really cute Latin boy's dick in a hotel room while the skinny tattooed girl, dressed in panties and bra, smokes a cigarette. Rob, bare assed, sucking some boy off in the bathroom.

Screen says, Coming Spring '00.

Homopalooza.

Kids dancing at a concert. Camera bouncing in the close quarters of a camper van. Three naked long-haired boys getting stoned in van. Boy in Phish T-shirt getting fucked from behind. Kevin peeing in the weeds by the side of a road.

Black screen.

Snow.

White Bitch Faggot

Tom Woolley

"Chulito" and "El Burro" are naked. Each stripped away their minimal clothing earlier in the scene setup. They are about to change into bathing suits when suddenly "Macho," who enters from who-knows-where, effectively redirects their motivation via the introduction of his hard penis into the frame. I think they are supposed to be in high school and on the swim team, though this seems too Caucasian a plot.

Macho walks over and sits on a bar stool, which, despite making no sense in a prop continuity way, is in the locker room with them. Except for his brand new Nike Air Max sneakers, Macho is naked like the other guys. He lifts one of his feet so that it rests on the topmost rung of the two-rung stool. The other is flat on the floor.

He places his left hand on the raised knee, which is shiny with cocoa butter or some other tropical de-ashing grease, and his right hand goes for his dick. He pinches the foreskin between fingers whose nails are miraculously clean. I thought they would be sort of dirty. Hoped they would be. He pulls his dickskin to show its length. The head disappears inside it. His lower back rounds as he cantilevers himself in an effort to push his pelvis under and upwards for presentation's sake. His position is perilous but inviting.

Focusing deep into the V of his crotch, I realize I can't see even a sliver of his asshole. It isn't so much that he is intentionally attempting to obscure his crack as much as it is naturally hidden behind his balls. His scrotum is slack. If it hadn't come to rest on the black vinyl seat of the stool, they would hang low. I want to see his asshole. I think the director should have made him show it.

Macho smiles at the camera. He is a charmingly innocent-looking whore. I think about the Mexicans who used to gather in groups along the streets of Los Angeles waiting for some contractor or another to pick them up for a day's labor. Maybe they would have showed me their assholes.

Chulito says something. I don't know what it means. I don't speak Spanish except for *Nuestra Seniora de Guadeloupe* which isn't really Spanish because *Nuestra* and *Seniora* and *de Guadeloupe* aren't Spanish words you can use during a Latin Scrabble game or anything like that. Then, *Chupa mi verga.* When Macho says it, I get its meaning, as Chulito or El Burro, one or the other, kneels to take Macho's brown wiener into one or the other of their mouths. I close my eyes. Macho's hairless straight-boy ghetto dick is in my mouth, too. For the millisecond it takes for the image to come and go, anyway.

Chupa mi verga. Just a fantasy....

PRM Light-skinned triplets, 17 y.o. gangbangers, fresh from juvenile detention, like to fuck each other while our mom's boyfriend watches the three of us and jacks his beer can dick. Looking for other roughnecks and homeboys to screw our identical Rican holes in a blistering frenzy of condom-free sex. Oh, yeah, also into kickin' it on the down lo. No fats, femmes, or white bitch faggots. Peace

It must be Chulito sucking Macho. El Burro (which I recognize from the Flying Nun television show as meaning the donkey, because that is what Sally Fields as the nun rode and what Carlos, the rich city nightclub owner, called it when he asked, "Sister, how did you get to the nightclub so quickly on El Burro?") is fully erect, and huge. Plus the addition of *ito* (as in Chulito) to any name means small, like burrito which I guess is small sandwich, not to mention that big dicks are never suck active.

So, anyway, Donkey Dick sidles up to Macho and stands beside him. Donkey's hip is against Macho's raised knee. I am certain the temperature at point of contact is about three thousand degrees. It's a stunning three-shot which makes me shudder: Chulito's head (with voice-over sucking noises), Macho from the knee up, and Donkey Dick from cock to shoulders. They left out his head. It's not so important.

As Chulito sucks (not as feverishly as the voice-over sucking noises would have you believe), Donkey Dick strokes himself. His penis arcs away from its root so that the tip, like a horn, points back to a place on his abdomen well above his belly button. The motion of his hand disturbs it less than that same motion would disturb a white dick. It is the skin, the extra skin he has. It glides up and down the darkening shaft. It doesn't jerk it or jack it or yank it. It is the lazy sensuality of another kind of penis.

Macho leans to his right somewhat, a lateral bend which, because of his youth, does not cause a fat roll to appear. Donkey Dick pushes his penis, so red now it is nearly black, towards Macho's mouth. It enters, sort of. Macho is struggling with it. Not really sucking it, or licking it, but performing something of a nibble. Nibble-ito. It looks like Macho hates that cock. Like he is tasting poop. I think it looks somewhat more edible. Brown sugah, I think, embarrassed at my own lack of ingenuity as that phrase comes to me. Chupa mi brown sugah verga you white cracker bastard. That's what Donkey says to me. And I do.

Chupah mi brown sugah verga you piece of shit pink-dicked cracker mother fucker. His words are like a song to me which he keeps singing... flat-assed chicken-head Nuyorican-loving pussy-hole maricone. His ejaculate releases in such a forceful and continuous stream I think he must be pissing in my mouth until the coagulated density of the liquid registers.

Just a fantasy....

GM, 23 y.o. Latino w/chiseled features, soft perfect skin, huge wet lips, deep brown eyes, muscular body with tiny waist, ripped abs, huge hairless tits with hot pink quarter-sized nipples, a fat fat fat hot-as-shit ass shaped like a basketball, a 14-foot cock, foreskin to my feet and nuts so big I need a whole separate pair of underwear just for them, looking for any one of any age and any size except white bitch faggots.

...because no white bitch faggot like me gets to suck hot Latino dick like that in the real world.

Excerpt from *Massage*
Henry Flesh

Randy, the central character of Massage, *is a thirty-two-year-old erotic masseur involved in an intense relationship with one of his clients, Graham Mason, a middle-aged, renowned novelist dying of an unnamed, wasting disease. Randy is drawn in by Graham's overpowering presence, fascinated by his fame and experiences, and tantalized by what little he knows of Graham's dead lover, Dennis Crawley, of whom Graham refuses to speak. In this excerpt, Randy is high on speed and, for the first time ever, alone in Graham's apartment. Randy does not expect him to return soon.*

Naked, Randy remained on the couch for nearly an hour, scarcely aware of time passing but acutely conscious of the apartment's murky gloom and of distant voices floating up from the street. The walls of the room appeared to be spinning into tiny waves. He found this strangely soothing.

A draft caressed his skin. He glanced behind him at the Hockney sketch of Dennis Crawley; Dennis's lips were fixed in a half smile. Searching for Graham's bottle of Dexedrine,

Randy turned away. On the table beside the couch he saw a photograph of Dennis in a bathing suit. He looked astonishingly beautiful, his hair damp against his brow, his chest lightly muscled, smooth and pale. Here, too, he was smiling halfheartedly, his expression compelling, a mystery.

The draft breezed past Randy. Shivering, he found the pill bottle, twisted it open, and tapped out a Dexedrine. He threw the pill into his mouth and sat still, his arms pressed against his chest. He decided he needed a drink. He waited a few seconds, then slowly rose to his feet. Proceeding carefully, he walked to the kitchen.

He switched on the fluorescent light, raising a hand to his eyes to shield them from its glare, and stood in the doorway, wobbly, adapting to the brightness. Once his eyes had adjusted and his equilibrium returned, he looked toward the kitchen sink and saw a half-filled bottle of Bombay Gin surrounded by half a dozen empty bottles lying on their sides and many used glasses. He moved to the sink and picked up a glass. There was a trace of clear liquid at the bottom, a dead fly floating on top. He turned on the faucet to rinse it out, seeing as he did a pile of dirty dishes in the sink, one caked with a moldy red sauce. A cockroach scurried across it. He ran the glass under hot water, and the sauce slithered apart. Mold slid down toward the drain, taking the cockroach with it. He watched, gripped by the insect's struggle, then filled the glass with gin and took a fast slug. After switching off the light, he returned to the living room.

He stood by the Hockney sketch, holding his drink, probing Dennis's face. He could feel the speed he'd taken earlier, joining the gin as it eased its way into his depths. Graham'll be back soon, he thought. He stared at Dennis's tenuous smile, enigmatic in the faint light. He wanted to know what he'd felt when he was with Graham, to learn how he'd lived his life.

Then he recalled the book he'd seen on his last visit, the one he'd thought was Graham's diary. It had been out in the open, conspicuous on the bedside table in Graham's bedroom. He wondered if it was still there. He wavered, his eyes on Dennis's face. At last, clutching his glass and cigarettes, he hurried to the bedroom.

The room was even more disorderly than it had been the last time he was here, blankets and dirty sheets tossed about, joining the clothing, papers, and used tissues on the floor. There was a stale odor in the air, not quite foul. He felt the draft. Chilly, he continued to the bedside table.

The book was gone, its absence making a framed photograph achingly prominent. He slumped onto the bed, placing his glass and cigarettes on the table, and studied the photo, one of Dennis at a club, flushed and laughing as he headed into a huge, strobe-lit crowd on a dance floor. Randy wondered when this had been taken and where.

He gulped some gin, then looked around him. He knew the diary had to be somewhere; Graham couldn't have thrown it out. Noticing a chest of drawers by a wall, he jumped to his feet and darted to it. He yanked the top drawer open and gazed inside, but saw only a mass of papers: bills, scribbled notes, a few prescriptions, and a manuscript. He tried the other two drawers. Again nothing, just sweaters and shirts in one, socks and underwear in the other. Turning around, he stared at the debris on the floor, searching. He returned to the bedside table, grabbed his gin, and finished it, then peered in front of him, sucking in air. There was a closet at the far end of the room. He rushed to it.

He paused by the closet's door before cracking it open. It was dark inside, but he could tell that the closet was spacious. A chain cord dangled from the ceiling. He pulled on it, and the overhead light came on. Hanging in front of him was an array of clothing unlike anything he had ever seen Graham wear: at least a dozen pairs of jeans, most expensive looking, a few worn and frayed; long shirts, some black, some white, others brightly colored or checked, all partially rolled up at the sleeves; five leather jackets, each appearing new; burnished black-leather pants. Randy was sure these clothes had belonged to Dennis. He moved inside.

He ran a hand across a pair of black jeans, fondling the denim, and raised the label on its back toward the light. It read Fiorucci. He drew the pants from their hanger and held them to his groin, then slid them on. They were tight—skintight, the way they were supposed to be, he knew. He edged forward, becoming erect, aware of the fabric of the pants rubbing against him. His eyes scanned the shirts and settled on a turquoise one, the most beautiful shirt he had ever seen. He took it from the hanger and held it to his face, sniffing it, convinced he could detect a trace of cologne on its collar. He slipped into it, savoring the feel of the soft material on his skin, and found that it fit perfectly. One shoulder fell down over his upper arm. He remembered that the shoulders of certain shirts worn in the early eighties had done this. As he tucked in the shirttail, his hand brushed his erection.

He returned to the bed and sat for an instant, then abruptly rose and raced back to the chest of drawers. He pulled the top drawer open. His eyes settled on the manuscript inside. *After Death,* he read, "by Graham Mason." He'd never before seen this title. This is Graham's new book, he thought. He touched the top page and let his hand rest there, stroking the paper. He finally gripped the manuscript and lifted it to him. He was astonished by how much of it there was.

Suddenly he saw from a corner of his eye something in the drawer that had been hidden under the manuscript—that book, the one he'd suspected was Graham's diary. In one brisk motion, he dropped the manuscript on top of the chest of drawers, leaned over, and scooped the book up. He sped to the bed with it and stretched out, then turned to the first page.

Before him was a full-page, black-and-white photograph of Graham and Dennis. This was a photo album, not a diary. It was leather bound and thick and did look like a lot of old journals he'd seen in period films. Even so, he couldn't understand how he had been so mistaken.

He examined the picture beneath its plastic sheathing. Dennis was dressed in a leather jacket and checkered pants and was slightly hunched over, his expressionless eyes veering off to his right. A mid-thirtyish Graham, more formally attired in a jacket and tie, stood beside him, an arm flung across Dennis's shoulder, his smile cold and effete, derisive. Randy could see other people in the room, women in glittering gowns, men in tuxedos, a few in leather. Abstract paintings were on the white wall behind them. He decided this was an opening and tried to imagine what it had been like.

There were four photographs on the spread that followed, all of a dinner party. Their colors were faded, so that they appeared older than the photo on the previous page. Graham was seated at the head of the table and was beaming in every shot. He looked as if he were in his late twenties here, fit and healthy, his thick, dark hair impeccably styled. There were three others at the table, two women and a man, and a birthday cake in the center. The women were dressed in colorful jumpsuits, the men in bright dinner jackets and ruffled shirts. Everyone was laughing. Randy was certain, because of the bottles of wine and hash pipes near them, that they were high. He recognized no one besides Graham at first, although he felt as if he should. He was sure these others had been famous; all of Graham's friends seemed to be.

Just then, in the background of the photo at the bottom of the right-hand page, almost hidden in the shadows, he noticed Dennis. He was much younger than the other guests, probably around seventeen, and was standing discreetly to the side, in the distance behind the table, looking to his right, downward, shyly. His skin was tanned and his hair long, falling past his shoulders, bleached from the sun.

Randy stared at the photograph, amazed that this self-effacing youth was the same person as the apparently confident Dennis he'd seen in other pictures. For a second the walls of the room seemed to move toward him. He focused his vision, then turned back to the first page, again noting Graham's chilly smile and Dennis's wayward eyes, which, dull and blank as they were, appeared bored by the scene around him. He returned to the photos of the dinner party. Dennis's diffident figure looked like a ghost's. Clinging tightly to the edge of the album, he turned the page.

In the next four pictures, Dennis was lying on a bed in his underpants. Randy took in the fine hair on his legs, then his face. He was pouting—seductively, Randy thought. Erect, he felt his eyes wander down to Dennis's crotch. He allowed them to rest there for a moment. Then he moved on.

He flitted through the book quickly, in a trance, glancing briefly at each photo, thrilled by the fact that he was looking at the past. Apart from the picture on the first page, the album seemed to be laid out in chronological order, and he could see how Graham and Dennis changed in telling ways from page to page. Dennis's hair became shorter and darker, Graham's sprinkled with gray. The ruffled shirts and bright jackets of the early pictures were replaced by tight T-shirts and pants, army-and-navy surplus items, combat boots and leather. Later, they wore clothes that Randy remembered from his early days in New York, jackets with wide lapels and sleeves, black shoes with polished toes, thin ties and thinner belts, square boxy shirts and suspenders. But the glamour of their lives was constant, Randy felt, the clubs, parties, openings, and dinners consistently alluring, their world charmed.

Three-quarters of the way through, he came to a photo-graph much like the one on the first page. It was in color this time, but was apparently taken at the same event, for Graham and Dennis were standing in that same crowded room, and from what Randy could make out, the people surrounding them were identical. This picture, however, was blurry, and Dennis and Graham's faces were maddeningly indistinct. Randy turned back to the first page, then started to browse through the album again, carefully this time, probing their expressions in each picture, realizing there was something he'd missed before, more subtle than their hairstyles and clothing, something he found hard to pin down.

For one thing, he could perceive a burgeoning confidence in Dennis as the album progressed. In a print that came just after the ones of him in his underpants, it was evident that he had grown more at ease in Graham's world. His hair had been cut, styled like Graham's, parted to the side so that it fell down over his forehead, and he was dressed in black-leather pants and a dark shirt, chatting with friends at a party, laughing and obvi-ously happy. The next few pages contained comparable photos: Dennis in elaborate outfits, strutting across a gallery, seated at a formal dinner, dancing at a club. Randy was awed by the exuberance of his eyes and by the huge smile that was always on his face. He could feel himself smiling back at him.

A picture near the middle of the album made him stop. Here Graham and Dennis were on the couch in the living room, a dozen glasses on the table beside them. Randy was certain there had been some sort of party going on. What grabbed his attention was the unmistakable anger he saw on Graham's face, a threatening gleam in his eyes that made Randy squirm. He was glaring off to his right, away from Dennis, and his hands were on his knees, locked on the kneecaps. He seemed to be trying to restrain himself. Dennis was glancing at him cautiously, and his eyes were downcast.

In the photos immediately following this one, they were still on the couch, but this time it was Dennis glaring at Graham, who was bleary-eyed here and clearly inebriated. Dennis's posture was upright and stiff, and Graham had wrinkled his brow so that he looked pained and disturbed. Randy wondered what had been going on, if Graham and Dennis had argued, and if so, why.

He moved on, then, several pages later, was struck by two shots that came just after the point where he'd stopped before, both shots on the same page. In the top one, Graham and two burly men, unfamiliar to Randy, were dressed completely in leather. Dennis was on the floor by Graham's side, crouched on his hands and knees, nude save for a leather jock strap and a dog collar around his neck, a chain leash attached to it. He was looking at the floor, his face hidden. Beside him, Graham was gripping the leash and grinning—sneering, Randy decided. He wondered what Dennis had been thinking.

The picture directly below this one was nearly as intriguing. Here Graham was lying fully clothed on the couch. His shirttail was out and his eyes closed, his mouth hanging open. Evidently he had passed out. A shadow, the photographer's, fell across his body. That must be Dennis, Randy thought. He found it odd that he had taken such a shot and tried to envision what had prompted him to do so.

He returned to the photograph above this, moving his eyes from the leash to Dennis's thighs, noting how strong they looked. He slid a hand under his pants toward his groin and let his eyes stray down Dennis's leg. Just above the calf, he saw a distinct mark, a purplish bruise. He gazed at it for several seconds, then, with a shock, realized it was a lesion.

He hurried on, hoping to erase this image from his mind. But shortly thereafter, in pictures that followed, he discerned a change in Dennis's complexion and overall aspect, an alteration that, slight at first, was more apparent on every page.

Dennis was getting thinner and paler, his skin taut around his cheekbones, his eyes hollow. His flamboyant outfits and leather gear, so prominent in earlier pictures, were gone, his clothing now restricted to old T-shirts and jeans. There was also a gravity in his expression, a weight there totally unlike the uninhibited demeanor he'd displayed before. Randy perused each photo assiduously, his stomach fluttering.

Near the end of the album were several shots of Dennis, painfully thin, sitting at a desk and writing. In the last of them, Graham stood by his side, leaning against the desk. He looked disheveled and intoxicated and was laughing, as if at Dennis. Frowning, Dennis appeared annoyed or possibly distraught. Randy remembered the stories he'd heard, how Dennis had started writing just when Graham had stopped. He couldn't imagine what had happened.

He saw only one more photo after this one, of Dennis, once again in leather, heading toward the apartment's front door, his head turned as he lifted an arm, waving over his shoulder, his eyes lowered, the set of his face rigid. His leather pants were loose around his hips, and his skin was pasty. He looked completely emaciated. Randy was startled by this image, seeing Dennis so ill, leaving the apartment, wearing the sort of outfit he seemed to have discarded pages before. He found it hard to take his eyes off him.

The next few spreads were empty. He flipped past them, ready to go through the album yet again, to study it even more carefully. But then, on the page just before the last one, under the plastic sheathing, he saw a manila envelope. He thrust a hand under the plastic, grabbed the envelope, and opened it quickly. There was a photograph inside.

He held this in front of him, his hands trembling, staring at a black-and-white glossy of Dennis, nude, strapped to a chair in Graham's living room, ropes drawn tight across his wasting body, his mouth gagged. His feet were tied together, his hands behind his back. His eyes were closed. He almost looked dead. Despite the gag in his mouth, he was smiling. And he was erect.

At that moment, a voice booming above Randy shattered the silence of the room: "What the fuck do you think you're doing?"

Randy twisted around and saw Graham by the door, rocking from side to side, his arms stretched out toward him, his clothing rumpled, his makeup smeared. He reeked of alcohol. Randy froze.

Graham stood weaving, glowering at Randy and breathing rapidly. Then he bolted up to him and whisked the photo from his hand. "Fucking cunt!" he screamed. He raised an arm and forcefully slapped Randy's face.

Randy pulled away, stunned, his head ringing. He lifted his hands to his chest and attempted to cover the turquoise shirt.

Seeing this, Graham cried, "Take it off, you little shit! Take it off right now! Christ, how dare you!"

Randy could not stir. Dazed, he tried to think of something to say. "Why...why are you here?" he managed to ask.

"What?" Graham moved back, squinting his eyes, as if distracted. "Why, that cunt Denise..." He stopped. Then, with a snarl, "What do you mean, why am I here? It's my fucking apartment!" He leaned over and gripped the front of the shirt Randy was wearing. "I said take that fucking thing off!"

Shaking, Randy unbuttoned the shirt and removed it. He threw it beside him on the bed.

"Everything!" Graham roared. He began to cough with an alarming force, his face turning red, then fell on his side next to Randy, curling into a ball. "God," he moaned.

Randy's vision started to blur. The room was spinning. He wanted a drink.

Graham lay curled beside him, coughing. His fit eased, and he sat up, taking hold of Randy's thigh, grasping the jeans he had on. "Take them off!" he shouted. "Get out! Go!" He pushed at Randy's leg.

Randy, quivering, stood and unfastened the pants. He felt dizzy.

His breathing labored, Graham stared at the photograph, which was still in his hand. "What a fucking sneak you are!" he gasped. "I can't believe you did this to me." He glared at Randy and cried, "Come on, take those fucking things off!"

Randy slid the jeans down his legs, then stood still. Everything was spinning around him.

Graham looked at the photo, silent. Wary, Randy watched him, afraid to budge. He thought he was going to faint.

Graham raised his head. "Well, what are you waiting for? Aren't you going?" Although his tone was still angry, his voice was lower.

"Please, I...I didn't mean..." Randy clutched at his chest. "I just wanted to know..."

"What?" Graham kept his eyes on him, his gaze deliberate. He peered down at the photograph in his hand, then back up at Randy, exploring his body. Suddenly he smiled. Then he giggled.

Randy felt himself flushing. The spinning stopped.

"Oh, right," Graham said, his tone softening. He seemed amused yet singularly intrigued. Still smiling, he lifted a hand to his chin. "You want to know about Dennis."

Hearing Dennis's name made Randy flush even more. It sounded strange, jolting, coming from Graham.

"But why, baby?" Graham's voice was now almost gentle. "Why are you so interested in him?" He narrowed his eyes. "Do you feel like you've been there, too?"

"I...I..." Randy looked down at the floor.

Graham glanced at the photo, then laid it beside him. He patted the mattress. "Come on, let's talk. Sit down."

Randy hesitated, then inched his way to the bed. He sat close to Graham, pulling his legs together and placing his hands on his knees. Graham smiled at him, weakly. Randy lowered his eyes. They settled on the photograph, next to Graham's hip.

"He learned, you know," Graham mumbled, following Randy's gaze, his words barely audible and slurred. "He learned that you can't escape. The world's just become a shit-hole. We're all monsters. I told him that a million times."

Randy focused on Dennis's thigh, seeing something there he hadn't noticed until then, a red mark. It was, he grasped, a welt, a deep one.

Graham motioned toward the manuscript sitting on top of the chest of drawers. "It's all in my new book, of course. I see you've found that, too." He laughed. "I hope it was enlightening for you."

Randy stared at the welt, oblivious to Graham. It appeared to be opening up before him, expanding across Dennis's thigh.

"But then you probably didn't read any of it, did you, baby? You never will, I'm sure. Let's just get high again, and I'll tell you all about it." Graham paused. Then, an edge in his tone, he exclaimed, "No, that's not what I'm going to do. That's not it at all. I'll just..." He paused once more, chuckling this time. "Listen, baby," he continued, impassioned, "remember when I used to talk about writing with you, what I told you then? Remember, baby? Show don't tell?"

Randy watched as Dennis's thigh seemed to vanish, engulfed by a swirling mass of red.

"But maybe it wasn't you I said that to, maybe it was him." Graham touched Randy's hip, kneading the skin between his fingers. "Anyway, baby, it doesn't matter." He stood. "I'm going to get the pills and some drinks. When I get back I'll..." He smiled. "Well, baby, then you'll learn all you need to know. Yes, baby, I'm going to show you everything."

When Graham returned to the bedroom, he was holding two glasses of gin and the bottle of Dexedrine, and his expression was grim. He seemed oddly melancholy. He sat on the bed and silently gave Randy a glass and two pills. Then, turning away, he found the photo album lying near them. He picked it up and leafed through it. Randy was afraid to look at him. Yet he felt at that point as if a fog were lifting; each instant of time became etched in his brain.

Neither spoke at first. Randy only clutched his glass as Graham, breathing heavily, flipped the pages.

After several minutes of silence, a half smile appeared on Graham's lips. "Yes," he whispered.

Randy glanced down and saw that he had come to the photographs of Dennis in his underpants.

"Yes," Graham said once more, still whispering, a remote yet pronounced tinge of sadness in his voice. He sighed. "And now it's gone."

Randy raised his head. Graham seemed lost in the album, his eyes glistening. Randy thought he could see the makeup on his face twisting into tiny red circles.

"What's that?" he asked.

Graham looked up, confused, evidently not recognizing him. His eyes were unfocused as he gazed past Randy at the wall. Randy wanted to touch him, lean against his frail chest, but found that he couldn't. The circles of red that he saw on his face were becoming larger, frightening.

Jerking his head back and glancing at Randy, Graham regained his focus. He frowned and took a slug of his drink. "Never mind," he said. He peered at the album, then in an abrupt motion, tossed it aside and jumped up. "Enough of this shit! We've got things to do."

Randy leaned forward and gripped his kneecaps. "Wha... what?"

Graham stood still, his hands on his hips, the smile on his face frozen. He waited for what seemed to Randy an eternity. At last he said, "I want you to lie on your stomach."

"Huh?" Randy stared at him, then muttered, "Oh." He lowered his eyes to the floor. "Oh, yeah." He thought that he understood. He lifted his eyes to Graham and, his voice quivering, asked, "Is...is it the belt?"

"The belt?" Graham's smile evaporated, replaced by an expression of an almost-exaggerated severity. Randy felt waves of fear, then excitement creeping across his shoulders and down his sides. He leaned back toward the mattress.

"Oh, right, the belt." Graham laughed harshly. "Well, I suppose that's a start." He gazed at Randy, murmuring, "Come on, baby, lie down."

Randy took a long breath. Then he stretched out, turning onto his stomach, becoming erect. He watched as Graham walked to the closet and moved inside.

A second later Graham emerged carrying a large duffel bag. He returned to the bed, set it by his feet, unzipped it, and pulled out several cords of rope. Kneeling on the floor, he leaned over Randy and pressed his lips against his buttocks, then slid his head down and slipped his tongue into the crack. He pulled back, laughed, and, leaning over again, bit Randy's left thigh. He pinched him, lightly slapped his buttocks, and stood. "Relax, baby," he purred. "I'm going to go put on some music."

"Yeah. Yeah, sure." Completely erect now, Randy closed his eyes.

He was lying across Graham's bed, his arms and legs stretched out, tied to the bed posts, thick ropes binding him tightly, music blasting from the next room. Above this, he heard Graham laughing.

"You're pathetic, you know." Despite his laughter, Graham's tone was almost tender. "Just a cheap little whore, a two-bit hustler."

Randy pressed his erection against the mattress and clenched his hands into fists. The rope chafed into his wrists.

"But that's why I love you, baby. Haven't I always told you that?" Graham unbuckled his belt and pulled it from his pants. "So then, are you ready?"

He listened as Graham snapped the belt against the floor, and beyond this, heard music: "Shatter me in pieces, you can't kill me."

"One. Two. Three." Graham paused. Then, with a terrifying force, he flung the belt across Randy's thighs.

Randy's body jerked spasmodically. The shock and the pain nearly obliterated everything. The ropes tying him to the bed seemed to tighten further. Panting, he waited for the second blow.

But it didn't come. All he could hear was the music: "Shatter me, shatter me, you'll never kill me."

Shaking, he peered behind him and saw Graham crouched over, reaching into the duffel bag by his feet.

"You know, baby," Graham said, smiling up at him, his right hand deep in the bag, "I don't think the belt is going to be enough this evening."

Randy gripped the ropes extending from his arms.

"No, baby, tonight I think we need something special." With a flick of his arm, Graham yanked a long, black whip from the bag. "Let's try this, okay?"

Seeing the whip, Randy coiled his chest up and pulled at the ropes. Sweat prickled his sides. He made an unsuccessful attempt to lift a hand toward Graham. "Don't hurt me!"

Graham giggled. "Come on! You've never complained before."

Panic leapt from Randy's stomach to his throat. He thought he was going to vomit, but, wriggling uncontrollably, forced his nausea down. The ropes seemed tauter than ever.

Graham stood above him, gulping his drink and chuckling.

Randy's heart rapped hard in his chest. He listened to a voice coming out of his mouth, not his own, he was sure.

"Cocksucker!" it shouted at Graham. "Motherfucking cunt!" Squirming, he pushed his groin into the mattress.

"Oh, baby," Graham laughed. "Baby, you're turning me on." Clenching the whip, he lifted it in the air and held it over his shoulder.

"Don't fucking touch me!" the voice cried. Randy heard the music in the distance, the lyrics no longer audible, its sound a wail.

Graham grinned. He started to lower the whip.

Randy's blood rushed through his veins, straight to his head. "Wait!" the voice screamed. He now knew that it was his. "Please!"

Nothing he said made the slightest difference.

He wasn't sure how long Graham whipped him, towered over him, flinging the whip across his back and thighs, screaming things like, "You cunt! You worthless piece of shit!" He knew he'd struggled, pulled at the ropes that restrained him, hurled himself from side to side, in shock and agony, enraged, yet erect the whole time.

It ended when Graham began to cough, a sustained hacking fit. He collapsed onto Randy's back, on top of the welts that had risen there, panting, but laughing, too.

"Fucker!" Randy shrieked, in pain. He heaved his hips up, forcing Graham off.

Graham rolled to Randy's side, coughing and giggling. "Baby, baby," he gasped. His fit died down. He slipped his shoes from his feet and took off his pants, along with his boxer shorts. He threw them onto the floor, then grabbed Randy around the waist. "Come on, baby."

No longer conscious of the pain, Randy tried to shove his elbow into Graham's chest, but found that he couldn't move freely enough to do so. "Motherfucker!"

Graham pinched Randy's nipple, climbed on top of him,

and pushed his erect penis against his buttocks.

"Eat shit," Randy murmured. He thought that he'd spoken in anger, that he'd spat the words out, but they came out as a moan, a caress. He felt himself move his hips up.

Graham let out a rasping cough and started to enter him.

Randy pressed up against Graham. He stopped. Moving quickly, he pulled his hips down. Graham's penis slid out. "Wait," Randy said, "don't you have any...?"

Graham grasped Randy's chest, pulling him back. "You're dying for my cock, aren't you, baby?" With a sharp movement, he again thrust his penis into him.

Randy felt as if he were being sliced open, as if Graham's penis were splitting him apart. He rammed his buttocks up against Graham's groin.

"Little shit!" Graham shouted, shoving down on Randy's shoulders.

"Shut the fuck up, cocksucker!" Randy lifted his groin off the bed, until Graham's penis seemed to be piercing his guts. This isn't safe, he thought, then nearly laughed. What is? The world's a fucking shithole.

Graham took a deep, irregular breath and stopped moving. Wheezing, his penis still in Randy, he placed his head on Randy's shoulder and sighed. Randy thought that he was going to cry. But he only lay quietly. Then he laughed. His hands crept up from Randy's chest to his neck, and he ran his fingers across his throat. "You know," he whispered in Randy's ear, "I could kill you right now." He fondled Randy's Adam's apple. "Then I could fuck your rotting corpse."

Not absorbing this, eager for Graham to continue, Randy cried, "Do it! Just do it!"

Graham moved his hands down to Randy's groin and grabbed his penis. "No, baby, that'd be too easy." He pulled out of Randy, then, with a frightening ferocity, thrust himself back in. "You're going to go with me."

"What?" Randy froze. He understood. Graham pulled out, then pushed into him again. Randy's eyes dropped. Lying beside him was the photograph of Dennis tied to a chair. He saw the rope stretched across Dennis's skin, the smile on his face, his erection.

With another quick thrust, Graham ejaculated. He lay on top of Randy, catching his breath. Then he stood. "That was good, baby. I'm just going to go pee."

Randy's heart was racing. He was desperate to move, to get up and dress, go. Graham's semen trickled between his legs. He peered at Graham, who was weaving by the bed, wearing only his mauve sweater and a blue shirt underneath that, his face pale beneath its running makeup, a hand cupped under his now-flaccid penis. "Untie me, okay?" Randy asked, his voice shaky.

Inching toward him, his movements unsteady, Graham grinned. "You want me to untie you?"

"Yeah."

Graham's teeth gleamed. "Well, all right. But first say 'please.' "

"Huh?" Randy stared at the streaks of mascara under Graham's eyes.

"Say 'please.' "

Randy was silent. Then, under his breath, he did what Graham had demanded. "Please," he muttered. He glanced down at the photograph of Dennis, then back up at Graham. The mascara appeared to have completely obliterated his eyes.

Graham continued to smile at him. "Make it 'pretty please.' "

Flushed, Randy complied.

"Good. Good boy." Graham leaned forward, so that he was directly over Randy. "Yes, baby, you're a very good boy." Giggling, he clutched his penis and released a stream of urine on Randy's back.

After Graham had untied him, Randy found that he was still unable to move; he felt glued to the bed, frozen. He didn't know why this was so. Just a moment before he'd wanted to leave. Now it was as if he had nowhere to go.

Graham fell down beside him. "I'm exhausted, baby," he muttered, his voice abruptly drowsy, weaker. He switched off the bedside lamp. "Let's just rest a bit."

Randy had no idea how long he lay there, smelling the urine on the sheets and on his back, listening to Graham's heavy breathing, his gasps, his hoarse coughs. Hours perhaps, or maybe just a few minutes.

Graham only stirred twice. The second time he threw an arm across Randy. "Denny," he whispered. Randy moved to him and pressed his head against his chest. He felt his skin's warmth. A cold draft blew past him; it seemed to be coming from Graham's depths. He slid away.

The room was dim, lit only by the illumination slipping in through the cracks of the blinds, coming from the street lamps outside. A clock on the bedside table told him it was a quarter before one. He sat quietly, watching specks of dust fluttering in the rays of light. Then he heard a sigh. He turned and saw Graham, suddenly wide awake, sitting up and grabbing the photo album. Randy wondered how well he could see it in the dark. His heart throbbed violently.

Graham sighed again, then started to sob. "Oh, baby, baby," he cried softly, peering up from the album toward a wall. "Baby, I'm sorry. Oh, so sorry!" He glanced back at the album, sucking in air. His breath caught in his throat, and he let out a piercing wail: "Baby!"

Terrified, Randy shot up from the bed and dashed to the living room. He found his clothes in a heap on the floor, his coat by the entryway. Once he'd dressed, he bolted out of the apartment and down the stairs, stopping at the bottom. He could still hear Graham's screams. For a second he considered returning to him. But then, in an instant, he knew that he could not go back, that he could never go there again. He threw the front door open and lurched into the night.

Excerpt from *Frontiers*
Michael Jensen

The year is 1797. When John Chapman's illicit relationship with a British major is discovered, John is forced to flee for his life over the snow-bound Allegheny Plateau of western Pennsylvania. Ill-prepared for the brutal climate, John nearly dies, but is saved by the mysterious and enigmatic Daniel McQuay. Suspicious of John and his motives, Daniel nonetheless allows him to winter over in his isolated frontier blockhouse. Daniel also agrees to teach John the skills necessary to survive this deep in the wilderness. Before long, however, John finds himself drawn to the brooding loner—and is surprised to learn that the feeling might be mutual.

With a mixture of horror and fascination I watched Daniel lie in the snow, then slide his entire arm into the elk's gut. Using a knife, he managed to quickly loosen most of the viscera, which slid free. He slit open the caul—the membrane containing the intestines and so forth—and set them steaming in the snow.

I found them oddly appealing, their slick textures, translucent colors, and amorphous shapes unlike anything I'd seen before. He peeled the caul free, spreading it over the snow. "Some salt, devil's weed, race, and a few hours boiling, and we got ourselves supper."

I wasn't terribly hungry.

"Next is the heart and lungs," Daniel said. "Lift so I can get in further."

His arm and shoulder again disappeared inside, but this time he continued pushing forward, and with a muffled "Higher, Chapman! Higher!" his head and neck vanished. Daniel now lay on his back, his hips arched upward as he squeezed further in. As he wriggled forward, his pants slid down, exposing not just pale, sensuous flesh, but the very top of the dark thatch that surrounded his cock. As if taking a breath, he lay flat for a moment, then flexed his back again as he thrust upward. Given the bloody work we were doing, I couldn't believe I found myself wanting to touch him.

A moment later, Daniel slithered free. Panting, he smiled up at me. His skin was slick and streaked with blood so that he almost looked like an Indian who had painted himself for battle. He reached back into the elk and dragged out something resembling a large red rock, followed by a pink, soft-looking organ that looked like an empty bag.

"This is the heart and a lung. We'll eat the heart tonight. Now it's your turn."

"What?"

"Come on, Chapman. If you're going to be a frontier settler, you need to learn this."

Shivering, I sank down next to him.

"First, drink," he said, handing me the jug. I swallowed. "Again," he said. After I'd passed the jug back, he reached over and rubbed my face. By now my head was spinning, though whether from the whiskey or his touch I wasn't certain.

"What are you doing?"

"You missed a spot," he said, gently working the lanolin into my skin. "I left the other lung inside for you to cut free. You've got to get used to this sort of work. Oh, and keep your eyes closed while you're in there," he said, using his knee to force the rib cage apart. At the same time, he guided my lanolin-coated hand, arm, and finally my head up into the elk's wet and still warm gut.

The experience was like being underground in a small slick cave. Moving under the animal's heavy flesh demanded most of my strength. Each of my senses reverberated, overwhelmed by the terrible intensity of the moment. Sweat burned as it ran into my eyes. My own breathing rasped in my ears. Sucking in what little air I managed, I couldn't so much smell the blood as I could taste it. The reek of it—the most base, elemental sensation I'd ever experienced—all but overpowered me, and I marveled at the oddity of feeling so alive while so bound up with death.

Without warning, bile rose in my throat. By swallowing repeatedly, I fought it down. More determined than ever, I sawed endlessly through whatever tied lung to elk.

"Chapman, are you all right?" Daniel hollered.

I opened my mouth to tell him I was fine, but found the side of the elk pressed down on my face so that I couldn't speak. I became dizzy as my nose and mouth again filled with the gagging, ironlike taste of salty blood.

"Chapman?" Daniel hollered again. When I didn't speak, he began to pull me out by my legs.

Determined to finish what I had begun, I kicked to get him to stop. He quickly let go.

With my strength beginning to give, I sawed and tugged with all the force I had. The lung finally tore free. Little by little, I pushed myself from the dark cavern until my head slid out. Exhausted, I lay on the ground, panting on my back, shading my eyes from the bright sunlight that blinded me. The air outside was cold; between the blood of the elk and my own sweat, I found myself shivering. I held out the lung to Daniel.

"After we wash up, we eat," Daniel said, stripping off his pants, then wrapping a blanket around his waist. He climbed up into the storeroom. "The way we reek, God Almighty must be able to smell us," he called down from above.

My head was already dizzy from the whiskey we'd drunk while butchering; the thought of Daniel naked, wet, bathing, made it positively spin. I recalled how, after I'd helped him with the beavers, he had washed my face and hands and arms. Look how bloodied I was now. What if he wanted to wash me again?

I downed another slug of whiskey.

A moment later he called out for me to give him a hand as he lowered a large wooden tub. Instead of being round, this tub was rectangular, almost long enough for a man to stretch out in. I reached up for it, saw up under the blanket he'd wrapped around his hips, and nearly lost my grip. Just knowing he was naked under there was enough to make me quiver.

Together, we pushed the table aside, clearing a spot for the tub.

"How's the water coming," he asked.

"It's hot." The way the blanket hung low around his waist made my heart surge like a river in spring.

"Good. That's how I like it. Get undressed. You can go first."

"No, why don't you? I need to use the necessary anyway."

"Are you sure? I don't mind waiting."

"I'm sure, Daniel. Go ahead."

After filling the kettle with more snow to boil, I went outside. I didn't need to use the necessary any more than I needed to bleed from my ears, but I dutifully wandered over anyway in case he was watching. A sliver of silver moon cast a faint, watery light onto the clearing, but not enough for me to pick out the dangling carcass of the elk against the backdrop of trees. A light breeze rustled the bare treetops, the only other sound was the crunch of snow under my feet.

Despite the peace and beauty of the night, I could think of but one thing: What was Daniel planning?

Stepping from the necessary, I feared going back inside. The truth be told, The Major and I had only slept together four times, and he'd always insisted on staying partially clothed and my doing exactly what he said and nothing more. Seeing Daniel naked, not to mention the times he had touched me intimately, had scared the living hell out of me. On the other hand, I felt myself stiffening as I remembered those moments....Starting to shiver, I reluctantly returned to the blockhouse.

Daniel stood in the tub, rinsing soap from his naked body. Wet, muscled arms and shoulders glistened in flickering firelight. I found it hard to breathe.

"Cold out?"

I nodded, desperately trying not to notice the black hair that covered his chest and stomach or the large cock swinging ponderously between his legs. As he slowly turned away, the white flesh of his ass gleamed.

He sighed and said, "This hot water feels goddamned wonderful."

"Glad to hear it."

"I'm finished," he said, setting down the cup he'd used to pour water over himself. "Your turn."

He was about to step out when I said, "Wait."

He looked at me.

Unable to believe I was about to do this, I took a deep breath. "You missed a spot. On your back." Taking the soap, I tried not to stare at him as I dipped it in the water, then scrubbed the blood that he'd missed.

Daniel's flesh was wet and hot and hard, and he smelled of soap and whiskey. I could've washed him for hours. Water danced down his body in gleaming rivulets as I rinsed his reddened skin.

Brushing his hair from his eyes, he turned to face me. "Thanks."

"Sure," I said, my voice trembling slightly. I dared to let my fingers brush over the warm, wet hair on his chest. He stiffened, trembling slightly, then stepped from the tub. "Your turn. Did you put more water on?"

Hastily stepping away, I nodded, worried that I'd gone too far, wishing I could take back what I'd done.

Still naked, he said, "Help me dump this."

Steam billowed into the frigid air as we poured out the warm water. Back inside, Daniel refilled the tub, then motioned for me to come over. Without speaking, he undid my belt and slid my pants down to my feet. Despite myself, my dick was beginning to harden, but he paid no mind.

"Lift your foot."

I did, but lost my balance and had to steady myself by leaning against his shoulders. The touch of my skin against his was so carnal that I would have been satisfied if nothing more had followed.

"Now the other one," he said, and I felt like a child. "Sit."

A moan escaped me as I sank into the hot water. My eyes fell shut. Little by little, the tension began to dissipate from my stiff muscles, aching arms, and sore back. At least until Daniel spoke.

"You know what I really like?"

I didn't open my eyes. "What?"

"To have my back scrubbed with a brush. Once I knew a girl in Boston who could scrub my back like nobody else in the world—if you know what I mean."

Not knowing what he meant, I said nothing.

"Look here, Chapman."

His hands were by his sides. In one, he clutched a wire scrubber, the cake of soap in the other, while his slowly stiffening cock hung in between. He made no attempt to hide what was happening.

"How about I scrub your back for you? If your muscles are half as stiff as mine, then you won't be able to do it yourself."

Even the scalding water couldn't keep me from shivering. "That's all right, Daniel, you don't have to."

"Of course I don't have to. An Indian doesn't have to get drunk, but he does." Before I could say anything else, he knelt down and dipped the soap in the water.

I would've jumped from the shock of being touched except that at that very moment every muscle in my body had locked into place. I'd gone from shivering to frozen in an instant, and I wouldn't have cared if Indians had come crashing through the door—I simply could not have moved to save myself.

"Lord, Chapman," he said, making me jump, the act of speaking breaking the spell that bound my muscles. "You're stiffer than the trunk of a hundred-year-old oak. You all right?"

"Fine," I croaked.

"Good, good. Just relax." His hands had a surprising gentleness as they worked the soap into my skin. Embarrassed by how hard I was, I leaned forward to cover myself with my hands, but he pushed me back.

"That girl in Boston I mentioned? She was a real Irish beauty." He snorted. " 'Course, she wasn't really Irish at all, but English and uglier than what lies twixt a cur's hind legs. She'd suffered the pox and had so many pockmarks that it would've taken half a day to count them all. Not to mention the two black eyes her employer usually left her with—all that's what made her an Irish beauty."

Daniel paused, and I hoped he was through. Each cruel word he blithely uttered turned my stomach.

He continued. "Now maybe her face was no treasure, but the rest of her? Let me tell you. She had red hair—beautiful hair—that she wore in a ponytail that I thought quite fetching. And the curves that tart had. There were more curves on her than in a bowl full of cherries." He traced his finger along the curve of my hip, and I forgot about the woman.

My dick had become so hard that it now rose out of the water, rigid as the barrel of a gun. Everywhere he touched tingled. Too much was happening at once, too much I couldn't control. Fear and loathing, excitement and curiosity, all coursed through my mind, confusing me.

"That girl," he said, his voice deep and throaty, "could do the most astounding things to my roger with the tips of her fingers. Makes me shudder just to recall them. Like this, for instance."

He leaned forward, his fingertips just brushing the tip of my dick. It felt so intense I had to grit my teeth. Even the Major had never, ever touched me there.

"She used to fondle my roger like this all the time," he said, idly doing it again. This time a ragged gasp escaped me. My breathing waned so shallow, I felt light-headed, as if I were starting to float.

His hands returned to my shoulders, massaging as he continued to talk. "I would come into Boston after a month of working in the coal pits. All filthy and grimy—just like us today—and she'd draw me a hot bath, then wash me as gentle as if I were a newborn baby." He worked his way down my body, scrubbing, massaging, until his hand disappeared into the soapy water. "Her name was Sarah, did I tell you that? Came from a small village in England called Greenhead. Beautiful country up there." His slick hands slid over my stomach, across my thighs, along the inside of my legs.

"Comfortable?" he asked, as I struggled to sit upright. Before I could answer, he cupped my balls in the palm of one hand, while the other eased back and forth over my rock-hard dick. Gasping, I closed my eyes and gripped the sides of the tub. The floating sensation multiplied over and over. Even though the tub was solid beneath me, I felt as if I were tumbling through the air.

"Do you like that?"

Too lost in the experience, I could only nod.

"Me too. No one could do that like Sarah." Daniel let go, and when I unlocked my eyes, he had stepped around in front of me, now standing in the tub. His dark, fat cock bobbed inches from my face. I took him in my mouth. The heat and hair of his groin pressed against my face, and he moaned as I caressed his weighty balls with one hand. I took in the sight of his narrow hips and flat stomach, an arc of that culminated in his hairy chest. My left hand teased his nipples.

Daniel slipped from my mouth as he crouched in front of me. To my amazement, he began kissing me roughly, his beard scraping against my skin, his tongue tangled with mine. A hand gripped me by the neck as he pressed his mouth ever harder against mine, and I felt utterly in his control. His other hand kneaded my shoulders and arms, rougher and rougher, but I didn't mind. Again I felt his hand grip me, then he did something extraordinary, something I'd never contemplated.

He lowered himself down, and at first thinking he was going to sit on my lap, I tried to move my rigid dick out of the way. Grunting, he pushed my hand away. I pressed against him, my dick bent a bit, then slipped inside him.

Eyes closed, moaning, breathing heavily, he gripped the sides of the tub and froze.

I sat there stunned, unmoving, my dick throbbing with a new-found intensity I'd never imagined possible. Unlike jacking off, where the pressure moved with my hand, this squeezed my entire dick at once. The sensation was unbelievable, unreal, like seeing a color I'd never imagined existed.

And then he began to move up and down on me. Flexing his legs and hips, he bounced once, twice, then lowered himself slowly until he was astride my lap with all of me inside him.

It was so bloody wondrous I thought I would die; dumbfounded, I barely felt coherent.

Leaning forward, he again kissed me. I kissed back every bit as hard, which served to excite him all the more. My hands wandered over his body, massaging his chest, his ass, slapping him once, then again. His nipples were hard, and when I pinched them, he moaned, then lifted and lowered himself more vigorously. When we stopped kissing, my mouth moved to suck on his nipples, biting and pulling on them. He moaned louder, bounced harder.

Sitting up straight, I gripped his hips tightly, trying to pull him as close into me as possible. He buried his face against my neck, and with each movement upward he tensed, then relaxed as he thrust down. An exquisite pain suffused my dick, my body, and I knew I was about to climax.

"Daniel," I said, fearful he'd be angry if I came inside him. "I'm going to…"

He pulled his head away from me, pressed his hand over my mouth, and began to bounce so hard his cock and balls slapped against my stomach. He stroked himself, his face a tableau of ecstasy. Softly stroking his balls, I watched in amazement as the head of his dick swelled and spouts of white jism erupted onto my chest and dribbled down to the waterline on my stomach. The sight of his swollen cock, his cum on my chest, and the feel of my dick throbbing inside him sent me over the edge. I gripped his hips as hard as I could while savage, guttural grunts and moans escaped both of us.

"Oh, God, Daniel," I cried, pumping into him, overwhelmed, as my dick swelled then exploded inside him, over and over.

After I'd finished, he slumped against me as I collapsed back against the tub.

In the Third Person: May 28, 1997

Aaron Lawrence

I think I have stepped onto the set of *The Silence of the Lambs*. My flashback to the movie is instantaneous. The killer is standing at the rim of the pit. At the bottom is an hysterical woman begging for her life. Ignoring her pleas, the killer commands in the third person, "The girl will do this," or "It will do that."

I have always been horrified at how he dehumanized her through his use of the third person. So when Adam greets me in the third person, I am surprised, to say the least.

"The boy will come in," he welcomes me.

Another idea occurs to me. Perhaps he has a daddy/boy fantasy he wants to act out. That could be hot. I've always wanted to try something like that.

The thought gives me mixed feelings. I do fantasize about daddy/boy role playing, but I do not want to be treated like a mindless piece of meat in the process. The way he called me "the boy" instead of "his boy" is creepy rather than erotic.

Although Adam is an average-looking man in his forties, there is something not right about him. Perhaps my discomfort comes from his voice. It is slightly effeminate with a touch of hyperactivity. Its tone unsettles me.

I shake my head to clear my mind and enter the apartment. Behind me I hear Adam close the door. Although it shuts with a light click, it sounds like the clang of a mausoleum.

"Daddy is pleased to see the boy," he begins. "Daddy would like to give a tour to the cute boy, but there is a special rule in this apartment. Does the boy know what that rule is?"

"No, what rule is that?" I ask. I'm not sure I really want to know.

"Oh, I guess the boy wouldn't know," he chuckles. "The rule of this apartment is simple. The person receiving the tour must be in the nude. The boy will take his clothes off so he can begin the tour."

Despite my unease, I strip of my clothes. Adam touches my body with his hands while I undress.

He must be able to sense my feelings because he tries to put me at ease. "Is the boy nervous?" he asks. "Daddy does not want the boy to be nervous. Daddy wants the boy to feel welcome."

"I'm okay," I halfheartedly reassure him.

Ignoring me, he continues speaking. "The boy has such a lovely cock. Does the boy have a name for it?"

"No, I've never named it."

"Then let Daddy name it. Daddy will call it Mickey. Mickey is the name of Daddy's dick. Did the boy know that?"

"No," I reply again. "I hadn't known that." Thinking about Mickey makes me wonder just how strange he is.

"Daddy's dick has been called Mickey for twenty years now. Daddy's first lover named it Mickey. So Daddy will call the boy's dick Mickey, too."

I am now twice as nervous despite Adam's attempt to put me at ease. I wonder if this is how all psychotics start.

"Now the Daddy is going to welcome Mickey to his apartment. Daddy always tries to make his visitors feel welcome."

Adam drops to his knees and gently kisses my dick. He reaches up and holds my semierect shaft to his lips before he gives it a large lick. He stares at its growing hardness for a moment before he slides it inside his mouth.

The sexual feelings help ease my anxiety. Unfortunately, just as I am beginning to enjoy myself he pulls back and stands up.

"It's time to begin the tour," he announces with a flourish.

Adam takes my hand and leads me several steps into his apartment. For the first time, I look around my surroundings. I am in a moderate-sized two-bedroom apartment with a balcony. The living and dining rooms are filled with overly ornamental furnishings such as statues and a waterfall.

He leads me directly to the waterfall. "Does the boy see this? Daddy is going to put the boy's penis in the water. It will feel very cold but then Daddy will warm it up for him. Does the boy understand?"

The boy understands Daddy's a crackpot. "Yes, I understand. Go ahead."

He wraps his hand around the base of my cock and slowly lowers it into the cold water. I involuntarily flinch as the water touches my skin. My erection vanishes instantly but he does not let go.

"Oh, the water is cold, Adam. Please let me pull it out," I say.

"Daddy knows the water feels cold on the boy, but Daddy does know best," he tells me. I am still uncomfortable around him, but he is right in one aspect. The sexual way he is doing this to me makes it bearable. My erection even slowly begins to return.

Finally he relents. "The boy can stop now." He picks up a nearby towel and dries the cold water from my body. Lowering himself to his knees, he puts his tongue on my balls. The numbness from the cold masks most of the feeling, but as he sucks on my nuts, I begin to feel familiar warm and wet sensations.

He sucks for a few more moments before he switches to my semihard cock. He holds it between his fingers then slides it into his mouth. Despite the return of feeling to my balls, my cock is still almost completely numb. After a few moments he stands up. "Daddy will continue the tour now."

I nod politely to cover my thoughts. This sexual encounter is frustrating for me. The way he orders me around is quite arousing, but his constant use of the third person is strange and disturbing. As much as I would love to act out a daddy/boy scene, he is not my image of a daddy.

To me, a hot daddy is a well-built, outgoing, and assertive person. He treats me firmly in bed but is respectful of my limits. Unlike my fantasy, Adam is skinny and awkward looking and is freaking me out with his role play. I am following Adam's orders only because he is paying me, not out of any sexual desire on my part.

Adam continues his tour another six feet into the living room. "The boy will sit down," he instructs, pointing at the couch.

I seat myself and spread my legs for him. He kneels between them, but to my surprise he does not begin sucking me. He grabs my ankles instead and lifts them into the air. Holding them far apart, he lowers his face into my ass and starts rimming me.

After two seconds he suddenly stops. I wonder if I an unclean down there, but I am sure this is not the case. A more likely reason is that he is living out the fantasy of a wild sex-filled tour of his apartment. The length of time spent having sex in each room is not important. Once we reach the end of the tour, we will have the actual sex. I am relieved at my insight. It helps me understand what is going on, which in turn means I can better meet his needs and fulfill his fantasies.

We move into the dining room. "Daddy would love to have a naked dinner with the boy." His reference to dinner makes me think of Hannibal "The Cannibal" Lector again. To my relief, we do not stay long in the dining room but move onto the balcony.

The balcony overlooks a large parking lot in the process of being repaved. I am surprised at his invitation to stand on the balcony in the nude. Fortunately, there is no one in sight. He kneels and begins sucking me for a third time. This time my dick is rock hard and ready for his attentions.

As I'd figured, he spends only a few moments sucking me. The next stop on the tour is an undecorated and shabby kitchen. He lifts me onto the counter and spreads my legs to give him an unrestricted view.

Stepping back to admire my body, Adam speaks again. "The daddy is pleased with the boy. He is much more attractive than the daddy's last boy. The boy is very beautiful."

Adam's reference to his last boy makes me wonder where he is now. Could something awful have happened to him? A shiver runs down my spine. Adam approaches me again and fondles my stiff cock. When he reaches out and touches my balls, I moan to conceal my uneasiness.

"Daddy" becomes more excited as the tour nears its end. He bypasses a guest room completely and gestures at a hall bathroom. "That is the boy's bathroom. If the boy needs to pee, he can use this room. Or he can use my bathroom in the main bedroom. Either bathroom is yours to use."

His slip from the third to the first person does not escape me. I think he may be coming out of his bizarre fantasy, but he quickly dashes my hopes.

"Oh, yes," he continues. "You can use my bathroom here. I would love to watch the boy pee in the toilet. Or maybe in the fountain in the other room. The boy will have to pee in the fountain next time he is here. If you really have to go to the bathroom, you should use a toilet but Daddy will wipe it for you. Just like a little boy, the boy will bend over while Daddy wipes his bottom."

I am thoroughly disgusted. He is not the first person to ask for a watersports fantasy, but his desire to wipe my ass totally repulses me. Now I want to leave and never return. I remain silent, because I do not trust myself to speak. I suspect the expression on my face speaks for itself.

The tour finally ends in the bedroom. Like the rest of the apartment, the room is overly furnished with tacky knick-knacks. In the center of the room is an unmade bed. A small pile of sheets and blankets sit off to one side.

"Daddy's fantasy is for the boy to be my houseboy," he begins in an odd mixture of the first and the third persons. "He wants to see the boy put the sheets on my bed while the Daddy touches him and molests you."

His speech is bizarre, but at least his request is harmless. I am more than happy to clean house for $150 an hour.

"Before the boy can begin," he continues in the third person, "he needs to remove Daddy's clothes."

I begin kissing Adam as I undo his clothes. I remove his shirt, then his pants, underwear, and socks. Finally, he wears nothing at all. Dropping to my knees, I take his soft cock entirely into my mouth, swallowing it completely. He moans and arches slightly against me.

Suddenly he pulls out of my mouth. "It's time for the boy to begin making the bed."

Although his style of role playing is odd, I comply as best I can. I step over to the bed and begin unfolding the sheets. I feel his hand rub my butt as I bend over. Making the bed continues in a similar fashion. Every time I pause to tuck or fold something, I feel a hand or a tongue touch my body.

Eventually the bed is made. Grabbing my shoulders, he slowly lowers me onto the bed. Reaching inside a drawer, he pulls out a bottle of lotion. He pumps a wad into his hand and reaches down toward my ass. He slowly penetrates me, sliding his finger deep into the tight center. I feel the lotion spread between my buns by the motion of his hand and fingers.

"How much is the boy enjoying this?" he asks.

"Oh, the boy loves, I mean likes, this," I exclaim, purposely slipping into the third person. I thought he might appreciate it.

"Is the boy ready to be fucked?"

"I'm always ready, Adam. You can give it to me as much as you'd like."

"It's not Adam," he admonishes me. "It's Daddy. Tell Daddy how much you like it."

"Oh, Daddy," I reply dramatically. "I love the way you are fingering my ass. I want you to fuck me, and I want you to make your boy feel really good." Although I can tell from the expression on Adam's face that I am saying the correct words, I feel self-conscious doing so. I find nothing erotic in this daddy/boy scene. I want to get it over with and leave as fast as I can.

Adam is unaware of my true feelings. He grabs his bottle of lotion and pumps several blasts into his hand. He reaches down and to my surprise rubs it all over the top of my pubic hair and on my stomach. "Daddy wants to lie on top of you and rub up against his beautiful boy," he explains. "It's his favorite way to come."

He climbs on me and lowers his body against mine. He begins humping me, sliding his dick against the flesh of my stomach. "Oh, beautiful boy, lie there and don't move. Oh, Daddy is so happy with his boy." I briefly wonder if he has a necrophiliac fetish. He humps me for no more than a minute before he loses control. His moaning and pumping crescendo as spurts of ejaculate cover my stomach. He quickly pulls off and leaves the room. I am glad my work here is done.

He returns a few moments later and hands me a towel. "I wish I could see you more often," he tells me. "You are such a beautiful boy. Would you be willing to make a deal? I could pay you less but give you a steady appointment each week?"

He has temporarily abandoned referring to me in the third person. I take this as a good sign. "To be honest. I'm not sure I can do that," I explain as I wipe myself off. "I really can't negotiate since this is what I do for a living."

"Well, think it over. I'll call you in a few days, and we can discuss it then."

Numerous replies race through my mind as I look him in the eyes. I want to tell him to go to hell, or that I wouldn't consider negotiating with anyone that wants to wipe my ass, but I say none of these things. Ever polite to the end, I tell Adam I will think it over.

Adam asks me if I would like to take a shower, but I respectfully decline. I've pressed my luck enough for one day, and I want to go home. It's safer that way. I still do not completely trust him. One never knows who the truly dangerous clients are.

As I get dressed, I realize my own daddy/boy fantasy will have to wait for another day. His fantasy and mine had nothing in common. Perhaps my fantasy will never be fulfilled through my work. Escorting requires I meet clients' needs rather than my own. I am unsure if the two are ever totally compatible. Then again, I've had enough unusual experiences to know nothing is impossible in my line of work.

We settle the issue of the money in the living room. He kisses me goodbye and lets me out the door. I'm off to home to shower before I depart for New York City for my evening client and yet another adventure. Perhaps the next movie set I walk onto will be more like an erotic film, less *The Silence of the Lambs*. I could get into that.

The Nether Eye Opens
Don Shewey

When Jerry called, I knew from his name and his tense, timid voice that I'd given him a massage once before. I found him in my client log, but the entry didn't churn up any detailed memories. The creature who arrived at my door might as well have been a total stranger. He was short and nearly bald on top, an out-of-shape blob of a middle-aged man with reptilian slits for eyes. My notes reminded me that he was "overweight and ashamed of it."

He didn't seem to recognize me or remember that he'd seen me in the past. So I pretended I didn't know him, either. He went to the bathroom and came back wearing only his white button-down shirt. He slipped off the shirt and wanted to hop right onto the table. I said, "I'd like to have you do some stretching before we put you on the table, to loosen you up." He looked at me like I was crazy.

Reluctantly, he took a step away from the table. As I directed him to close his eyes, take some breaths, and become aware of his body, he followed my instructions, but he acted like a little kid annoyed at having an adult make him do stupid things, like walk downstairs one step at a time.

When I had him stretch him arms up to the ceiling, I noticed he was holding something in his right hand.

"What's that in your hand, Jerry?"

He showed me the white plastic inhaler.

"No," I said, feeling shaky. "I don't use poppers."

He said, "You don't have to."

I said, "I don't mix poppers with massage."

He said, "They help me relax."

I said, "I'm really a good masseur. You'll be plenty relaxed."

He dutifully deposited the tiny bottle on top of his clothes, which he'd left on the chair next to the massage table. As he lay on his back and I stretched out his arms and legs more, I tried to lighten the atmosphere with some chitchat. He didn't respond. He kept his lips pressed together tightly. He seemed to be pouting about having his poppers confiscated. It made me nervous. I felt guilty for shaming him about using poppers.

He resisted a lot of the massage. He seemed restless and impatient with my slow tempo, scratching himself and coughing. He never sighed and sank into the pleasure of being touched. I got the picture that he's someone who's used to going to masseurs for a half-assed backrub and a hand job, no questions asked. Perhaps at the beginning I could have broached the subject of his real desire and made some accommodation. Often I do say something like, "What's the experience you'd like to have today?" Not that anyone ever says, "A half-assed backrub and a hand job, please."

Guys like Jerry who crawl around in a snail shell of sex-shame rarely have much experience at asking for what they want. They either expect you to read their minds, or they're masochistically resigned to whatever you want to dish out. In my desire to be conscious about sexual touch, you'd think I'd have developed a smooth routine by now of letting shy, sexually undernourished guys like this know what they're in for with me. For instance, I could say, "I'll get around to focusing on your erotic body, but first I'm going to spend about forty minutes massaging the muscle tension out of your back and your legs and your feet." I refrain from being that direct because I want to avoid sounding too much like one of those wholesome Danish sex-education films. Rather than tease clients up to my level, I suppose I tend to sink down to their level of inarticulateness.

In any case, now I was launched into my usual massage routine, and there was no way of stopping it gracefully. I knew giving him a thorough massage had value. I also suspected that he couldn't give a shit.

Everything changed when I got around to his butt. My notes told me I had done butt work on him before, so I felt confident in moving in for close butt touch. When I spread his cheeks and lightly brushed the coarse black hairs and the shiny pink skin around his stretched-out butthole, he twitched as if shocked by an electric current. When I rested the palm of my hand against his pelvic floor and rocked him back and forth, his erection swelled out from under his ballbag, the snail poking its head out of its shell, antennae first. Even if I'm pretty sure that someone wants butt massage, I like to check. Sometimes people have hemorrhoids or loose bowels or some other condition they'd prefer to conceal. I leaned in close to his ear and said, "If you like, Jerry, I could put on gloves and do some more massage around your butt."

"Okay," he said.

I stepped over to my supply cabinet and grabbed a pair of gloves and a tube of K-Y. When I turned around, he was reaching for the inhaler he'd left on top of his shirt.

I was on him in a flash. "If you insist on using poppers, Jerry, I can't continue with the massage."

"What?" he said. I couldn't tell if he was hard of hearing or just selectively so.

I retreated from my ultimatum. "I'd rather you not use poppers during the massage."

"Okay," he said again. He returned his head to the face plate like a child scolded.

"I want to invite you to keep breathing and taking in all the sensations you're feeling, Jerry. Does that sound okay to you?"

He shook his head yes, face down, buried in his shame.

I climbed up on the table and knelt between his spread legs. The sight in front of me—the hairy back and flabby butt of a middle-aged man—wasn't the most appetizing I'd ever encountered. I wasn't turned on but I wasn't turned off either. Some people can't imagine touching let alone giving an erotic massage to somebody they're not attracted to. For a lot of young gay men, the idea of having anything to do with a guy like Jerry would be absolutely unthinkable. I don't mind. In fact, I like it. I like the feeling of control, of being entrusted with another human being's vulnerability. I have a hard time only when clients assume that, because I'm touching them erotically, that we've suddenly moved into some kind of reciprocal sex mode and they're free to grope me.

I guess that sounds awful. Like, "Don't kid yourself. I'm the attractive one around here. I'm the one who gets to touch and have power." Well, it's true. I want it to be clear that I'm in control. I want them to behave. There's definitely arrogance on my part. But no contempt. Anyone who presents his tender butt for loving touch gets a big gold star in my book. He can rest assured I'm going to take good care of him.

With Jerry, I felt like a spelunker ready to hunt for treasures in the secret cave. I pulled on first one white vinyl glove, then the other. The latest box of surgical gloves I bought were the smallest size, and they're skin tight on my hands. They make me look like Mickey Mouse in evening wear.

In contrast to his lassitude during the back massage, the man on the table now began to respond to my every move—

the cool breath on his tight butthole, the firm pressure of three fingers over the opening, the cool slipperiness of lubricant being rubbed rhythmically over the folds of skin covering his sphincter. He jerked and twitched whenever I hit an especially sensitive spot. I knew I wasn't hurting him. I knew he was flinching because he wasn't breathing smoothly enough to distribute the intense sensations. So I coached him to breathe all the way down to his toes.

I went into him easily, one finger then two. I brought him up onto his knees with his head resting on the table, his butt in the air. He wrapped his feet around my calves. When I slid the length of my middle finger across his swollen prostate, he groaned with pleasure. "Deeper," he requested. I adjusted my posture so I was a little higher and slid a third finger into his ass all the way up to the last knuckle, held it there, and vibrated it. With the other hand (whose glove I'd peeled off), I stroked his inner thighs, circled his balls, and tugged on his hard cock. Then I reached around and put my left hand on his lower belly just above his pubic bone and pressed inward, so his prostate received pressure from both sides.

To be this deep inside a man is about as physically intimate as you can get. The quality is so different from fucking, in some ways much more intense. Articulate, multijointed fingers can reach places inside the body that a hard cock cannot. They can increase or modify pressure on the sphincter or the prostate at will. And while someone who's fucking often has to keep sliding in and out to receive pleasure and to stay hard enough, a hand can stay put when it hits a spot that produces moans. I know when I'm fucking, I can get very mental about the state of my erection, wanting to please my partner and prolong my own pleasure at the risk of losing it altogether. Doing butt massage, I'm liberated from that anxiety.

Touching Jerry, fiddling with his erotic knobs like an engineer tuning up a delicate machine, I felt detached, distant, powerfully in control. Like the most beneficent of gods, at once servant and master, giving exquisite pleasure and requiring nothing in return.

Once he was accustomed to being penetrated, I picked up the pace. Now I was fucking him—with my hand, anyway—in and out, pumping his butt. Wordless murmurs issued from his throat. He raised his butt higher. With my free hand I slapped his big rump hard, first one cheek then the other, again and again. He jerked and cried out with each slap. His cry did not say "Stop." The sound of bare hand against bare butt excited me. I escalated the strength of my slaps. Then I paused and ran my fingertips lightly over the reddening skin. I reached down and wrapped my fist around the base of his bulging cock and balls and pulled them toward me.

"Do you have your whole fist in me?" he suddenly asked.

"No, not quite," I said. "Three fingers."

"Can you fist me?" His voice was quiet, not timid but hopeful.

"Have you ever been fisted?"

"No. But I'd like to try."

"Let's see how it goes," I said. I put some more lube on my hand and slid all four fingers inside him. He groaned with satisfaction. I could feel his belly, his bowels, his rectum, his insides breathing with me, letting go. When I slid my hand back, a few bubbles of air pressed their way out, relieving the interior pressure. Without clenching or clamping, his ass wrapped itself around my hand, like a starfish on a rock.

I got off the table and stood next to him. I ran my free hand up his back and stroked his shoulders, his neck, the scaly top of his bald head. I leaned into his butt, which opened slightly wider. He sighed. Now I slid my thumb into him, so my hand formed a wedge that pushed all the way in until my knuckles rested against his sitz bones.

I noticed that he was no longer hard. It occurred to me that he might be hurting. He might have had enough. But the gurgles he released whenever I bore down on his prostate told me he had entered a deeper zone, that altered state of erotic experience that is beyond erection and ejaculation. It's a mystical place, akin to dreaming or nearly dying, where the membrane that separates matter from spirit becomes very thin. Memories and emotions slither up from the murky depths. The nether eye opens to what's usually hidden. The roof of the planetarium slides open, and the infinite beckons. I knew he was travelling through space, like those scenes in *2001: A Space Odyssey* where suddenly the spaceship would be hurtling through a blur of stars. Only this was inner space, a tunnel of quiet dark. Vaulted ceilings. Echoey stairwell. A horse's eye. I hung out there with him.

Almost an hour and a half had passed since he got on the table. "I'm going to slow down now and start coming out of you, Jerry," I told him. One finger at a time, I brought my hand out, cupping my palm over his hole before releasing it entirely. Then I laid him flat on the table again, cleaned his butt with a Baby Wipe, and toweled off his back before turning him over.

"How are you doing?" I asked him.

He looked up through his slit eyes and said, "Good."

I knelt at the end of the table looking at his face upside down. I saw his stubbly chin, his thin lips (relaxed now), his fleshy ears.

"You've been on a little trip I think."

"Uh, huh," he said.

"Uh, huh," I confirmed. I rested my hands on his shoulders and looked down into his steely green eyeballs. They were the eyes of someone on a trip, who has seen something from the other world and not averted his gaze. He didn't seem confused or shy or embarrassed.

"Did any images or memories occur to you during this session?" I asked.

"Yes," he said immediately. I was surprised. I like asking the question but usually people don't relate to it.

"Tell me," I said.

"I remembered that my father used to take me over his knee," he said slowly. "He would pull down my pants...and pull down my underwear...and spank me."

"And that was exciting to you?"

He nodded.

"Did your father know it excited you?"

"No."

"Did you get a hard-on?"

"No, not at the time."

"But later when you thought about it...?"

"Uh, huh."

I let that memory sink in. Inside me something large and dangerous moved, like a giant octopus tentacle flopping across the room. When I started slapping his big hairy butt, little did I know that I was stirring up his oldest erotic fantasies. Or mine: the forbidden daddy-love-touch.

"There's something about an older man, your father, taking an interest in your naked butt that's very exciting and forbidden, isn't there?"

"More forbidden," he said.

"Ah," I said. "Many things that are forbidden are exciting."

He was quiet for a minute.

"Anything else?" I inquired.

"Yes," he said.

I was overjoyed. More!

"I was in Morocco once," he began. "Have you ever been to Morocco?"

"No," I said. "I'd like to go."

"This was many years ago," he said. He spoke slowly, as if in a trance. "I was there with some other people on business... and we were all taken to this bathhouse....There were men and women there....I got separated from the people I was with....I saw some stairs....I went up there....It was a little room....I met a Moroccan guy....He was big...well, not big. Stocky."

He paused.

"Then what happened?" I said, barely controlling my impatience to hear the whole story.

"There was a bench there....He pulled it over to the middle of the room....He had me get up on it...the same way you had me do...with my butt up."

Aha.

"And then he...you know, he fucked me....And there were two other guys...Moroccans...Three of them all together."

"They all three fucked you?"

"Uh, huh."

"One right after the other?"

"Uh, huh."

"That sounds hot," I said. My dick grew in my pants. To tell the truth, I was jealous.

"It was," he said immediately. "The other guys were walking around the place....I didn't know where they were....Men and women...."

"Oh," I said, "it was a place where everybody was there having sex, men and women?"

"Yes," he said.

"But they could have walked in at any time and seen you?"

"Yes."

We both quietly took in the thrill of that scenario.

This guy had more going on inside him than I ever would have suspected by looking at him. I got up and sat on the table next to him. I picked up his arm and let it rest against my chest as we continued talking.

He wanted to know more about fisting. "Do you think you could get your whole hand inside me next time?"

"I don't know," I said. "For fisting it's a lot easier if you're in a sling, because your whole body is able to relax. When you're on a table, your muscles unavoidably maintain a certain tension."

"Do you have a sling?" he asked eagerly.

"No," I said. "Some people have them in their private playrooms, and some sex clubs have them."

"I couldn't see myself doing it in a sex club with just anybody," he said. "But I could do it with you. What if I lay on my back?"

"That might be easier," I conceded. I started feeling slightly apprehensive. I've never fisted anybody. This session was as far as I'd ever gone in that direction. I didn't want to set myself up as an expert. But his eagerness to explore touched me. He didn't seem like a numbed-out thrill seeker. From the stories he told, I understood that intense body play connected him to his deepest erotic fantasies and memories. What else can you call these things but experiences of God, memories of heaven? In those moments, brief and eternal, you feel most alive in your body and most spiritually connected to the tempestuous energy of the universe, that mystery at once so physical and so invisible. How many saints and monks, meditating days at a time on their dusty mats, have dwelt on just this, remembered or wished-for episodes of ecstatic buttfucking?

"We need to stop for today, Jerry," I said.

"Can you help me get off?" he asked.

"You want to squirt?" I asked, a little dubiously. I thought he'd gone way beyond it. I thought he'd had a sacred-sex breakthrough and realized that you don't always have to ejaculate to have a powerful erotic experience.

"Sure," he said. I looked at his dick, which he'd been idly toying with during our conversation, and I saw that it was stiff and dark pink. I oiled him up and stroked him. He had a medium-sized dick, maybe five inches long erect, circumcised, with a big split down the middle, a thick frenum. Pressed flat against his belly, his cock looked like an arrowhead—or a devil's tail. As I worked on his cock, he started running his hands over my body. I found myself tensing up, afraid that he was going to start invading me and grabbing my cock. I didn't invite him to touch me, and I wasn't at all turned on at the moment. I wanted to finish up the session and get rid of him. Sacred sex is sacred sex, but after an hour and a half your time is up.

I pumped his cock with one hand and reached my other arm under his neck and around his shoulders. He lifted his arm to pull me down to his face. I resisted, but eventually I allowed him to press some stubbly kisses against my face.

As I pressed my hairy chest against his, his thin lips smacking against mine, I became for a moment that angry daddy pulling down his underpants, that stocky Moroccan towering over him and swallowing him up, the horned god appearing by magic in the forest clearing where the chubby boy lay on mossy grass pleasuring himself. The world turned upside down with a lurching sound like a train pulling out of the station. Blossoming flowers erupted from the earth. Waves of air pressed into his lungs until he burst.

How do I want you to touch me, Daddy? I like having power over you. I want to be somewhere you can't hurt me. I like it when I can see you and you can't see me. I can see every part of your fat hairy body. I see your scar under your shoulder blade. I see the razor line of your barbershop haircut. I see the curled callous on the edge of your big toe. I see your pink balls peeping out from under your thighs. You're face down, so I can spread your cheeks and look right into your wrinkled butthole.

I can see where your sallow skin turns rosier, the color of the inside of a velvet cape lined in silk. Whorehouse pink—not garish but muted. I could write on your butthole with a Magic Marker. Little hieroglyphics. Sportina Cheese. Marco Wuz

Here. Close Cover before Striking. Bad Advice. Liar. I could slide the Magic Marker in and out of you, like Midwestern boys caught fucking themselves with pencils. I've turned the tables on you, Daddy. I'm fucking you.

I don't want you to notice or say anything. Not right now anyway. Later I want you to tell me I'm wonderful and give me some money. Right now I want to squeeze a pile of slippery goo onto my rubbery fingers and slide them into your butt, so you feel me fucking you, you feel me towering over you, planting a seed, mowing your lawn, making you pregnant, making you moan. You reach out and grab my leg. Suddenly I feel like Don Giovanni in danger of being dragged to hell. What do you want? Let me go. Let me go! You want something from me, something more, and I don't want to give anything more. I want to say no without saying no. I turn you over, and you look at me with your slanted reptile eyes, dark green, from just under the surface of the water, you alligator with the crooked smile (no lips) and hairy belly. You reach up to touch my cheek. I lean in to your ear; you turn your head to kiss me. I open my mouth, and our tongues press together like cheese and burger. We fry. I'm kissing you, Daddy. I always wanted this.

We're both hard. I'm running my hands through your hair. Now I've given up shame. I have no restraint. I strip down to my jockstrap and take that off too. I wrap it around your neck. I climb on top and slide into you without stopping. I pump into you and pull the jockstrap tighter around your neck. Your eyes bulge. Your dick swells. It's unbelievably huge. It's like a big balloon. It's a baby lying between us. It's a baby boy growing out of your crotch, and the longer I fuck you, the bigger he grows. Now he's sucking on your tit, and I'm fucking you, and your face is getting redder, like fire around your watery eyes, and I flood you, I flood you, your banks overflow, blood trickles from the corner of your mouth.

I take the baby and wrap it in your T-shirt and run. I run through the snow looking for a taxi. There's no one on the street but me. We get to the airport in no time. I don't have any luggage. They let me walk on board with the baby, both of us naked and crusty. I sit in first class, order a beer, and toast you, Daddy, love of my life.

Kim:
Little Friend of All the World

Ishmael Houston-Jones

"I'm not good at this," I think through the graceless minutes between the exchange of cash and the nakedness. Reared by a Black Baptist mother, I want to offer him tea or a soft drink. I do offer a choice of music, although he doesn't seem impressed by my selections.

"Hey man, this is your scene. You be in charge, okay?" Sure, sure. I put on a CD that I hope will be neutral enough that he won't think I'm totally pathetic. Something hip but retro with queer references but not obviously faggy. He looks bored, and we've only just begun. "That the bedroom through there?" Why yes, so it is.

I see his face, and I don't know what to make of it. It seems so predigested and predictable. A cliché from movies or magazines or pop songs. In reality I am more focused on his moods and their tiny shifts within such a minuscule range. As I said, he starts off bored. More than bored. Annoyed by this apparent waste of his very precious time. I catch him sneaking glances at the clock on the VCR. Once the clothes come off, which takes about twenty-seven seconds, he switches into something like that fake TV sitcom acting. You know, when one character is trying to keep something from another while a third, who is in on the caper, is present.

That is, he pretends to be hot for what's about to come in a way that is sure to let me know that he really is not. Too much lip licking and pouting.

"Nice bed." Yes, it is, I guess. He stretches out both bare skinny arms in a totally inauthentic gesture to welcome me into his embrace. I accept fully and fall into him, close my eyes, wait.

"There, there. Now, now." He's doing the maternal thing. Rubbing a circle on my back with a palm that barely touches me. He smells like Cuervo Gold and Marlboro Mediums. I still have on my underwear. Now it's me who's eyeing the clock. Monday, 11:07 P.M. Better get started.

He makes it clear that he doesn't want to be kissed on the mouth. I make it clear that I want to kiss him. It's a buyer's market as I tongue among the teeth and loose crumbs of corn chips. I bite his neck, and he butts me away with his head. "Watch it. No marks, remember?" I don't remember. That is, I don't remember that being part of our contract, but, whatever. I grab his wrists with more force than I need to raise his arms above his head. He pretends to resist. I burrow my nose and mouth into one, then the other of his sparsely haired armpits. He wriggles and quivers as I tickle him there with my tongue, as I pull and suck loose strands of pit hair. Thankfully he doesn't wear deodorant but is reasonably clean anyway. I suck on his nipples, which gets less of a reaction than I expected, so I move on down.

I continue the theme of burying my face into his other damp hairy crevices. And yes, I kiss his long bony feet and the backs of his knees. Sometimes he's with me, sometimes not. Most often he watches from far away. I feel too active and frenetic. He has become the embodiment of stillness, almost Zen.

I can jockey him around like some nude G.I. Joe doll. Reorganize limbs any way I want them. But like the toy soldier, his face always stays the same. It's the one thing about him that I need to change. The phrase "by any means necessary" pops into my head, and I shudder at the implications— physical, sexual, political, criminal.

I had a perverted subletter earlier this year who left behind in a bag of toys, among other stuff, a bottle of poppers and a twelve-pack of surgical gloves. I haven't been into amyl since the mid-'70s, and I've never worn hand rubbers, but right now I'm superconscious that I might be boring my naked hireling, and I think, "maybe this will entertain the little shit." I snap a glove onto my right hand and begin to glide it over his back and butt. It's frictionless. "Hmmm, that feels good." I slap his ass. "So does that." I lift his passive little behind up from the mattress and spank him again and again and again till I begin to get bored and his buns have reddened. I reach for a tube of Super-lube that the perv left behind and bathe my gloved hand with it. I slather a liberal amount in his ass crack, and still I get no reaction, so I probe with my middle finger. I'm reminded of the yearly embarrassment when during my prostate exam my young doctor nervously performs this exact act with the shy apology, "You may experience some discomfort." I always involuntarily smirk and chuckle a bit which makes Dr. Mike even more tense. Here in my own bedroom I could be poking a rolled medallion of raw veal for all the response I'm getting. I twizzle my finger around, feeling the wrinkled walls of his insides. Occasionally my fingertip comes across unmoored bits of stuff. Curious. I withdraw part way then add one, then two more fingers. His head turns quickly to look at me, then looks away. He gathers some pillows and clutches them to his chest. Is this the reaction I was waiting for? I'm not sure, but for now it will have to do. I braid and unbraid and rebraid my three fingers inside him. I hear a change in his breathing. Or is it mine? I think that I should say something so I place my ungloved left hand on the small of his back, which is now beaded with sweat.

"You okay?"

He responds with a grunt that sounds like it could be a "yes," so I continue. I've never done this before; I'm a little apprehensive. I'm also spellbound by the act, and I need to keep it going. I glance at the VCR and see that contractually there are twenty-five minutes to go. I pull back my three fingers and prepare to squeeze in the fourth. I rummage left-handed in the bag and gather six wooden clothespins. I slowly, meticulously decorate his dainty dick and scrotum. He silently flinches as each pin is added. Good. Good. I uncap the vial of poppers with my left hand and my teeth and place it under his nose. "Breathe in." He does and in slide my four fingers, my thumb tucked into the fold. I'm in as far as the last knuckles which surprises and scares me. I pause. He says nothing. He's breathing loudly. He's clutching those pillows as he would a flotation device after a water landing. I push the vial under his nose again, though no more forward progress seems possible. I think, I want to feel his bleeding heart beating in my hand. Then I think, What for? He takes the poppers from me and inhales once, once more, then again. I've been twisting my hand around and back, around and back. He adjusts his spine, snakelike, supple. Slowly my hand is sucked in beyond its hump. His asshole is braceletting my wrist. I feel light-headed and woozy. I'm not sure what to do now. Again I ask how he's doing. Again I get a grunt in reply.

That I'm aware that the CD has changed, that there's a drip in the kitchen, and that a car alarm just went off. It troubles me. Those extraneous sounds should be banished from my brain by the feat of reaching up inside a man's belly and being shackled there by his anus. But no, I remember that my American Express is overdue; Mother's birthday is next month. The room smells like a giant fart. He told me his name was Kim which I'm sure is a lie. With my free hand, I reach clumsily for a disposable camera on the night stand and take a picture of him from the waist down. I wonder if I'll have the guts to get it developed at the corner Fotomat. The clock says we have eleven more minutes. I prepare to liberate myself. I smear my naked left hand up and down in the pool of sweat caught in a deep furrow of his back. Slowly, slowly, slowly. Then suddenly I'm out. He utters an even more guttural sound than before. "Are you all right?" The greasy glove is flecked with his shit. Now he's whimpering, but he hasn't moved. "Are you all right?" He rolls to his side, facing away from me and chokes, "Just let me lie here and talk to myself for a minute."

I get up to dispose of the glove, smelling it first, of course. There is no blood so I feel confident that I haven't caused any permanent damage. Physically at least. There's an opened 40-ounce of Budweiser in the fridge. I take a long swig then get a roll of toilet paper that I bring back to the bed. He's still murmuring to himself, folded tightly around my pillows. I put the Bud and the TP on the mattress in front of him. He takes the bottle and nurses it as if he were its baby. He won't look at me. I look at the VCR. "Uh, officially we're off the clock now, right?" He nods in my direction. I'm still in my underwear. I change the music and go to my desk and begin to write this.

"I'm not good at this," I thought through the silence in the minutes before his clothes came off. Reared by a Southern Baptist mother, I wanted to offer him tea or a soft drink....
I smoke two American Spirit Lights, make a cup of coffee, smell my pits, and play some Solitaire before I finish with:

I changed the music and went to my desk and wrote.

It's been an hour and twenty minutes. I've been so wrapped up in the chronicling of the night's events that I've forgotten that there's an actual person lying in my bed. He's still cocooning around my pillows, holding the empty beer bottle. He's motionless, which spooks me. I touch his shoulder. His skin is icy cool. I flash on two words: "Man/One." Then there's a slight rise and fall in his rib cage. I shake him lightly, then some more. His body minispasms. "Hey, Kim, time to go." His head and eyes drift toward me. Hazy but alive. He unravels a winding string of words that includes questions concerning the time and whether he can stay just a little while longer. He curls away from me, closing his eyes. I take the empty from him, "I'll get you something to drink." He shrugs his whole body. In the kitchen, I drop the bottle into my recycling box and pour him some filtered water. Back in the bedroom I sit next to him. "Here." He's snoring softly. He defines calm, peace. I rub the cool sweaty glass between his shoulder blades. He shudders away. "Kim...Kim." Since I'm convinced that that's not his real name, it's me who's doing the bad acting now—World War II British army nurse to wounded American soldier, "Kim, you must wake up now." No, he's a giant, contented baby, snoozing serenely, with big feet and a greasy butt.

It's late. I'm tired. I'm seduced by his apparent tranquility. There's dancing under his eyelids as his lips suckle mutely. I begin gathering the detritus of our debauchery. I put the vial of poppers, opened package of gloves, and tube of lube back into the toy bag. Gingerly defusing a bomb, I unclip each clothespin from his puny genitalia. There is no explosion. I cover him with Aunt Bonnie's crazy quilt. I stuff an extra twenty into his sleeping fist, take one pillow away from him and a blanket from the floor, and go to the sofa and crash.

Breakfast.

Hey, Stud

I should've charged you extra for that little scene. I'm too nice a guy, I guess. I guess I lack certain business skills. I can't find one of my socks (not important) or my black baseball cap (muy importante). I think they might be under you but I don't want to wake you up. If (when) you find them you know how to find me. Or I can get them when I come over next time. Hint, hint. Anyway, it was weird but hot.

Friends to the end,

Kim.

P.S. I started reading what you wrote but it was like hearing my voice on the answering machine. Maybe when you get famous you can give me a free autographed copy. Or when I marry a rich senator you can use it to blackmail us.

Anyway, whatever, K.

P.P.S. Oopsie. Your door doesn't lock without a key. Hope nobody comes in and kills you in your sleep.

K.

Shooting Stars

Luis Miguel Fuentes

I could feel his beard stubble rubbing against my cheeks kinda like sandpaper. I close my eyes, and imagine it's really Kevin insteada this outta-towner...Ted, Fred, whatever the fuck he said, it probably ain't his real name anyway. I arch my back like when you stroke a cat, tryin' to give him a dislocated tongue. He's been eatin' me out for like ten minutes already....Fuggit, it's his time, and he's definitely payin' for it. I usually drift, dream, and end up in this semiconscious state where I can kinda hear the traffic fourteen stories below my usual sleaze-bag whore hotel where I so often bring Teds of various lands sizes shapes colors...drift...as he spreads my cheeks with his hands and sucks, his stubble trips the events....I'm smelling air that's fresh with flowers, honey fills the air and tickles my nostrils....I smile to myself 'cause Ted becomes Kevin every hour on the hour. His mere stubble becomes a full beard....I'm standing by the pond on Kev's property, and he picks me up 'cause I'm still kinda small. I wrap my legs around his back as our tongues chase each other...licking tops bottoms sides and parts of your mouth that have never had the pleasure. His hands under my ass dipping fingertips into my shorts and touching so gently what I want him to really dig into. It's erotic to fantasize that I'm his pauper peasant boy and he's the king. Erotic for him to think of me as a gentle faun when I'm an anxious tiger. He touches me with his fingertips as an artist strokes his canvas, gentle at first and fierce at times…heating with passion. Trace the trail of my face from my forehead gently down to my chin with your other hand pawing at my cheeks as you lick a line from my chest to the head of my dick which you take into your experienced mouth as loving as possible savoring each second for you for me.

I usually only let Teds fuck me if they pay big or I'm wrapped up in one of my Chicago fantasies and Ted becomes Kev once again pushing into me pulling outta me and filling me with love (juice). I time his clicks with mine. A stroke of the prostrate and we come at exactly the same time…kinda like synchronized ejaculations.…He likes to kiss me more than fuck, I think. He's suckin' on my tongue, and I bust a nut that mats the hair on his belly. I grab his ass and push him as deep into me as possible as I come. I feel his cheeks tensing and then relaxing. As his ass tenses his dick expands, he's stretching me to heaven, my love assassin.

I like to lay out on his lawn in the back on a summer night. Sometimes I bring my lover Miguel with me. We share a blanket and a bottle of wine. As I lay on my back fingering the stars, ya know like putting 'em between my fingers and closin' one eye as I kinda measure the suckers…, I kinda hope to see a UFO or at least a shooting star. Kev rolls us up some joints 'cause we ran outta Phillies. He likes to roll 'em, but I never seen him smoke. He likes to watch me and my baby smoke and press our lips together exhaling and inhaling each other. We stroke faces and stroke our hard dicks under the moonlight as we slowly undress…a vision of naked boys dancing in the darkness. Kevin jerks himself off watching us sixty-nine until he can't take no more and turns sixty-nine into seventy. We come into the sky as I finally catch a shooting star.

...And the maid is knocking or rather pounding at the door. It seems I overslept....Sunlight is trickling through these $1.50 curtains that looked like they was robbed from a funeria. Fuckin' red velvet? The pounding is annoying me so I yell in Spanish, "Yay, ya cono!" I get up and slap on my last-night jeans which are waitin' for me in the corner like a fuggin' dog at feedin' time. Ted's gone....I slip on my jeans and tuck my T-shirt in so it don't come out the bottom of my sweatshirt. To be messy in my line is like way outta line. Fuckin' Ted...stiffed me and my loot. I seen like eight Teds the day and night before and was packin' $420 under the sole of my Jordans...gone .... I open the door to a young maid....Mexican.

She keeps yellin' at me all the way to the elevator where I press the button and then take a step to the steps where I jet down fourteen flights of piss scent. I want to cry at my stupidity, but I can't, I can only cry at my ignorance. I worked all night and gotta jump a turnstile to get home..., so I say fuck it and spend another dreaded day at the Deuce.

The Whole Bloody Story of My Life from Beginning to End

Shaun Levin

Just listen to this. You're not going to believe it. I was on the tube, right, coming home from the studio, right, and there was this guy on the train. We were eyeing each other like fucking animals. And I just knew something was going to happen. I could tell he was really into me. I could tell he really wanted me. I knew exactly what I was wearing, and I could tell it was making him hot. He was so fucking gorgeous, and he just couldn't keep his eyes off me. And I let him, fuck, I let him stare as much as he wanted to, right. And then he got up, and it was like he had some fucking dog collar around my neck. He yanked me out of my seat, and I was off. After him. We were way past King's Cross, past the Angel. But I wasn't going to let this one get away. He was fucking gorgeous, and I was shaking, I was, I was so fucking nervous I thought I'd shit in my pants. In these new fucking cords. I thought I was going to die.

Anyway.

His place wasn't far from the station, but I could tell I'd never be able to trace my way back later. I could tell there was no way I'd find my way back to the station. It's not like I know my way around London after all these years. Take me to a part I've never been before, and every house and street looks the fucking same to me. Identical. But I was being led by him, right, fucking dragged along like a dog. His boots were thudding on the pavement as if they were saying: Fuck you all out there. I don't give a fuck what you all think. I live here. This is my fucking street. I've never had that, you see. I've never had that feeling in any place. So it was like I could feel it through him. Fuck, I could have carried on walking behind him forever.

But then we got to his house. Just this regular fucking house. He opened the front gate as if he didn't give a fuck whether I was behind him or not. He unlocked the front door, and we walked up to his flat on the first floor. One of those converted houses with about six fucking flats in one house. He said his brother owned the whole place. He said his brother felt sorry for him. He said he felt sorry for him and let him stay in one of the flats. And then inside. Inside there was no light. The blinds were down, and he kicked the door shut behind him, and there was this dead fucking silence. Like: Shut the fuck up, nobody talks from this point on.

I knew he was going to turn round and lash at my face with a fucking knife. I knew it. I thought: This guy's going to whip out a fucking chain from his back pocket and fuck my head in. And I thought: What the fuck. There's no way I'm going to get out of here so just fucking enjoy yourself. And did his place stink. Fuck, that place smelt foul. Cigarettes and dirt and smelly clothes, and I just thought: You English are so fucking grimy. You're all fucking slobs. And that was when I knew this guy would never hurt me.

He came at me, grinning, grinning like some fucking evil fuck, but I just kept my eyes on his. I let him play his game. His face was this close to me, this close, and he put his mouth on mine. He held the back of my neck and pushed my mouth open with his tongue as if he wanted to dig through me. He was quiet, not a word, and I wasn't going to risk saying anything. I wasn't going to make a fool of myself by saying something really stupid. Then he bit my bottom lip, here, look, look what he did, left his mark on me, and then he stepped back. He stepped back to look at me and started to undress right there in the fucking living room. In that fucking pitch dark living room that stunk of wet ashes, armpits, and shit-stained underwear. He knew I was watching him. He took his time taking off his jacket, unbuttoning his white cotton shirt, massaging the hair on his chest, pinching his nipples. He stood there in his boots and jeans, and I knew with every pore in my fucking body that this guy was going to fuck me and it was going to be so fucking good.

He was like a fucking animal, I'm telling you, thick and hard and covered in dark red hair. He left his clothes on the floor and walked into his bedroom, sweat glistening on him like fucking dew in a spider's web. You can't imagine what it was like. I just wanted to go down on my knees and lick his whole fucking body. I did. I was ready to lick the fucking floorboards his shoes had stood on. I imagined looking up at the fur on his shoulders and his chest and stomach and him pulling me to my feet and saying: Boy, I'm going to fuck your pussy.

Fuck it, you know how smooth I am. You know how sometimes my body feels as soft as a cunt and I'll do anything to get a man to fuck me. I'll follow him into his bedroom and beg him to stick his cock inside me. I'll call fucking strangers on the phone and leave the door open for them to come in. That's what was going to happen here. But no begging this time, right. He was fucking hot for me. He was going to fuck me like a fucking wolf, and there was nothing I could do about it. I took off my All-Stars and my cords, then my T-shirt. I left them lying there in the hallway and went into his bedroom and lay back on the bed, just watching him take off the rest of his clothes. He stared at me while he undid his trousers and scooped out his cock. He looked at me as if he could kill me and he said, "I want your arse so fucking badly. Show it to me. Lie back like that and let me see. Let me see where I'm going to stick my fucking cock."

And I did just what he said. Fuck. He was so fucking hot for me.

"I'm going to fuck your arse," he said. "I'm going to fuck it so good. I'm going to fuck your arse like it's the only thing in this fucking world."

This guy couldn't get enough. Can you picture it. Can you picture him there talking to me, saying, "I want to be inside you, man. I want to fuck you so hard and long and sore. I want to fuck that soft smooth cunt of yours. Come on, show me. Spread your arse like that. Yeah. Let's see."

By then I'd propped myself up on his pillows, holding my arse open and watching him pull off his boots, then his trousers and socks. He wasn't wearing any underpants, and his cock stood out like a fucking flagpole, jerking up and down every time he said "fuck" as if his prick was some fucking worm-monster waiting to get stuck into my fucking arsehole.

He came at me with a vengeance. He did. He pushed those cushions off the bed and jerked my legs over my head and buried his tongue up my arse like there was no fucking tomorrow. I wanted his whole fucking face in there. I wanted him slobbering all over me, making noises with his mouth so it'd feel like the sounds were coming from inside me. His tongue pressed against the lips of my arsehole, and I lifted myself up and held onto the back of his shoulders and pulled him into me deeper. And he made those noises, those fucking animal noises, as if he couldn't get enough. Like a mangy fucking mutt caged and starved for days. He whimpered and growled and chewed into my arse as if he didn't care what was going to happen.

And his bed was like ice. Believe me. I'll never forget that. Like ice. Sheets like a fucking ice rink. But smelly. Fuck, did they stink. Damp and creased and smelly. I could feel the fucking cum stains melting under my back. And his hot tongue between my legs.

"Open up," he said. "Open." And I swear I could have screamed or fallen in love between each syllable. "Come on, baby," he said. "Come on. Open up for me."

I could have ripped myself in two for him to be inside me. I pulled my arsecheeks apart and felt his face push further into me. I don't know if you've ever felt this way. I don't know if you've ever trusted someone like that. Have you? Have you ever trusted someone to do to you whatever they wanted, and you knew they'd never hurt you?

And when his tongue wasn't enough, he tucked his shoulders under my knees and brought his cock to my arsehole. He stared at me without blinking and slowly made his way into me, chiseling his cock inside, jerking it back and forth. He was in. He stopped. He closed his eyes and let out this gush of air that was a scream and a sigh. Then he drew his cock out to the tip and slid it back in and kept whispering, "Open up, open up, open up." And I watched him moving in and out of me, and he looked so fucking tormented. Fucking deranged, believe me.

He was sweating like a pig, right. And grunting. Every time he stuck his cock into me he'd snort like a pig, like a desperate fucking animal that had lost all control. His body became darker as the sweat made his hair a damp mat on his skin. My legs were aching as if I'd been holding them up in the air for fucking ages. I needed to lower them, so I slid them off his shoulders and made them a ring around his back. I put one arm around his neck and clung to him like a baby. I pulled myself up and filled my mouth with his hairy nipple. I sucked on it and drank sweat out of his fur and told him to fuck me.

"Oh, God," he said. That's what he said. He said, "Oh, God, I'll fuck you. I'll fuck you. I'll fuck you so hard. I promise."

With my other hand I wiped the sweat off his back and rubbed it into my chest. My skin was already slippery from the sweat dripping off him. He pushed me onto the bed and stared at me. His face was beautiful. I touched his cheek and stroked his forehead and ran my fingers through his hair and traced them down his spine. His body tensed as if he was about to pounce. I clung to his arsecheeks and drew his cock deeper into me, slowly, reassuring myself. I wanted to say: Look. See? I've got all of you inside me.

Are you listening? Are you listening? Can you imagine this? Can you imagine what this was fucking like? In the middle of fucking nowhere with this stranger inside me, and I knew it was going to be fine. I knew that all he wanted was to fuck me. That he wanted me to lie there and take his big fat red-haired cock up my arse.

Then he said. He said, "You like it, don't you?" He said, "You love me fucking you."

"I do," I said.

"You do what?"

"Love it." I said. "I love it."

"What do you love?" he said.

I said, "I love you fucking me."

And then, just like that, he lifted his hand and slapped me across the fucking face. Hard. The pain shot from my cheek to my arsehole like a dart ripping through me. Then he just grabbed my legs and yanked my body down onto his cock and hugged his arms around my knees and shoved his cock into me and used my body to pound into as if I wasn't there and he pulled my arse towards him over and over. And I just let go. I just closed my eyes and let go as if I was doing some fucking yoga exercise, some kind of meditation, right. Fuck, I don't know, some mind and body split. I was looking down at myself and thinking: Fuck, this is amazing. I'm nothing. I feel nothing, and I'm fucking loving it. And then he fucking snorted up this big wad of gob from the back of his throat and spat into my face.

And I could feel again. I could feel how soft my arse was around his cock. I could feel how tight his arms were around my knees. I could feel the fur on his chest rubbing against my legs. And I wished he'd slap my face again. God, I fucking prayed he'd hit me before he came. Because I knew he was close. I knew by the way he was grunting and roaring and then his cum shot into me and dripped from my arse down to my back and he just dropped my legs and fell on top of me.

My face was under his armpit, drenched with sweat, and fuck knows how long since he last washed. He was gasping like he'd just run some fucking marathon. I put my arms around his back and stroked him. His skin was coarse and slippery. I ran my fingers up and down his back, combing his hair, until he rolled off me, slowed down his breathing, and just stared at the ceiling.

"Okay," he said. He said, "Okay. Okay." He said, "You can fuck off now."

I was lying there and there was nothing inside me and I thought: How the fuck am I going to get out of here. I wanted to ask him if I could stay. I wanted to say to him: Let me be here with you. Let me stay here at least until it gets dark outside. Then I can go. I don't want to be out there where everyone can see me. Please, I'll lie here and be still. And when it's dark, I'll go. I should have said that to him. I should have. All I wanted was to be near him. But I kept quiet, I kept hoping he hadn't meant what he said, or that he'd fall asleep and forget. I should have said to him: You don't have to be afraid. You know that. I don't expect anything from you.

But he got off his bed and moved into the living room. He gathered up my clothes and walked with the bundle to the door. He opened the door and chucked everything onto the landing. I walked past him and was going to ask if he really wanted me to go but he stared at me with such disgust I couldn't bear saying anything to him. I couldn't but I still wanted to and I felt my cock go hard and I just said, "Let me stay with you. Please. Let me stay."

His face wrinkled up as if I was the juice at the bottom of the rubbish bin. I should have said: I can love you more than anyone in this world. I can love you like nobody can. But I didn't. He held the door open with his foot and stood with his arms folded across his chest. I looked up at him, at that red fur covering his chest, at his massive nipples above his hands. Then he grabbed his cock and wiped my arse juices from it and onto the wall outside his place. He stepped back inside and slammed the door. And that was it.

I put on my top, hoping someone would come up and see me naked. Fuck, maybe he was even watching me. I tied my laces, my trousers still round my ankles, my arsehole facing his door. I walked back the way we came, looking straight ahead, making sure I didn't see the street name on the corner wall. I know what happens when you come back for more from these guys. I took a left, I think, I think it was a left, and I kept walking. The sun was still out but the air had turned cooler. I love this kind of weather, the kind of weather we've been having lately, that crisp brisk-walk kind of weather. It reminds me of when I was a kid. Going fishing with my grampa. Sitting in his boat at the mouth of the river before the sun came up.

I wandered around for ten minutes before I saw the café. I was sure I'd been there before. The name looked familiar.

Maybe they'd done the place up since I was there last. It was bright. Yellow and orange walls and this bright blue furniture. The guy behind the counter stared at me. He just stared at me, and I thought: Aren't you open yet? Was there a sign on the door I didn't see?

"You alright, mate?" he said.

"Could I just have a coffee," I said.

"Anything else?" he said.

Because I remember him asking that. I remember him asking if I wanted anything else. And I remember him calling me "mate." I think he did. I think he said: Anything else, mate? Because when he said that, I knew I had to get out of there. I knew that if he asked me one more question I'd answer him the way mad people do when they latch onto you at a bus stop. I'd end up telling him the whole bloody story of my life from beginning to end.

I said just tell me the way to the tube, and he frowned and said, "Coffee's on the house, mate." He said, "Stay. Drink it before you run off." I said I had to be somewhere. I said I'd forgotten that I had to be somewhere. And I did. I did have to be somewhere. I had to be here with you, didn't I? The ride home's a blur now. Maybe because I kept my eyes shut on the train. Maybe because no one ever looks at you in this city.

I had a quick shower at home and changed into some clean clothes. When I looked at myself in the mirror everything seemed fine. I looked fine. I hadn't eaten all day, and my face always looks better when I'm hungry. More defined and chiseled, right. I like the way I look sometimes. Jesus. Thank God for that. I never have to worry too much about going out and looking a mess. And then I came here. And here we are. And I'm fucking starving. So let's order some food.

Bonehead

Lawrence Ytzhak Braithwaite

You have two ways of leaving this
establishment—immediately or dead.
HUGH O'BRIAN in *The Shootist*

Pasnem told; he wasn't any more than violence. The acts and what had been done to him vindicated his desire to perpetuate a certain cruelty and disregard upon his nature. It was unnatural, shameful, and brutally vulgar. He stole Pasnem's lighter, and everybody laughed.

He went to move out of his place (they lived) to clean the hazard of him. All he could think about was all the wicked thing—the idea of deadness. Pasnem and Bat and Uggy and Crocket, they're getting things done—moving's a shoot down. Pasnem couldn't remember how the couch got in the place, but he remember that it wasn't there to begin with—True brought it in. He charged him nothing, and then he moved further up island so he could take over a town. He took the pickup, too. So they had to get Uggy to do the move.

Him and Louis, they shot inside, on this couch. It was all inside them. It ran straight up their hearts and drunk punched their lungs—no shit to clean up or anything. Pasnem left him shaking, and they slapped each other's palms for getting there like that. They say girlies can only do that but they wrong—just an untrue.

Under the couch was something choice when they moved it—was a flap of meth. Pasnem lost that fukker over three months ago. He couldn't find it for fuk, but he wanted to; real grave. It cost him a twenty, and it was about two points. He got Bat to close the door, and they smoked the rest. Uggy went with, to the bathroom, for awhile, and came out pretty stokt. He got junkie sleeves year round. In ninety degree summer days, when he changes his mind, for a few months, that swell runs through more of Pasnem's e-oil....it got more than fourteen-thousand IU's—it all cover over, there.

Louis never was comfortable doing anything unless it involved force and aggravation. So sleeping starkus on hot nights like that would never be considered. The boiling in the blud needed to be sustained. Nothing to do with passion, or passion for Pasnem, just only a distance in the relief of discomfort and added discomfort of sharing an enclosed space that limited his need to cool his body.

They got all his stuff moved quick after, and nothing could stop them, not even the tree daemons scraping the top of the van with their twig fingers.

Louis didn't see the beasties, like Pasnem did, the first time, on this evil island. He took him to the woods and kept trying to make him watch the diddlers have sex. He'd go, "Look." But Pasnem wouldn't (cause of the cammed agents hiding in the trees trying to spook all the woodsy guys from going at each other). Nobody saw the beasties around...scary, sitting in the tub, with affecting fluttering badness somethings, like that overhead. He's got water to duck under there, and beasties, they don't like water—they dirt things. His heart quickened, and Pasnem couldn't get excited over anything, but the chill was doing him good, not that he could ever get off when Louis would stress him out so much.

Louis'd hang with tuffs in puff jackets whispering threats—mock boasts of gargantuan times of dada coons that could have been. He had an awkward seriousness about him like a boy in a ill-fitting shirt. But his eyes revealed a hesitation which rendered his stature bathetic. Anyone familiar with a hard life, beyond the conditional cruelty of gangland parents, would have tagged him spot on. He was a joke to Pasnem and to Bat.

Pasnem and True, then Pasnem and Louis, they going to do big deals and head off to Mexico——just like Bobby Blake. Thing is, when True bailed and he found out about Louis and Pasnem, he said,
　　—He'd probably pimp you to the howies—

Louis got it all started, on that night, when he and him first came into this bonanza of uptown joy and they chased it with bourbon and Guinness, in the glasses they stole, from the welly pub down the street...and it was just hot. The landlord never turn the heat off, and the outside was freezing piss. So everything was shut up. Louis went to the bathroom for awhile and came out with nothing. Pasnem looked up from the table and saw him in the big chair. He didn't know that he would look that way. His legs overwhelming him. They framed, perfectly, all the stuff in between. He looked sweet. How could he upset it.

Louis figured, with Pasnem, the way he is,
　　—We'd just have to figure a way round that, then—

So that didn't kill the thought none at all. It was all up to Pasnem, and Pasnem, he waited for the big oops!

He could only get the smell of a lunch box or brown paper bags when Uggy, Crocket, Bat and him, walked into his new place. It's always cold, first, but he didn't feel that he had to bring the debugger to clean out the baddies and beasties from the crib.

It's what Louis did.

Pasnem never smacked him with the towels. They just wrapped them, and some blankets, around themselves and sat there on the couch, laughing and listening to the Wailers and Rancid. Louis knew every word—of Rancid. Pasnem pointed his finger and mouthed, "hypocrite."

True and Crocket gave Louis a slash across his face once— True, before he left...then Louis, he went too, to his mother's farm.

When he, when Louis, took Pasnem for a walk in the woods, he held his hand...this magga high yellow jackass, he came on to Pasnem, there. Pasnem didn't watch him much. He tried to touch Pasnem in front of the tree witches and daemons. The chill was making him feel better but Louis always stressed him, and this dandy was stressing him. The man, he screamed at him that Pasnem didn't like Blackness. Pasnem did. The hyello wouldn't come to the conclusion that Pasnem didn't like him, is all—he just ugly.

Louis and Pasnem, they were making plans for murder.

Louis lost an eye in a fight. Bat says so. It was True and Crock that did; for shit Louis said and took from Pasnem and others and them.

Pasnem and Bat and Uggy and Crocket, they lay down on the bed, in that room, that's better than the one he just left behind, because of the badness there. No sticky twinkling stars on the ceiling. Pasnem found a pack of matches, and Bat and Uggy and Crocket all smoke a cig and passed it back—Pasnem, he got his own.

…he was only once with Louis in this bed. It was the morning, the next day, after figuring a way around it. He woke up and he pulled Louis' legs apart and watched him. Louis told him,
    —FUK. I'm still asleep—

Louis made some magnificent noize and breathed out. He did, and Louis told him and he watched him and he did and he did.

A Beating

Karl von Uhl

"Evening, Ross," I said. I had planned a simple night out, even dressed simply—leather pants, vest, no shirt, sap gloves, engineer's boots and jacket—to ensure a night of socializing. The bar was pleasingly dark, and the music's mechanized pulse was insistent and sensuous.

Ross stood at his customary spot, wearing a white T-shirt, torn jeans, and combat boots, a stripe of black rawhide circling his neck and dangling midline down his chest. He had recently trimmed his Vandyke.

"Good evening, sir," he said, catching my eyes briefly then lowering his gaze deferentially to my boots.

"Are you having a good night?" I asked, looking at his close-cropped hair, sleek and lambent in the blue light from the bar.

"Yes, sir, after a difficult week, sir," he said, raising his head, but keeping his eyes lowered, obeisant.

"Sorry to hear it was a difficult one, Ross. Would you get me another," I said, handing him my empty bottle.

Ross was an excellent boy, a fine example of what leather can do for a man. He was obedient in the best sense of the word, humble, appreciative of a strict code that is paradoxically liberating. In a world where meaning is popularly forced, Ross was reliable, reveling in the dance of graceful, pleasing causality and respectful indoctrination.

Ross returned, holding a bottle. "Sir, your beer, sir," he said, never taking his eyes from my boots.

"Let's go out to the patio," I said.

A scream pierced the night's camaraderie. I looked to the exit, my reflexes alert. Abandoning Ross, I ran to the door and threw aside the heavy leather curtain. Just outside was a young crew-cut blond with a bloodied mouth and nose and the start of a black eye. A man in black latex propped him up. "Where?" I asked.

"In a red jeep," said the blond, his speech muffled with edema and a missing tooth. "Three of 'em. One that got me had a baseball cap and a Niners shirt."

"Call nine-one-one," I said to his companion. I went to find the vehicle, in hopes of getting a license plate number. I strode quickly up the street and cut down an alley. There were headlights at the other end. I eased my pace a little, but paid careful attention. About sixty yards ahead of me was a pool of darkness between the Victorians, their languid regularity divided by the corrugated sheet metal gate of a pipe-fitting and glazing concern.

I reached for my keys as if looking for my truck but kept approaching. A voice called out, "Hurry up, dude!"

"I'm going as fast as I can, shit!" said a voice from the dark.

As my eyes adjusted, I could make out a figure. Male, maybe 5'8", slim build, a baseball cap clearly visible. As he leaned into the light, I saw a numeral eight stenciled on the back of his T-shirt. Steve Young's number. Running, I grabbed him.

"Shit!" he cried.

The jeep's lights flared as the engine roared. From the jeep, a shout, "Some fag's got Seth!"

"I was just pissin'," said Seth, trying to squirm out of my combination half nelson and hammerlock. "Fuckin' let me go!"

"No," I said. I lifted him easily and slammed his feet against the corrugated metal bordering the sidewalk. His cock, still leaking, dripped on his pants.

"Guys! Guys!" he yelled. The jeep yanked into reverse, backed out of the alley into the street, then roared off. "Fuck!"

"Shut up," I said, quietly.

"Fuck you, faggot!"

I twisted his arm further up his back. Seth yelped.

"I said, shut up." Keeping hold of him, I said, "I saw what you did. Don't try anything." I released his right wrist from the hammerlock; he shook that hand a few times but otherwise kept motionless. I unbuckled my belt and slowly removed it. "Give me your hand." He didn't move. "I said, give me your hand." When he did nothing, I flexed my elbow up to increase the pressure on the half nelson, keeping him in line. With the belt in my hand, I took his wrist again.

"Oh, god," he muttered.

"Give me your other hand," I said.

"Who the fuck are you?"

"Give me your other hand."

"I can't," he said. I eased the pressure, controlling how much he could lower his arm. I shot my hand forward, caught his left wrist, brought it behind his back, and lashed it to his right. After making sure they were secure, I took my hanky and, threading my left arm up through his in an awkward embrace, caught one end of it in my hand, twirled it, and tied it around his head, covering his eyes.

I took hold of his wrists. "Walk with me," I said, heading for my truck.

"My dick's still out," he said, strangling a whine.

"This is San Francisco. Who's going to notice?" I said. "Open your mouth." I stuffed in a glove to shut him up. I walked him stiffly to my truck, sat him down, and locked him inside. He sat still. No one noticed him on the drive home. Needless to say, I took a circuitous route.

"Are you a cop?" he asked. He was in the middle of my playroom, tied to a wooden chair that was missing a large part of its seat. His arms were behind him, ankles lashed to respective chair legs. He wasn't bad looking; maybe nineteen or twenty, brown eyes, buzzed head, a jaw that would turn square when the baby fat melted. His cock still poked out of his fly; he was uncircumcised.

I stood beside him. "Would it make a difference if I was?" I said.

I had converted my playroom from a storage area under my house, added a couple of floor drains, soundproofing, a workbench, and extended plumbing and electricity.

Seth was still clothed. A video monitor provided the only light in the room; images of Marilyn Chambers eating out her costar flickered past, the light but not its substance reflecting on the leather I wore. He stared blankly at the screen, his cock stirring to attention at the sight of a female tongue on female parts.

"You brought me here to show me pornos?" he asked, scornfully.

"No." I put my hand on his cock. He flinched. I watched as the tension leaked into his stomach and chest, through his shoulders and down his legs. "What's the matter? Never had your cock touched by a man?" I asked.

"No," he said, flat and hard.

"Not even a doctor."

"Okay, a doctor," he said, sullen and sarcastic. "But he wasn't a fag."

"How do you know?"

"He wasn't."

"How do you know?" I asked, squeezing a little. His cock fit easily in my hand, the pale flesh contrasting with my black glove. I stroked the tip of his glans lightly with my thumb. "I'm circumcised. That's one difference between my generation and yours."

"Shit! You wanna suck it, suck it, faggot!" he said, his anger peaking.

Tightening my grip on his cock with my left hand, I punched him hard in the gut with my right. "Takes one to know one," I said. He breathed hard. "Another difference between our generations is that mine was more optimistic."

I stood and turned on the light above my workbench. Various floggers and whips hung from a Peg-board. Below were drawers labeled T/T, C/B/T, and so forth, containing clothespins, clamps, sterile needles, scalpels, the detritus of a life committed to power exchange; a place for everything and everything in its place. I grabbed a pair of EMT scissors.

"Your name is Seth," I said.

"Yeah. So?" he said absently.

"I want to make sure I know what to call you."

"And your name's faggot," he said, candid and direct.

I slapped him hard, then yanked his T-shirt out of his pants and made quick work with the scissors, making sure to poke him in the throat with their rubber-coated tips and exposing his smooth chest and almost pinpoint nipples. A thin trail of hair slithered over the faint web of his abs and led below his belt line.

"Seth, let's get something straight. You think you know why you're here, but you don't. So shut the fuck up. I'm calling the shots. So shut the fuck up. And if you don't shut the fuck up," I said, walking to the bench and grabbing a belter, "you'll get this," and struck him hard with it across his chest. It left an imprint, white at first, then pink, then red, a sunset of the shades skin can offer.

I set the belter down and changed tapes in the VCR. Two men in various stages of leather and undress came on the screen, accompanied by a synthesized rendition of Stravinsky's "Firebird."

"Watch it," I said.

Seth turned his head away. The belter slapped against his chest. "Watch it," I said. Seth kept his head turned. Twice the leather slapped his chest; Seth gasped and turned his head to the screen. One man sucked the other's cock. Seth had gone soft.

"The worst fag bashers are always gay themselves," I said. "I think that's the case here."

"I'm straight," said Seth, rallying defiance, watching one man gulp greedily at the other's cock, seeking whatever nourishment was there.

"You don't believe that," I said, hitting his belly with the belter. A network of red and white lines crisscrossed his torso.

"Quit hitting me! It hurts!" he yelled.

Smacking him hard with the belter three times, I yelled back, "Do you think so?!" I wrapped the thick leather strap around his neck. "You stupid, arrogant little punk. You think you can get away with fucking someone up? Not with me," I said, tightening the strap with my hands. "What did you expect to find at my home? Ugly plus-size gowns, tattered wigs, and show tunes? See what stereotyping gets you?"

Seth's breathing turned rapid and shallow. I looked at his crotch and saw his cock stir. "See?" I said. I dropped the belter and yanked at his pants; they were baggy and difficult to manage, but I soon had them over his calves. Underneath he wore pale red boxers. He sat expressionless as I pulled them down. His cock unfurled lazily, pointing along his leg, his balls drawing up against his body. "You're getting hard," I said.

"Fuck you," he said, quietly.

"I'd be the sweetest piece you'd ever get," I said, slapping him open-handed on his belly. "You don't even struggle."

On the video screen were the two men, one fucking the other slow, deep, and hard. Seth's cock twitched again, but he obediently watched.

"You've never felt that? Never felt a cock up your ass?" I asked.

"Fuck no," he said, surprised that someone would ask.

"No teenage sex play with your cousins? No Boy Scout blow jobs?"

"Fuck you," he said, derisively.

"You're the one getting hard. That just proves my point."

I walked over to my workbench, selected a pair of adjustable alligator clamps, and removed the rubber tips. Seth tried not to change expression as the jagged metal teeth bit into his nipples, but apprehension crawled slowly through his face. "You can't fight the sensation," I said, "it'll happen. Every man has the same nerves." When both were attached, I increased the pressure slightly. Seth clenched his jaw, fought shutting his eyes. With a gloved finger, I stroked the underside of his glans, sliding my finger underneath his foreskin. With my forefinger and thumb I pinched his frenum and pulled it forward, seeing how far it could stretch; it would pierce nicely.

"Is this what you always do?" he asked. "Hurt guys?"

"No," I said, "just you," and kicked the chair. The chain on the clamps jumped; Seth whimpered.

Back at the bench I fetched a razor and a can of shaving cream. As Seth watched the video, I kicked the back of his chair hard. He screamed, spilling face first onto the concrete floor. I walked over to a sink, ran the water hot, and filled a bowl. "Time for Daddy to teach you how to shave, son," I said.

The wide hole in the chair's seat framed his ass neatly. I wet his crack and slowly applied the cream. His legs tensed every time I brushed his hole. "Feels good whether you want it to or not," I said.

I worked the razor carefully around the ruddy corona of his hole. The hair came off in short, easy strokes. Seth held perfectly still, made no sound, though I could tell from his breathing he was still conscious. His legs no longer tensed when I touched his hole, now smooth, the satiny flesh glistening from being rinsed so many times. I kept shaving, following the line along his perineum, and stopped short of his balls.

Using my foot as a fulcrum, I wrenched the chair back onto its four legs. Seth stared impassively at me, as though somehow he could evoke pity, his right cheek seriously abraded and swollen, dotted and streaked red and brown. Dried blood lent a matte finish to his complexion. My cock swelled, pushing against my pants, held fast by the leather.

"You're not watching the video," I said. He looked at the screen. Two new men this time; one rusty-haired and bearded, was smearing the butthole of another, blond and bearded, with Crisco. The rusty-haired one dipped his fingers liberally into the other's hole, his thick peasant fingers glistening, the hole accommodating eagerly. Four fingers disappeared, emerged, disappeared. Without warning, the entire hand went in; the blond man opened his mouth, moaning, delirious.

I picked up a set of clippers from my workbench. "Bet you never knew your butthole could do that," I said.

"Let me go," said Seth, quietly.

"What?"

"Please. Let me go."

I knelt in front of him. "On one condition, Seth." Clippers buzzing, I sheared the hair from his balls.

He made a face, a little disgusted. "And what's that?"

"Admit the truth. Admit you're gay."

He threw his head back. "I told you. I'm straight," he said, wearily.

I slapped the welts on his stomach. "Watch the fucking video," I said. The hair around his semihard cock dropped away. I followed the trail of hair up to his navel. "You don't seem to mind this part, Seth."

"I've shaved before," he said, a trifle relaxed and asserted.

"Not for bodybuilding."

"No," he said, a little defensive. "You don't have to be a bodybuilder to shave. For swimming," he added, with a note of pride.

"Ah. I was a linebacker in college," I said. After a casual conversational beat, carefully measured for its awkwardness, I said, "So you're a swimmer."

"Yeah."

"Does shaving really help?"

"Some. Reduces friction. I get better times when I shave," he said with authority.

"Coach tell you to do it?"

"He says we don't have to, but says it helps."

"You know, I would have pegged you for a boxer."

"Nah, that's no sport. No finesse, no technique," he said.

His pubes were the merest stubble. I looked him in the eye. "Now, see? We can have a nice, civilized talk. And we can do it when we're both hard."

"I'm not hard," he said, affable.

"Look south, Seth." I grabbed his cock, fat against my hand, a little over six inches. "My cock is hard in these pants. It wants out, but I'm not going to let it out. I don't want to make yours shy," I said.

I jacked Seth's cock slowly. "It feels good. It feels good whether you want it to or not. And if I tug on this," I said, taking the chain between his nipples, "it feels even better." He gasped, and his cock jumped out of my palm and stood stiff, pointing from his groin.

I stood, leaving him to the video. "You know," I said, grabbing a bowl and a box of dental alginate from a drawer in my workbench, "a study was done not long ago. About homophobic men and their reactions to gay porn. Virtually all of them were turned on by it." Seth watched as one man plunged his arm into the other's hole, the hairs on his arm slicked by Crisco, sweat, and butt juice. Seth's cock never wavered.

"So?" he said. "You're gay, right? And that first video you put on was straight porn. Does that mean anything?"

I waved my hand. "A wiser man than I once said that if you process too much, you get Velveeta. All I know is you're hard."

"But I'm not gay," he said.

"You're hard."

"You can get hard for other reasons," he said abruptly, frustrated.

"Like what?" I asked. "Stargazing?"

"No. From fear," he said, discomfited. "Or other kinds of excitement."

"No doubt you read that bullshit in your high school sex ed class," I said, dumping a measure of alginate into the bowl. "At least I have the guts to say why I'm hard."

"I'm not shitting you," he said. "You ever see pictures of hanged guys? They all have bones."

"Homosexuality and necrophilia," I said. "This is getting interesting." I walked over to him. "You mean to say you're just afraid of me. Nothing more."

He nodded.

I slapped him hard, then grabbed his throat. "You don't know what fear is, asshole. Fear is not knowing who your friends are if you tell them who you really are." I could feel his carotid arteries dance feverish and monotonously under my fingertips. "Fear is having no job security on account of who you really are. Fear is the needle in your head telling you a walk down an alley could end in death." The muscles surrounding his trachea were slack against my fingers; his throat would make an easy fuck. "Fear is thinking your life isn't yours." I slapped him again. His stomach clenched. "I have to go upstairs. If I come back and see you aren't watching that video, I'll kick your ass. Is that clear?"

Seth nodded, measured and deliberate. He learned quickly, was trainable, malleable; here was Ross in the rough. My cock throbbed, swayed by the power of an autocracy built for two.

Upstairs, I went to my refrigerator, grabbed a quart of milk, and took a quick swig. From a cabinet, I took a tall disposable plastic cup. I descended the stairs quietly, making sure Seth was doing as ordered; he was. "Good boy," I said, scratching his head. At my workbench, I began cutting out the bottom of the cup with an X-Acto knife.

"Is this all there is in these videos?" he asked.

"You want plot in pornography? Two men meet, they fuck, they're much edified, the end. Like Susan Sontag said, 'there's only one dirty story,' " I said.

"Who?"

I kicked the chair. "Watch the fuckin' video!" The two men were joined by a third, dark-haired and bearded man. The rusty-haired man on screen wrapped a thick leather belt around his arm and sank his hand and arm into this man's ass. Elbow-deep, he started pulling the belt out, gently plunging his arm at the same time. The dark-haired man squatted on the cheap foam rubber mattress, his mouth in an open grin, supported by the blond.

I fit the erstwhile bottom of the cup over his cock, securing the edge with surgical tape. Seth's cock tapped against the inside, a drizzle of dick spit oozing along his foreskin. I tugged the skin down, exposing his moist glans, and tied a small noose of fishing line just under its edge.

"What the fuck's this?" asked Seth.

"Nosy bastard," I said, mixing a little water with the alginate. "Ever been to the dentist? And he made an impression of your teeth? I'm gonna make one of your cock." I took the end of the fishing line to keep Seth's cock centered and poured in the alginate, tilting the chair so the alginate was level in the cup. Seth hissed as the cool liquid swelled around his cock.

I brought my face to his. "Keep it hard, asshole." I kissed his forehead, tasting his salt and musk, a faint trace of nicotine, an acrid bite of something metallic. "Boy's gotta keep his cock hard for Daddy." Sweat rolled down Seth's face. "Prettyboy cock gonna stay hard, keep it up for Daddy," I said. "Think of that boy's hole you saw in the video, stretching wide open, those fingers sliding in and out, all that grease and juice feeling good, slicking up your insides. Make that hole slick and smooth, keep your pussy ready and wet for Daddy, give that cunt to Daddy, make him happy, keep his hand warm and safe in your guts. That's what you wanna do. That's what you need to do, just open up, just give it up, and say what you want, open up and suck it up your pussy, your pretty little boy pussy, tell your Daddy what you want." Carefully, I reached down and increased the pressure on the tit clamps. Seth looked directly at me, perhaps hoping to divine a message from my eyes. "Feels good whether you want it to or not, it all feels good, whatever Daddy does feels good, and you want to make him happy, make his dick happy, make his balls happy, 'cause Daddy makes you feel good way up inside, makes you feel good, makes you feel safe, makes you hope your dick'll get big as Daddy's." I licked my lips and inhaled Seth's sweat. "If you're bad Daddy'll whup you. But then he'll make it up to you, kiss away that hurt with more hurt, see what hurt his little boy can take, and Daddy's boy does anything for Daddy. You know deep down you came outta his dick, he gave you life, and you're afraid he'll take it back unless you give Daddy what he wants, what you know he wants, what you want to give him 'cause you owe him so much."

Seth's eyelids were heavy, burdened, and his breathing was deep. The alginate was set. I grabbed the X-Acto knife. Seth twitched when he saw it close in on his groin. The plastic cup cut away easily; I nipped off the exposed end of fishing line.

"You may go soft now," I said, tugging at the mold. Seth panted. "I said you may go soft," smacking his head. Seth looked up at me, puzzled.

I grabbed a bottle of Liquid Heet from the workbench. "Damn shame I couldn't prepare for this scene," I said. "Sometimes I fucking hate improvising." I swabbed his balls with the reddish fluid. "It takes a minute," I said. I reached up to the clamps; "Take a big breath," I said. As he inhaled, I removed the clamps. His moan stretched into a series of yelps as the blood rushed into the dented flesh. I dabbed his nipples with Liquid Heet.

"Fuck fuck fuck fuck fuck," he said, squirming in the chair, almost jumping.

"You soft?" I asked.

"Fuck yeah!" he said, spitting through his teeth.

"Fuckin' hold still!" I yelled. Seth continued whimpering, the menthol and camphor cutting into his scrotum and nipples. I carefully lifted the mold away from his reddening groin; his cock slipped out like a slack eel. A few hairs stuck in the mold, but otherwise it was a good impression.

"Fuck!!" yelled Seth.

"Shut up!" I responded, punching his stomach hard. Seth's mouth was agape, his eyes wild; his lungs would not swallow air. His chest and shaved belly heaved, hiccuped, yet would not draw. I felt dick spit leaking inside my leather pants, a familiar buzzing in my nuts. Seth strained against the rope and chair, the sinew thickly corded as only the fear of death can make it. He turned pale. I watched, knowing his brain was racing at infinite speeds, thinking I'll never breathe again I'm gonna die I'm gonna die. Suddenly the air sucked in, filling him deep; his color returned, flushing his face and neck, as if he were a creature of black and white bleeding into brilliant hues.

"It still burns," he said, weakly.

I unzipped my fly and pulled out my cock, eight inches, longer but not as thick as Seth's, with a slight upward curve. I flicked my middle finger hard against the underside, stinging my frenum, a strand of fluid sticking to my finger. My hard-on subsided as Seth watched, whimpering from the heat still slicing into his nuts and nipples. A sudden spurt of piss, then another, flew from my cock, landing on Seth's face. As the stream grew stronger, I sprayed him at his neck and down to his scrotum, nipple to nipple, soaking him good. "It'll cut the heat," I said. I left him dripping. Seth's head was down, as if he understood this as an act of marking territory, and felt ashamed.

I turned on a hot plate on the workbench; a small saucepan on it held paraffin shavings. "Ever read *Deliverance*? Or see the movie?" I asked.

"I saw the movie. Long time ago," he said, a little vacantly, panting.

"Did you like it?"

"Yeah. It was good, I guess," he said, still trying to catch his breath.

"Squeal like a pig, boy!" I said in my best north Georgia redneck drawl. The paraffin melted slowly, disappearing into itself, opaque into transparent. "So what do you think it's about?"

"*Deliverance*?"

"Yes."

"It's about testing yourself against nature. Finding out what you can do if you have to. Like Hemingway, in some ways," he said, warily.

"And what instructor told you that?" I asked. "*Deliverance* is gay porn made safe for straight men. There are clues everywhere; in the beginning, Jon Voigt's character fucks his wife in the ass as some forbidden delight before he leaves with his buddies and in a couple parts really gets into describing Burt Reynolds' muscles and cock. The other guy, Ned Beatty's character, gets fucked in the ass by a couple inbred freaks, the only men twisted enough to want to fuck a man's ass for sport, but only when Jon Voigt thinks he's absolutely powerless to stop it. In other words, all the vectors by which pleasure could have entered have been carefully and pointedly eliminated. And, in the book at least, in the end, one of the sheriff's deputy's is named Arthel Queen. Which means his nameplate reads A. Queen. What more do you want?"

The paraffin had melted completely. I took the mold of Seth's cock, carefully poured in the paraffin, and set it aside. I grabbed some lube and exchanged my leather gloves for latex.

I knelt in front of him. Over my shoulder he watched the rusty-haired

man gliding his hands into each man, as the other two, the blond and the dark-haired pair, kissed deeply as their holes were expanded and plumbed. I smelled my piss on him. I poured some lube into my right hand and slicked it through my fingers.

I reached under the chair and began massaging Seth's hole. The pucker was tight, but Seth didn't flinch. I smeared the lube around in small circles, smoothing out the folded flesh of his sphincter. Seth's balls drew up. "It's just a finger, Seth. I want to see what you're made of," I said. "Watch the movie. You know it can be done." I pressed my forefinger against the clenched muscle, vibrating it a little. The tip slipped in. "Feels good whether you want it to or not," I said, softly. I rewet my hand with the other one and kept pressing. "It's all muscle control. Let me in."

A squint flashed on Seth's face, growing more apparent as I worked my finger in. "That's it. Suck it up."

My finger slipped inside suddenly; Seth flinched, then relaxed. "Please. Let me go," he said, softly. "You can fuck me if you want. Just let me go."

"I don't want to fuck you," I said. I began circling my middle finger around the other where it entered him and slid it quickly inside. Seth caught his breath.

"You can fuck me if you want," he said again, absolutely still.

"Last time I heard that it was from a Marine, who then told me I couldn't kiss him 'cause he wasn't queer," I said. Seth's prostate was easily palpated. I rubbed my fingers across it; his cock jumped and began to swell but stopped midway. "I want to see if you're one of the big boys, Seth. I want to see if you can squirt," I said. "Are you gonna squirt for Daddy?"

"I can't," he said, garbled. His sphincter clenched onto my fingers. I continued rubbing his prostate. Dick spit oozed freely from Seth's piss slit.

"You don't think so?" I asked, pressing hard on his prostate.

Seth made a strangled grunt, dread focusing on his face and chest as though projected through a lens. I pressed again, rubbing up and down, maintaining pressure, insistent. "What we have here is a failure to communicate," I said, pressing ever harder, kneading the smooth wall of his rectum. Seth squeaked a few times, and his cock lolled up to his belly. He grunted again; his sphincter unclenched. His foreskin peeled back, and white fluid drooled from his cock. He shivered.

I pulled out my fingers and stood up, snapping the gloves off. Seth was choking back tears. I licked his face, licked the abrasions which had swollen and darkened nicely, tasted the salt. I dragged two fingers through the jizz on his belly, stuck them in my mouth, then stuck them in his.

"You shot quickly, Seth. A gift of youth," I said. I grabbed his head in both my hands. "Keep watching the movie," I said. Seth obeyed.

The wax casting was still warm, but solid enough to be removed from the mold with a little coaxing. I knelt behind Seth this time. "Daddy's real proud of you. You can squirt like the big boys. Daddy's gonna make you happy," I said, smearing lube on the wax dildo. "You're queer for cock, boy, got a sweet boy pussy, sweet slick pussy for hard cock, fingers, anything." I positioned the replica's head against his hole. "Ride it out, boy, gotta ride it out like Daddy tells you, let it slide up your pussy, make that hole feel good." Seth's sweat drained onto my piss, renewing that scent, which mixed with the slight, dark undertone of Seth's shit. "Smell that, boy? That's your pussy opening wide, that's your hole taking whatever Daddy gives it, smells like sweet fresh pussy." Seth kept his face forward, eyes on the screen, his shoulders trembling a little. "Sweet little queer boy I got, sweet little faggot son." I swabbed a little Liquid Heet around Seth's hole and relubed the wax cock. "Sweet faggot hole, boy's got a sweet slick faggot cunt," I said. Seth's hole relented, and the cock slid in to its hilt. Seth cried aloud, openly, trembling, whimpering, squeaking. "Sweet boy cunt, best faggot cunt Daddy's seen," I said.

"I'm straight," he said, a drooling, watery, lacrimal whisper.

"Of course you are," I said. I went upstairs to jack off, leaving him to expel the dildo on his own.

Shortly before dawn I returned him where I found him, transporting him blindfolded and cuffed, his cock inside his pants this time. I kept the wax cock. Seth may believe what he wants about himself. I know I will.

Thugs

Matt Bernstein Sycamore

Luce says, "Skinheads are the caviar of thugs," and I think that's brilliant 'cause Luce has a thing for skinheads but he's way too vegan for caviar. Everyone thinks he's talking about how he wants trade, how he can't wait to get his hands on some butch cock. So everyone laughs, they know what Luce means.

But of course, I'm not part of everyone, and Luce wants to please me, most of all, so when I start laughing, he's in hysterics, and we're sitting at this way-too-snotty dinner party just about to die. I mean cry. I mean we're having an amazing time.

Luce pulls me into these escapades, and I pull him into me. He's daring me—it's my turn to raise the stakes—so I pour a glass of wine on the person next to me. Just like that. I don't even know who it is, or who Luce is, for that matter. This second guy screams, he's wearing Prada no doubt, and I'm thinking thank God it's white wine because a few drops got on me, too, and dammit I'm wearing that one-dollar used powder blue T-shirt that makes me look buff and queeny at the same time: priceless.

Luce is still now—I'm definitely winning. I say oh my God I'm sorry, I'm so sorry. I swear the guy has a hard-on in his khakis. Well he didn't have a hard-on until I started wiping his crotch, now he's looking at me with the pupils right in the center of his eyes, boom.

I want to get on my knees, but no one's drunk enough yet. This story is about Andee, he likes skinheads, and I wrote the first line thinking about him but then I knew he'd get angry at me for creating his quotes in my fiction. So I used Luce, a character in a Robert Glück story, who says, "Your daisies are the eyes I've been waiting for. Let's do this stud 'til he's a dud."

This guy's no stud, but then he's certainly no dud either and neither is what's underneath his khakis, bent. I say, "This is Luce, Robert Gluck's lover." But then shit, I remember Luce wasn't—and isn't—Robert Gluck's lover at all, especially not after I've changed his name. Luce and Bob are close close friends—right?—they call each other at three in the morning.

Like Andee and me. I've known him for at least sixty-five years, he's a close close friend but still he can't hug me good-bye. So I introduce Luce, who opens me up until I'm swallowing my own juice. Luce reveals my Dustbuster, sitting in the corner all alone. What do you do with a Dustbuster in a loft space?

Back to the party. This guy in khakis—Andee's his name—he wants me but he isn't ready to say, "I loved the way you spilled wine on my shirt, then wiped my crotch." That's Luce's job. Luce whispers, "Now why do you have to call them both Andee?" I tell Luce to stop whispering. Loudly, I say, "From now on, I'll call Andee 'Candy.' "

Now this causes quite a storm at the party, everyone's toasting to that because I guess Andeeboy here is the stud-dee-dud everyone's lusting after; roomful of queens and here's this specimen of manly wonder among us. We all fall for that shit.

Just like I thought at first that Andee had on Dockers but looking again I see they're clearly size thirty-two Merc Staprests that Andee brought back fresh from his trip to London, mind you—yes it's all they say it is—make that size thirty-six because damn those pants run small.

Luce kisses me on the neck, guess he's going for the groin because I've outdone him tonight, but once I'm on, honey I'm on, and I'm not about to stop now. When this DandyAndee says to me, "Wanna smoke some killer weed," I almost slap him, but then I realize I need some killer weed to get through this party, so I say, "Only if I can suck your cum through a straw, baby."

Everyone gasps, Luce is back where he belongs—in hysterics—and I'm stiff as a boardroom brawl.

Straight-acting RandyAndee dares to say excuse me, and with that I'm on my knees, lips at his zipper, and he grabs my head—oh, drunker than I thought—and then I've got his dick out, in seconds he's hard. I'm sure everyone's watching now, but I've got my eyes closed when Andee's dick slides into the back of my throat.

But ouch, what was that? A stone in my throat. Shit I'm having a food allergy attack, it must have been the tahini, I shouldn't have eaten any hummus. I stand up and rush to the bathroom, don't want anyone to think I'm choking on dick when it was really that fucking hummus. Luce is behind me, or wait now he's in front of me, but I'm coughing, and he says what's the matter, can't take the mod-boy's cock?

Then Luce is on his knees for me, sucking my dick but damn I need to piss, and I say to him, in between choking, "I need to piss." There's gravel in my throat—maybe it was the sunflower seeds, yeah the sunflower seeds, tahini's too sludgy to get stuck like this. Luce says, "Piss in my mouth," and at first I'm kind of freaked out because no one's ever asked me to do that unless they were paying me, and certainly not Luce with the khaki Merc pants brought fresh from London. Wait, that's Andee. But what about Candy? She prefers black.

So Luce with the worn-out army green thrift store trousers is on his knees and I've stopped choking but I'm too hard to piss, then somehow I just let it go and Luce is moaning and then he starts choking and pulls away, I get piss all over the floor. He stands up, and he's kissing me madly, and I can taste my piss on his tongue—salty—actually it's kind of good.

I say, "Now what am I going to do about the floor?" Luce is sweating, his T-shirt looks moist, and I'm sweaty too but luckily I'm wearing that shirt that dries fast—there's lycra in it for sure—and then I start cackling because we're in a house full of yuppie wannabes and there's no air conditioning, ten points for hipster realness. Luce points out the cabinet full of Kiehl's products, and I'm cackling, because yes I am the wicked witch of the West Coast, stuck in New York City. I'm crouched on the floor in my own piss, and Luce leans down to pet me.

I start licking the floor to gross Luce out, but mostly so I can say— "Did you like that piss, boy?"—as loud as possible. Luce puts his hand over my mouth, gasping and giggling, but when he says, "What about your Home Health Antifungal lotion?" he's way way way behind, I grab his crotch and say Virgin Sol Tea Tree Burn Relief. And we're both in each other's hysterics, someone's knocking on the door, saying, "You boys okay in there?"

I rub the rug over the floor to dry off the piss, and Luce says "Yeah, the wife's water broke so we're fixing the pipes." Turns out it's John outside the door, what kind of khakis is he wearing? Luce grabs John's crotch, and John says, "You're drunk." Luce says, "On your credit card, baby," and we go back into the living room.

I guess we've been gone for hours and the straightboy—no way was he *straight*—is gone. We were the life of the party, so obviously, without us the party is dead. Luce starts singing about chantilly lace, the place for good face, damn he *is* drunk; four guys are comparing Nikes—they've all got on the same ones. I say, "That's enough to fund an entire sweatshop," and Luce screams. "Bitch you are on!" And then he's on me, we're making out on the sofa, and I swear that when I wake up, I mean make up, no sit up, there's some fashion victim pretty boy—one of thirty-seven in the room—telling me that I'm wearing a whole cow on my feet.

But that bitch doesn't know what's coming for her. I gasp. Luce clears his throat of mine. Andee would know—CandyAndee, that is, who first showed me the Merc mod pants, "Sta-prest trousers, babycakes. That's what they're called." And then he showed me the boots I'm wearing now, just like the used combat boots I've been wearing for years, steel-toed and all. The bitch who doesn't know what's coming for him smirks, and I say, "These boots are vegan."

With that, it's over for me and Luce at this party. He downs another cocktail, and we're outta there. I smile like Madame Tussaud before she became a name on a wax museum and say, "Thanks." John tries to be amused, actually he is amused but he's still trying. I kiss him goodbye, and Luce says, "Later, man." Dead ringer. I slap his thigh on the way out and—what—he's *hard*.

Luce grins at me, and I've got that soppy look in my eyes. I wanna say it, but I'm stuck, and then he says it. The elevator comes, and Luce throws me against the wall. I love him, and we look at each other—"seven floors down"—and then we've both got our pants below our knees and we're jerking off furiously and I kneel on the ground so I can spread my legs more and Luce gets down there with me and when we come we're crazed, zip up our pants: we're sticking together.

Finding

M. J. F. Williams

Vermont.

October.

Some home magazine for bored upper-middle-class house-wives with too much time and money has a picture of a country garden, resting under a blanket of fresh snow. Jon thinks it must have been taken after the nor'easter last February; he's sitting in the common room of an empty dorm flipping through the gardening magazines Maria leaves around to civilize the place.

Valentine's day. There's a gazebo at the far end of the garden. Not really a gazebo, but something much more intimate, a covered bench, just big enough for one to sit and one to stretch out. February. March. Spring. Jon envisions sitting on the bench with Troy, talking about everything and nothing, taking turns resting in one another's arms, changing places when the hard maple slats begin to take their toll. February ... the two of them bundled in coats, bundled together. Confessing the sins and secrets accumulated over twenty years. Or. Catching up? Yes. Catching up on what the other has missed out on since they last spent time together, what seems so many ages ago, or only yesterday. Perhaps. ...

The silent idyll of imagination is punctuated by a low, basement rumble, then a crashing, wooden thwap, then a low rumble again of wheels on concrete.

"Not this shit again." Jon is irritated, throws his magazine on the coffee table.

"Look, Skaterboy, could you *please* stop this shit. God fucking damn."

"Dude?"

"You do this all the time, and this is supposed to be the quiet dorm."

"Dude? I'm like sorry," Troy says in a low but audible drawl, barely above a mumble, as Jon walks to the stairs. "Dude?"

"Whatever."

"Dude, wait."

"What?"

"I wanna show you something."

"Okay. Fine"

Troy, excited, grabs Jon's forearm and walks his audience of one over to a small musty corner next to a sleeping giant of a furnace. "Dude, I can finally land a pop-shove-it." He runs to the far corner of the musty space, with the excitement of a five-year-old riding a bike without training wheels for the first time. He pushes off. Picking up speed and turning a corner, his erect tall body leaning into the turn like a sailboat mast leaning into the wind. He crouches in preparation for the jump. He pops the board with a sudden jerk ... sending it up into his body, like a clumsily dropped lunch tray in reverse. He lands running, struggling for balance. Swimming through the dank air. "Damn. I can't do shit now. Last summer I was pulling off phat ass no complys on the grindrails."

Jon snickers.

"Dude, you're not popping it, you're doing an ollie. If you ollie up a pop-shove-it, then it's a no comply."

"I didn't know you could skate, bro."

"I can't."

"But this chick told me that you ollie it up, and I was like, whatthe-fuck?"

"What do chicks know? If you ollie up a pop shove it, the board's too close to your body when you kick it around for the 180 and you just hit yourself in the balls."

"Like, how'd you know that?"

"I used to when I was twelve. I can't anymore."

"C'mon, bro. I know you can."

"Dude, I can't"

Troy picks up his well-worn board by one end, and offers it to Jon. "Dude … try. Okay?" Jon takes it and tries to balance himself, overcome by self-conscious awkwardness. Troy puts his hands on Jon's hips with the casual familiarity of a big brother, the cotton of Jon's khakis folding under the adoring tightness of his grip. Jon's chest tightens at the touch. This welcomed invasion. He can't breath. Thoughts race.

"You know what, fuck this," he says, stepping off the deck. "You wanna help me kill that bottle of gin from last week?"

"Sure, bro."

They proceed to Jon's room, with the smirks of boys on a treasure hunt. Jon pours stiff drinks as the late winter sun sets, a pink and orange fanfare, a Delius score, then fading chords of first heliotrope and then indigo, then … silence. Christmas lights strung from the ceiling glow softly, the low drifting wobble of a Stereolab moog fills the room, they sit next to one another on a single-size bed, leaning their backs against the wall with the bottle tucked between them.

"I'm trying to find a old school deck, like a old school H-Street Matt Hensley. If I can find a old school Matt Hensley H-Street board, I'll be able to skate bad ass. Skating these new school decks is hard…'cause like when I try to do a high ollie, like, it does a kickflip, and kickflips ain't me."

"What about a woody? Wouldn't that work. None of my friends who skate woody skate slicks."

"Thing is, dude, I want something big. Ha ha. Something for a man. I thought about getting a longboard or the Powell flames deck, 'cause my fave tricks are the no comply tricks."

The gin takes effect. Tension turns to laughter.

"You know, there was this place in California…."

"Yah?"

"I don't know. They had a web page, and they had a big variety of sizes."

"Dude! Cool!"

"Yeah, 'cause you're kinda tall."

"Like old-school decks? Oh, fuck!"

"Yeah," says Jon, shirking from the weight of Troy's arm now over his shoulder.

"Dude, thing is … I'm used to old school decks."

"You have to do a search for it though … "

"These new-school boards are kinda hard to ollie."

"… since I can't remember where it is."

"I know the Powell flames deck is nice and big. Nine inches wide, thirty-three inches long. My bro told me that longboards are hella fun on ramps. Like the terminal velocity board. Dude, they're long as fuck."

"Dude, see, I don't halfway know what you're talking about."

"I ollied a longboard once, and like it was the highest ollie I ever did. Longboards are, like, long as fuck. Ha ha. Perfect for bombing hills. That's my fave part of skating."

"Damn, dude. You're badassed."

"Badassed? Bombing hills is fun! If I get a longboard deck, I'll be like 'oh shit! I'm getting speed!' Down this massive hill.

Dude, I'm trying not to break anything again."

"In '89, I used to like skating down parking garages. That was a blast! Dude, doing slides and shit. Dude, one time I got a bumper ride. Went thirty miles an hour and slammed hard as fuck."

"Were you okay?"

"Ha ha. I was fine. After a few weeks. But I had a blast! Dude, I wanna go to that glory hole spot I've seen in old skate videos with a longboard. It's that huge pipe. Like, if you slam on that bitch you're fucked! And, dude, on longboards, you, like go much faster."

"Man, that would rock."

"I know ... like, why the fuck does Core-Games have street and vert, but no longboarding shit? Longboarding is under-ground."

"I don't know. Dude, when I saw rollerblading, I decided that I hate that show."

"Me too."

"You know anyone that skates a old-school board?"

"Nah. Dude you're too hardcore."

"I'm not hardcore. I suck at skating."

"Yeah, right."

"Well, dude, like, technical skating I suck, but, if I'm on a big hill, I'll bomb it without thinking of it."

"You're so way better than me, though."

"Whatever."

A nervous laugh. A lull in their chatter.

Then Jon pulls Troy's lanky torso close to his own. The stubble on Troy's cheeks rubs against his face. He reaches one arm around to the small of Troy's back, while the other explores the softness and unfamiliar curves of the back of Troy's head. Jon whispers, "You are better."

"Whatever, dude." Troy pushes Jon down on the bed straddling his friend's abs between his strong legs, pressing the weight of his body into Jon's shoulders with outstretched arms, supporting his tall frame. "You can probably do more tech stuff than I can." Then he falls limp next to Jon like a house of cards in a breeze.

"Dude, I can't do shit."

"Dude, whatever. You can."

"I didn't skate the whole time I was in high school. Then, I could barely ollie. Now, dude I can't do anything."

"Yes you can, bro. Just takes practice."

"The only trick I can land on a new school board is a boardslide on a small short metal rail at the skatepark. We can go to the skate shop tomorrow and get you some kneepads."

"Dude, scabs piss me off. I hate that cream you have to use."

"Ha, ha, bro. Scabs rule. Get kneepads and wrist guards. No worries, bro."

Their laughter trails off, like the fading sound of a car as long missed visitors drive away down a country road, into the distance of past memory as they lay next to one another half asleep.. They listen to another song.

"I'm really drunk, man." Troy responds by moving his body closer. "It's so cool to be here next to you."

"Yeah bro, me too. It's cool to find someone you like and not have this gay-bi-straight-political bullshit stand in the way of hanging out with someone you like...I missed you so bad when you went home last summer. It hurt. Dude, I didn't think you'd ever like me. Like, you always treated me like I was bugging you."

"Well, that's because you were."

"Dude? What do you mean?"

"Dude, I just thought you were stoned all the time. I was like, 'Goddamned fucking stoner, everybody at this fucking school is stoned, even the profs are stoned.' And then, that time I was running late to class and you *stopped* me in the hall, and I was like, 'What the fuck do you want now, Skaterboy,' and all you said was 'I love you, Jonathan.' It weirded me out. Like ... why?"

"Dude, I don't know. I just do." To touch, hold, be held, kiss, fall asleep next to, caress the folds of one another's ears with one's eyes until they become dunes of sand on a desert night, undulating, curving around to a natural rhythm, in an arc that seems so timeless. I don't know, bro. I just do."

Jon listens as Troy's breaths go from the long, slow, inhalation of rest to the short staccato of nervous agitation. "What's wrong dude. You can tell me."

"One time, like, I ate a bunch of pills, dude. In hopes of dying. I tried to grind down a fifty-step handrail, and I said 'If I die I'll be happy. If I make it I'll take more pills and do it again.' So, dude, I get onto the handrail and I fall and I fall onto the ground and I think I'm dead. But, dude, like, I wake up and find out I'm not dead. Dammit, dude... I was pissed."

"See, I don't understand this shit. Wait. Well. Actually I do. Sorry. I'm only mildly bipolar and have only been in the hospital once. You get tired of fucking mood swings for no reason. I mean if your parents died in a car crash, that would be a good reason to be bummed, but when you feel like shit like that for no reason at all, you get tired of it." Jon shifts in the small bed, laying his head on the softness of Troy's hoodie, wrapping an arm around his rangy torso.

"Yah."

"I think you're rad, though."

"Thanks."

They stop talking for a while and just lay there together listening to a song play. Long, minimalist riffs, modulating, then repeating, then evolving into something else. "I don't mind the mania episodes.... It's when I get depressed that I can't stand it at all."

"Oh, I think the mania is great. The manic part is like boarding down a mountain for a week straight, but then it wears off. That's what sucks."

"I love you, dude."

Jon's heart stops. His mind stops. He doesn't know what to say. After all the years he waited seemingly in vain for someone to say this, these golden words come from the last person he was expecting to hear them. Troy gets restless again. Jon kisses him on the cheek. They stare long into each others eyes with shocked awe. What the hell is going on here? Is this a surreal dream or a nightmare. There's still a way back from this fantasy. Perplexed, they look.

They kiss again. This time with fervent passion. Arms probing bodies. Seeking. Searching. Finding curves of muscle and bone. Bodies pressing. Wanting. Hands feeling, loving. Holding tighter, closer. Lips finding ears, tongue, neck. Needing. Having. Needing to fall into one another, two becoming one. Hard cocks pressing. Bodies pressing so hard. Hoping that by pressing so hard they would dissolve into each other. Swimming deep into each other. Drowning.

They stop. Exhausted.

"You're not going to tell are you?"

"No, dude. We're friends now."

Destroying the space between. This space of which they have suddenly both become extremely conscious. They hold on to one another to destroy the space between, to live as two alone in one world no space. Between.

"Don't tell anyone?"

"I totally promise."

"When I was sixteen, dude, I was hitching once. This old dude picks me up. He's like my dad's age. We drive down the road a little, and then when we're getting closer to the house. He pulls over. I was like, maybe he has to take a piss. But he's, like 'I'll give you twenty bucks, you let me suck your cock.' I was scared as shit, dude. But I just said 'No thanks.' He started grabbing my cock, so, like, I punch the motherfucker in the nose and run all the way home. Dude, I cried when I got home. I felt so sorry for hitting the guy, but I was six-fucking-teen. I just cried. I felt so sorry. Dude, that's what made me decide I'm not gonna be gay. I don't want someone associating me with some queen that I hate because they're trying to get with sixteen-year-old kids in their cars."

"Troy, stop, okay? It's cool now. It's over." Tears. So pleasantly happy, so pleasantly mournful, so sad. "Dude? Are you okay?"

"You promise, like, not to tell anyone, dude? You promise...not to hate me?"

"What? Dude, I'm here for you. Always. I love you."

"Whoa, man, I love you too."

"Get up!"

"What, dude?"

"C'mon, get up. I have something to show you. In the bathroom."

Close. Holding closer. "Look. This is us."

"Ha, ha. I like it."

Wind whispers loving words to trees in eternal courtship, words spoken with the lightness of a good bye kiss when you know someone will be returning tomorrow. Gray branches, barren, sway in the embrace of the wind, arms reaching out in return. Short, quick kisses of evening that become increasingly passionate as evening progresses into night into morning. They sleep. Entwined. Close. Warmth. Together, entwined.

It begins to snow.

Spike

M. Christian

Matching, same, identical—Spike and Spike were fooling around behind the barn.

No, that's a lie—no, that's merely a location slip. They were definitely fooling around—Spike sucking on Spike's cock while Spike fondled his brother's quills of starched blond hair—but they weren't cock sucking, getting cock sucked behind no barn. Urban equivalent: Spike opened his throat, in an abandoned mattress factory in the Mission District, and took eight inches of his brother's pale dick meat down till it danced with his very well-trained gag reflex. Just the two of them and the skittering dance steps of invisible rats in the walls—urban equivalent of mice, cows, and horses.

The mattress factory was one of their favorite fuck spots. Yeah, rats. Yeah, plaster dust like a liquid itch on whatever rubbed against it. Yeah, it smelled—fuck, no—it fucking reeked of crackhead piss, butane, wine. But it was their place, and it was close enough to Bebe's so they could suck and fuck themselves into a quaking-kneed palsy then stumble over to sack out on his sofa. It was close to the 24th Street BART station, too, so if Bebe was being bitchy they could jump the gates and head out somewhere else.

They had this thing for the place, aside from its handy conveniences (like a whole room that acted as a piss hole). It was a fog of dust, lath showing from crumbling holes like a whale's ribs, and carpeting like the surface of a swamp. There was something about its decay and mold that made it; it always put them in a fucking mood to fuck.

Spike and Spike were tall and thin, skeletons dancing in bags of pale white skin, navels done (steel), eyebrows done (one gold, one steel), septum done (big steel), tats of primitive sunbursts around their right nipples, and PAs done (steel).

They were wild boys, feral kids. They had some money, just enough, but more important than cash or a place without rats to crash, they had each other.

Fuck that, they were each other. It was a damned art to them, to mix, merge, switch, combine and, every chance they fucking got, to fraternize with each other. They weren't just twins or anything like that—smiling goofs from some commercial. They were a young guy who happened to be in two places at once. It was a point of pride between Spike and Spike that they didn't use first names (tell one, tell both) and that no one (not even Spike and Spike) could tell which was who or who was which—just Spike, man, just Spike....

They took an extreme delight in their similarities, sharing everything with each other and trading back and forth so often that even in the rare instance of them being apart you could never, ever, be sure which one you were with—and it didn't matter, because if you were with one today you would be with the other tomorrow.

This time, they almost came at the same place at the same time. At least as far as coming went.

Spike was just about at the crest—kneeling at Spike's feet, his mouth wide open to catch his hot jism, he furiously worked his own long, pale cock. Nothing got Spike more worked than tasting Spike's cum. It got him so juiced, in fact, that he was way ahead of Spike on the wave.

Spike could tell that his brother was gonna beat him to the punch and come way fucking sooner than he was—and he was supposed to come in his fucking throat. Didn't seem right, Spike figured, for Spike to get so hot and come from just the idea of swallowing his milk and not from swallowing him. A little pissed, he reached down and grabbed Spike's head, impaling his thin, blood-red lips around his long, pale cock while skillfully kicking his brother's hands away from his throbbing dick.

Moaning at having his brother's long thin cock down his throat, Spike swallowed and rolled his hard tongue around it and locked his hands tight (so fucking tight!) on the taut backs of Spike's lean-muscled thighs.

Spike, meanwhile, groaned the good groan and lifted a leg over his brother's head—twisting around to show Spike his asshole and try and reach down to lock a sweaty palm around Spike's pulsing, bobbing cock.

Gravity won, in the end, as Spike reached back for his brother's member, lost his balance and collapsed on top of him into a natural (though slightly bruised) sixty-nine. Spike plunged his mouth onto his brother's cock just as, at the other end, the same was being done to him.

Mouth/cock, cock/mouth, they moaned, sucked, slobbered (it's really good when you don't care you're drooling) and rocked back and forth—feeling at the same time as sucking, sucking at the same time feeling their own cocks getting sucked. Coming, like that, was prime in keeping them glued together as Spike.

They came together, or at least as close as they could get: Spike jetting into his brother's face, cock jerking as it spurted sticky cum down onto his laughing lips, Spike coming up towards his brother's also-smiling face, but his cum's trajectory different because he was on the bottom, so it splattered the plaster-dusted floor of their hideaway with white abstract.

They broke for a moment, knocking back huge swallows of cheap white wine from a bag. Breathing heavy, they kissed—mixing salty proteins (cum) and an acidic high (wine) with their steamy mouths. Quickly, cocks were tapping again at their legs and thighs, quickly they were stroking each other to an iron strength with the lube of their still-slippery cum.

Spike was the first to go down on Spike. Shoving his long, pale legs out from behind him he swallowed his brother's sword without a blink, with never a hint of teeth or of bend of throat. To Spike, receiving, it was dipping his cock into an intimate, hot, tunnel that gripped him with all the dexterity of his own—or his brother's—hand.

Giving, Spike snaked a long-fingered hand down to his own cock and rolled over onto his side so he could stroke himself as he sucked off his brother.

On the good ride to a second come, Spike bent back, catching his rapid descent just in time with his hands. Now propped, he watched with sexy joy his brother sucked him up and down and up and down—his shaft gleaming with spit and friction.

Then...it...happened.

Spike, the sucking, stuck a finger into the asshole of Spike. Now it should be noted that Spike's asshole wasn't exactly what you'd call virgin territory. The act of having a finger eased into it, and him, wasn't—in itself—all that shocking. But it is what Spike did with it that caused...Spike stuck a finger into his brother's asshole as he sucked him off, a mad hydraulic machine. Then, with his finger deep in his brother's puckered hole, he swiped it around, relishing, playing with, the contours of his anus. Then he managed to get his finger just far enough inside to feel around for, then find, his magic button.

Maybe it was the quality of the blow job. Maybe it was the surprising skill at which Spike managed to find Spike's p-spot, but whatever the cause, Spike's cum jetted into his brother's mouth, filling it with salty, sticky, protein.

Then he got mad.

"Where the fuck did you learn that?" Spike said, standing, pulling his still-hard cock out of his brother's mouth with a cartoon pop.

Spike sat back and shrugged, his blond quills all but rattling on his head. "Dunno...."

"We haven't done anything like that."

"Just thought it might feel good," Spike said, shyly, reaching again for his brother.

"Bullshit! You got that from someone else! Who have you been fucking?"

Spike smiled, this time slyly. "Fuck off."

"I will not fuck off! Who the fuck have you been fucking!?"

Spike got to his feet. They were twins, so one was the same height as the other. Still, standing, Spike seemed to tower over his angry brother. "Fuck off. It isn't important."

"Fuck that shit! We're supposed to only fuck each other, right? Isn't that how's it supposed to work: you fuck me and I fuck you, right? So who else have you been fucking!"

Spike's reply was a clumsy but effective swing. Catching him in his pale stomach, Spike's fist knocked Spike off balance, and he fell to his knees, clutching his shocked, throbbing abs. Spike watched him gagging and all but puking at his feet for a beat—two—then knelt down and grabbed him by his short blond hair and lifted him up just a few inches. "I've been fucking bored!"

Spike obviously wasn't all that hurt. He stood and swung in one quick motion, aiming for his brother's jaw. But Spike was clearer headed than his brother and saw it barreling at him as if in slow motion. One quick little dance step (plaster crackling underfoot), and Spike's straining fist shot by his ear. As Spike gazed at his flying fist, he slugged him again in the stomach.

Spike dropped to his knees, gagging and clutching his brother's thighs.

Looking down at his brother, Spike panted as well—but not from exertion. His cock suddenly was hard as a, what—fuckin' rock—and thumped firmly against the top of his brother's head. Reaching down, he grabbed Spike's hair again and pulled him up just enough so that he was staring at it. "Suck, and make it good, or I'll fucking kill you," he said, pulling Spike's head onto his cock.

Spike swallowed it, over the lips, into the mouth, down the throat, sucking on damned skin-coated steel. Spike had never felt his brother so hard before. Distantly, as he sucked and sucked, he was aware that his own cock was also a skin-wrapped rigid rod; he started to stroke himself.

Moaning, Spike hauled his brother to his feet. "You're a fucking boring lay," he yelled into Spike's face, as spit rolled down his face. "Boring!" He slapped him, hard, and watched the skin of his lips and mouth vibrate with the impact. Spike whimpered, but his cock stayed as hard as his own, pressing against his own throbbing balls.

"Boring!" Slap!

"Boring!" Slap!

A few drops of blood flecked the corner of Spike's mouth. Spike bent forward and kissed them off his brother, tasting copper and brine. Then he hit him again.

Spike grabbed his brother, spun him around, and threw him off—to the plaster-dusted boards. He landed hard, groaning when his hard cock slammed onto the floor with him. Spike knelt down quickly, wrapped a hard arm round his brother's waist, and hauled him up into a kneel. "You're..., " he screamed, sure as shit someone would hear, "a fucking...," and bust down the door, "boring fuck!"

He slapped his brother across the ass, at first about as hard as he'd slapped his face but then—when he noticed that Spike didn't react—a lot harder.

Under him, Spike moaned. His asshole, juicy, puckered, and relaxed with the anticipation of each impact.

Spike's slaps became a to-and-fro applause, striking one cheek on the foreswing and the other on the back, the sound rolling through the factory, building like a standing ovation at the end of an opera.

In fact: "Thank you thankyou thankyou thankyouthankyouthankyou" —from Spike, his ass coloring from pink to red to blood crimson.

Spike jerked and twitched with the impacts, bucking and humping his straining cock against a section of worn rug.

Spike's hand really started to hurt—especially his fingertips, which were absorbing the backstrokes. He reached to where their clothes lay in a denim and cotton heap and pulled loose his belt.

The sound was like a shot in the room, and Spike half-expected to see a window blow from the percussion. The heavy leather slammed into Spike's flaming ass cheeks like a fist into a sandbag. Spike screamed, shrill and sharp, and tried to scoot away. Spike stretched out a skinny corded arm, grabbed his ankle, hauled him back, smacked him again with the belt, and again, and again.

Spike's screams evolved into a long wail—a stuck siren— then melted into a stream of deep grunts. Spike's ass was deep cherry, stoked by an internal fire, blood venting from a tiny cuts sliced by metal studs on Spike's heavy belt.

"Maybe the next time you'll try and be a bit more...imaginative," Spike yelled at his brother, putting his back, shoulder, and whatever remained in his arm into five final swings, hypnotized by the sight of Spike's ass jiggling at the blows, drunk on the power of giving his brother so much enjoyable pain. Spike had progressed beyond moans and groans; now he roared.

Spike's own cock was doing its own kind of aching. With a snap, he looped his belt around his brother's waist and hauled him up from his sprawl on the meanly carpeted floorboards. Getting up on his own knees, he pulled Spike's ass and asshole right onto his own ache, scored flesh meeting ready cock.

Spike and Spike had never been hotter, tighter, harder. They fucked like the real meaning of the word, hammering and getting hammered. They slammed into each other, fucker and fuckee, till they couldn't keep the stopper in anymore. Spike on the bottom jerking off in synch; one rocketing onto the floor and the other into his ass.

Then they passed out, one on top and still in, the other under and still hard.

Later, afterwards, Spike and Spike, identical twins, could be seen walking down the street, any street. No, that's a lie—no, that's merely a definition, not an observation. Afterwards, after that day in the barn (lie), it was easy to tell Spike from Spike. Spike and Spike walking down the street: Spike leading Spike, towing him around by a chain, a leather thong, a cord, some rope, or just an ordering crook of pale finger. He was always the Spike in control, the one with the gruff voice, the snap to his tone.

And, behind him, there was the Spike that was always there, always smiling a satisfied smile, always the bottom.

After that day, you always knew Spike from Spike.

Strictly Professional
Francisco Ibañez-Carrasco

Is Heaven a physician?
They say that He can heal;
But medicine posthumous
Is unavailable.
EMILY DICKINSON

A morphine surge tongued me inside out. It takes about sixty seconds for the blood to circulate once through our entire vascular system. The origin of that elation was his hand that thumbed the end of the syringe; a gush ran wild through my veins. I was falling and falling in a spiral, a carousel so intense I holler in my head, whoop-de-doo! I didn't actually utter a sound for the sheer pleasure of suffering in silence. I held on to the stretcher railing as the world turned around, and probably my face transmuted through various shades of pale. He said, "Shit, you told me you weren't allergic to morphine." I thought, I have told you so many things, as I filled up a kidney basin with acidic stomach fluids. Then I could hear him behind the curtain say something to a nurse. A lost soul shrieked nearby, it was Halloween, and a frantic pace reigned in the ER. The nurse sternly responded she couldn't go and help, too many men, too little time. Grudgingly, he came back with another syringe, it's Gravol, my favorite. His articulated hands fumbled, unskilled at the needle; he, after all, would never have to do the dirty work, he would be the doctor. He stretched my arm (I had it drawn against my chest as if clutching pearls), and my hand was positioned squarely under his crotch; he was nervous, I had the shakes, bad scene. The liquid was not getting through so he asked me to pump my hand, open close, open close, while he tried to hold me back onto the stretcher. His embrace was tight, but I resisted like a child who is enjoying the ride too much. Eventually, my body dutifully complied and the fluid merged swiftly into the maddening traffic of my blood. As soon as Gravol completed an entire circuit, with a neigh I let the railing go. I lost my other grip on his crotch and fell into an orgasmic stupor thinking about the lengths I have to go to see him, to have him talk to me and touch me.

I had made my way through a packed waiting room, a gridlock of midnight traffic: intoxicated ghouls and witches, young men in ridiculous mumus and slutty lingerie. The only night on which straight blond boys give free rein to their desire to wear women's clothes; it's pathetic. I had psyched myself up for a long time, planning every detail, plans where everything was designed to go wrong but not fatal. It took more than simply watching *General Hospital* on TV. It takes work to be a victim, a martyr, a serial killer, or a lover, and I am a bit of every one. The first time I had seen the young intern, and he had come back to say, "I'll get you through this," I knew he was sincere, innocent (a flaw more fatal than ignorance), and that he had seen more TV than I had. He was a catch.

My having AIDS is incidental. Not that my life has been simple, but after years of fighting every freakish opportunistic infection, every shooting pain, and every consuming dull ache, intermittent or chronic, every torturous treatment, I am used to being sick. I am savvy; I know what I am doing. The turning point in my adult life wasn't a diagnosis, it was meeting him when I landed in the ER at 2 A.M. I fell in love. I learned later that what I had was septicemia, irrelevant indeed, it could have been pneumonia or anything else, all I knew is I was high on fever, drenched in sweat and almost delirious. I had called a loyal friend, and he had taken me to the hospital. I was so sick that I was spared the admitting process. I was plunked on a stretcher and wheeled into one of the cubicles. There I laid moaning and waiting. Going in and out of my mind I waited until I woke up thinking I was an odalisque surrounded by veils, which in fact were the curtains they demurely draw around you to preserve a silly trace of modesty. My friend and a chunky orderly had prepared me for this ritual as they exchanged 'I-know-which-way-you-swing' looks. Fortunately, and unlike having sex with strangers, when one has to bear it all under naked bulbs to be appraised like a cow at a cattle market, in the ER one is allowed to wear a virginal white robe. I was there like a kidnapped Helena, listening to the sounds of the battle and the fury around my tent ("This part is unavoidable," said my friend. "There is always too much need and too few people working in public hospitals." I had no idea what this warrior was talking about.) A nurse came in and took my vitals, awful stats, and wrote them in her chart. Before she left she told me that the intern would be along any time now.

Another forty-five minutes elapsed during which I gave free rein to all kinds of personal expression. I cried, sorry for myself, I cried in pain, in anger, I yelled, and cried some more. I grabbed my good friend's hand and asked him to feed my cat and not to take any of my CDs unless I was terminally ill. He got tired of the scene and softly told me he would go for a coffee and come back in half an hour or so. Bullshit. He was on his merry way to chat the chunky orderly up. That's when he, the intern, appeared amidst the veils, like a Valentino (or a Fabio?) bursting into my tent planted in the hot desert, ready to save (or conquer) me. The cussing from the adjacent stretcher broke the spell, but the young healer paid no attention. With a lovely preamble he introduced himself and drew so close to my face I could feel his breath, so inspiring, I cried some more, but silently. The nurse came in, he told her to inject five CCs of morphine right away. A minute later I was drowning in his vast blue eyes, two pools of calm water suspended in midair. My anchor, the grip of his hand, was firm yet warm. I thought he would make a good surgeon. I thought I would let him shred my body into ribbons of flesh and blood and claim victory over my land. I thought....

I woke up when they took me for X rays. I didn't understand their polite explanation, but I politely nodded my approval. They hung me like a parrot in a trapeze, I couldn't stand on my own, twirled me, first this way, then the other. I passed out. When I woke up I was changed, I didn't care, I wasn't afraid or reluctant, anxiety had abandoned me, I had abandoned my body to their care, *his* care. When they brought me back from the X-ray room he was there to tell me that I would probably be admitted to the hospital. It was 6 A.M. I would have to wait for the next available bed. I asked him whether he was leaving, he said he wouldn't leave until he made sure I was admitted, he said, "I'll get you through this." He asked me if I was in pain, I nodded yes. On a scale from 1 to 10? 15, I mutter, but this was really my appraisal of his magnificence, and he ordered more morphine. I remained in this calm oasis while he asked me questions about my ailments, whether I used street drugs, what I did for living, a list of my medications. My answers came out deliciously, like a purr. He asked, "What is your 'risk factor'?" Last time a doctor asked me that I laughed in his fucking face! How come they can't bring themselves to say something as simple (and good) as, "what kind of sex do you have?" so I can respond, "I was fucked up the ass." Let me spell it out for you, fucked-up-the-ass. (Oh '70s joy!) This time I bit my tongue and humbly stretched the phrase "a-nal-pen-e-tra-tion," and he didn't blink once.

Then a flash of genius came upon me. I said that two months earlier I had a herpes outbreak in my rectal area. "I'll have to do a rectal check," he said. I struggled to prevent my grimace from mutating into a grin. I used to get healthy hours of anal action before I got so sick and full of technical difficulties that made it impossible and annoying to be fucked. Fisting was never my thing but a good deal of traditional fucking and ass playing were always the dish du jour on my sexual menu. My lover had died, my fuck buddies were either too dead or too sick to do anything. I played solitaire most of the time with plastic prosthetics that could never replace the moody, yes, overrated, but immensely necessary phallus. He rolled me on my side, and the sound of the latex snapping against his ample palm crowned with strong fingers made me salivate. His voice slurred on, that it would only take a second, to calm down, to relax. This was more than many gay men, always too hasty to get their fucking rocks off, had done for me in a long time. It had to be a straight guy of course, in a clinical way, but such strictly professional relationships (like prostitution) tend to be far more humane and tender. He gently slid two thick fingers smeared with cool water-based lubricant into my ass (all in absolute accordance with safer sex guidelines; one can't even get that in a one-night stand these days) and glided them around, exploring, asking me what I felt, ("tender"), if it hurt, ("hmmm, not really"), probed a bit further, ("a bit"), and kept searching. I gave mixed signals, small jolts, a brief trembling, a subtle tightening of my anal muscles, all interspersed with a few verbal hints. I sighed hugely when he withdrew his three fingers (three?). I rolled on my back and pulled the blanket up so he wouldn't see my hard on, I think he didn't see, if he saw he pretended he didn't. Liberal middle-class blond men can be so respectful and proper. He said there might be something "up there," but it was hard to tell because I was too agitated. Then he checked the rest of my body with his warm hands, sat me up to sound me with the cool stetho-scope (an occasion I used to vomit again, which wasn't gracious but I couldn't help it), then he tapped my chest and my stomach and pressed my groin and my testicles and asked about the lesions on my legs. For a while he ran his hands over them, which was more than the pity or the disgust I had gotten from the few men I had gone to bed with in the last four years. Men who were so gay, so out, so understanding but could not allow themselves to think about bodies which were not primed, young, and immaculate. But I digress....

He left and returned with a group of students and the doctor in charge of the ward. They stood around like farcical penguins exchanging proper little nods, lifting the sheet up as if in a morgue, pawing me, never looking me in the eye. He stood out in this curious lineup, with his wild mane of blond hair, probably twenty-four, if not younger, with an impeccable accent and fluoride teeth, strong neck and nose, and a clean-shaven sharp jaw, surely exemplary DNA. I was his case, his patient, a true relationship of submission; I was his, I was his slave, he could determine what was to be done to me, what could happen to me, he could inflict care or pain, delay the process or rush me through another set of questions and tests. I had wasted my time looking for an S/M relationship in all the wrong places, thinking one would arrive with more aggressive men, who turned out more often than not to be racist old white folks or young plastic studs who didn't have the first idea about controlling someone (or getting a hold on themselves). Often they wanted to be cruelly fisted, abused, and disposed of before their high wore off, so they could forget about the night and go on with their lives: sound-bite love, internet roadkill. Until the day they were diagnosed with HIV, when, shocked, desperate, they would start mouthing about fucking civil rights and government neglect. They would have a fucking epiphany and cry wolf about the AIDS phobia and sexual discrimination within the self-absorbed so-called gay community when they had done all those things in their own private lives all along.

It was ironic, but not surprising, that I would so amorously submit to a heterosexual man with a well-fed body, authority, and scientific knowledge. It is the secret of a queen's eternal desire; we camouflage its manifestations in various styles. I wanted to be treated like a wounded animal, a precious and fragile object, even if it was just a clinical appeal, a need to touch me, to look at me, to scrutinize, to listen to the drum of my heart, the croaking of my bowels, the cracking of my bones, and to attentively hear about my savage sexual practices, strictly professional. As subtly as I could I prolonged my answers to let him know of the things my body could do, the arching and releasing, the highs, the abandon. I looked for a glimpse in his eyes, and I got it, imperceptibly so, the way a man looks at an animal at the zoo and wonders who has really trapped who. That night, when the penguins left the cubicle, he stayed behind and wrote in his notebook and slightly squeezed my hand as he was leaving. It felt like lightning. I was too tired to say or do anything. He said goodbye and good luck. My friend was there back from his coffee and was instantly mesmerized by this Christian tableaux vivant, a saint holding a sinner's hand. When the young doctor left my friend said that he was jealous, and I said I knew why. He said he would let the doctor have him any time, in fact he thought he could be gay and that he had made some kind of eye contact, a second longer than it should, not strictly professional. I said, "Wishful thinking honey!" I didn't feel threatened or humiliated by my friend's lust like I had felt before, knowing too well that he could get the men I couldn't in a million years. He was young, gorgeous, firm, and healthy. He was HIV positive but he could still pass, and passing is the trick these days, having a undetectable viral load. I was beyond passing. Fate is queer. My last close sistter friend is now dead, poor thing; he exploded like a supernova, viagra and poppers, while harpooning fresh underage fish in Bahamas.

An hour later I was taken to a room on the ninth floor, from where I could see the light blue velvet of the early morning caressing the city with a winter drizzle. As the two sublingual Ativan worked their deep sleep magic on me, I imagined the doctor, young and tired, getting home in a nice neighborhood, stepping out of his sports car, turning off the lights left on all night in the living room, making his way to the bedroom with a glass of milk in his hand, brushing his gorgeous smile, taking his clothes off almost inaudibly, just a rustling noise as they brush against the soft pelt that covers his tight skin, a noise one can only hear in the movies, revealing his sturdy body, releasing the smell of his deep armpits, then laying next to his blond girlfriend, sound asleep, touching her hips for a moment, letting her respond by stretching herself between the sheets like a lazy cat, but dedicating his next thought to me, his challenging case. As I fell asleep in the ward, with the IV ticking into my central line and the nurses puttering around, I dedicated my last thought to him, and I wondered what it would take to see him again.

So I starved myself like a Catholic school girl who has fallen in love with her most handsome young teacher. No one could understand what was wrong, since the infection that had brought me to the hospital in the first place had been defeated, albeit in a rather dramatic way, by inserting a catheter connected to the superior venocaeva underneath the clavicle, where it stood out under the skin like a little microphone. Now I was bugged, he could have free access to the intimate contents of my fluttering heart. I also was taking an expensive course of drugs trumpeted as the cure for AIDS. Bullshit. I was advised over and over to drink lots of liquid so my kidneys wouldn't suffer, because the drugs had a high content of Calcium. I was told that kidney stones are tortuously painful to pass, a pain comparable to giving birth.

I didn't drink. Strategic phone calls to friendly male nurses who owed me for past favors, my humble hipodronic weed operation at home, gleaned precious information about him— his schedule. I knew I could not stalk him, that was absurd and kind of psychotic, so passe anyway, not really conducive to true love, so I approached him on his own turf, nothing too threatening, straight men are not afraid of queers as long as they know they can be on top, never at risk of being penetrated. I spent some cold evenings sipping coffee in a shop across the street from the hospital (the caffeine actually contributed to my dehydration), checking his comings and goings. After his shift he was picked up by his girlfriend, not a blond but a generic, unattractive, brunette type. She drove a Volvo, the most anal retentive of cars, and dressed conventionally, no makeup. Her flaws were points in my favor on an imaginary checklist, a *Cosmopolitan* personality test. I would look at him in awe every time he waited for her. He was tall and wore loose corduroy pants, wool sweaters, and a Gap coat, walked briskly holding a brown leather bag, the stethoscope always around his neck. He was a vision even when I wasn't high on drugs (although I am often stoned to endure the pain of chemotherapy and other weekly medical procedures). I saw him get in and out of the car a few times, never embracing her but giving her a fleeting kiss (sometimes only in the cheek!); she would smile, he just looked okay, they didn't burst into conversation or laughter. The red light right in front of the emergency entrance was great help, it allowed me to observe a bit longer.

After a month of fieldwork and fantasy I was ready to see him again, but my health wasn't worse. I had lost a lot of weight and all my hair, but I looked more butch than ever without even trying. I surely wasn't sick enough to rush to the emergency room. From another call to friend at the hospital I learned, much to my chagrin, that he would leave in a couple of weeks to be part of a ward team on the second floor, completely unrelated to AIDS, something about accidents, thus making my access to him more improbable. I panicked; for two days I didn't eat and had constant diarrhea but didn't get fever or a seizure of any kind. Damn it! On Halloween night I decided to implement plan C (or D), the spookiest, something radical—I slashed my wrists. I was so high and horny I didn't feel a thing; it was a clean job, and then I called 911. My machinations almost backfired, the paramedics, busty blonde girl and to-die-for calendar guy, wanted to take me to a different hospital, farther from my neighborhood but less congested with fucking goofy heterosexual youngsters who had been beating each other senseless in cars and bars in the night of phantoms and witches. No way, this could not happen to me, I was on a mission of love, bleeding like nobody's business, and no fucking testosterone fest would take the spotlight I needed shining on me. I made such a fuss about being taken to that particular hospital because of AIDS, because I always went there every time I was sick, because they had my file, you name it; I called out racism and homophobia, effective liberal battle chants, until they finally gave up, muttered a curse, told me to be quiet and took me where I wanted to go to rendezvous my destiny.

In the midst of a masquerade of vampires, skeletons, Batmans, Martians, Marilyn Monroes, and other celebrities, I made my grand hysterical entrance, pulling away at the temporary tourniquet and bandages they had put on me in the ambulance and clamoring for the grim reaper to come and take me away. They immediately led me into the ER, not into one of the cubicles separated by curtains but into one of the small separate rooms. Fast track they call it; all covered in white tiles and only one other stretcher. The guy next door had a huge blade wound in his thigh. He looked like a whore from the waist down, although the red net stockings weren't his color. A nurse came and tore them open and away unceremoniously, cleaned a bit the wound, put a big patch of gauze over it, and exited leaving him there all bruised and naked. His sheet had fallen to the side exposing him, gorgeous. I took a long and hard look at him, which he obviously resented, but was too sedated to do anything about it. I said, "I could let you fuck me good but I'm here to see someone else." He blinked twice, astonished, and fell into a coma or something like that while grabbing on his blanket for dear life like a big baby. The next obstacle came after the nurses had bandaged me, hooked the IV drip, and taken my vitals: another doctor, no less gorgeous, but looking dangerously like a priest, came to see me and explained in officious words that he would have to report my "situation" to the police stationed at the ER due to "its nature." This was trouble, I didn't want to be committed or anything, far from it. I was babbling some lie when fate dealt me a good card, the young doctor stepped in the room to ask the older doctor, obviously his senior, something about somebody, took a glance at me, kept on talking to him, took another look, bingo! He recognized me. There weren't any bells but the beeping of the heart machine gave all kinds of noises. He smiled and asked me what had happened, and the other doctor grabbed him by the arm and took him outside to explain my "situation." When he came back he was very serious and asked me to tell him what had happened to me. I told him I was sick and tired of life, AIDS, people's pity, everything, he held my hand and said, "However, you seem in better shape than the last time I saw you." I thought, You should say that, there is nothing that a bit of starvation can't accomplish. I used to be overweight due to liquid retention and overeating caused by enormous amounts of pot smoking. I gripped his hand, I felt like Maria Callas after her comeback as slim as a nymph, and I told him right there and then that I loved him (why wait?). He smiled, and I swear that before I lost consciousness he gave me a kiss in the lips.

It may sound limited to some, but for me, with a short life expectancy and a narrow range of possibilities, our relationship means a world of difference. The young doctor completed his stint at that hospital, completed his courses, and graduated. Without a word, without as much as a gesture, and no explanations, I followed him to the suburban building where he set up his first office (general practice) with another blond partner. He has married, has a child—another on the way, a four-wheel drive family van, and a cellular phone. He has turned thirty, plays squash twice a week, shops for groceries on Sundays, visits his in-laws once a month, and spends most of his time at work. I see him every week, same place, same time. If I am very sick I go to the hospital; I have a little bag always ready to go: toothbrush, toothpaste, comb, the few things one needs when one is in there. I know the routine. Someone calls the young doctor, and he shows up in the ward. If I am bedridden at home, he sometimes comes over. He politely exchanges a few words with the nurse, the homemaker, the volunteer buddy, or whomever is there. He closes the bedroom door on his way out after having examined me in private, strictly professional. I fall asleep, tired, with a bittersweet taste in my mouth, like a fairy in a cabbage of crumpled sheets.

About Rapture
Ferd Eggan

About Rapture

Whatever good Paul or Jefferson or Freud really meant
pales under a nearly full moon over Fire Island.
I crash through the undergrowth,
enraptured by the luminous circle above the shadowy dunes.
I slide loose pants down the white muscles of a '90s tribal queer
     boy.
The surf booms. Exhaustion comes.

Flesh is dependable extasis, rarely disappointing even in these
     shifting sands.
We are generous and squeeze a shoulder after.
Here is the deciduous Whitman geography. O, camerados!
What a privilege to be in this moist green and not the dry
     crackle of LA.
I touch and can imagine nothing better.
Here all the men are beautiful even when they wear their hats
     backwards.

Although maybe not: the sad chunky boy goes to the
    Belvedere,
we time-share at Debris Jr.

The shock when Robert takes my hand on the wooden walks
    of the Grove
under the drunken hunter's moon, transformed in the
    greenwood we're Robin and John.
Or we're Mary and Martha, intent on welcoming the beautiful
    Jesus
as he comes, one of us distracted by tasks. Robert's shrink
tells him he's depressed because he's bored with sex,
which he'd counted on to carry him through since childhood.
And I counted on being good. Two strategies that didn't pan
    out.

Recently I notice the thrilling access to sentimentality
or perhaps to real feeling—the difference
between the Belvedere and Debris Jr. is our lack of compassion.
It's scary to be real, even scarier to notice that real is only real.
Audible even in the deep thickets: the music of the spheres,
the clack of the wheels of the railroad, the nut-numbing shock
    of the surf.
My shrink says it's like glasnost: what do we do if we don't
    just do what we've done?
Facile oppositions don't cut it. Robert's hand,
the moonlit down on the butt of that boy in the sand.

Reply to About Rapture

1/27/95
Hi Ferd:
    I thought yesterday was the twenty-seventh, and now I am
completely confused. See, I couldn't afford the brand name

refill for my filo-fax, so I purchased a cheap imitation....I don't deserve this perverse New Covenant. It's beyond my modest means of memory. (I also don't like being forced into group activity—at least not with people whose names I might be responsible for remembering.)

Thanks for your note and for sending me *About Rapture*. I always get a chance to expand my vocabulary when reading something of yours. You make me pull out my dictionary—it's a cross between *Drummer* and a really thick 1925 Webster's that works my biceps into a frenzy of torn and rebuilt muscle tissue.

About *About Rapture* (sorry, but when you publish this little ditty, it's a given to any literary critic): I think our emotions, as individually informed as they may be for the most part, melded together on a bed sheet at the beach. When you were writing, Mary Ellen was reading, and I was trying to change the color of my skin (or at least prove my Portuguese heritage through the melanin of my ancestors who were darker). I wallowed in great pleasure from being with you and M.E. You, on the other hand, the hand that received mine, are a fantasy of mine that stems from the simple thrill of being desired and knowing (I know you know me and usually this would be immensely disconcerting to me, yet from you it always means comfort and security, in a very sexy way that smells of sweat and tastes like sugar.)

I have a problem remembering events in any factual sense (a fancy discourse for denial, you might say). I believed I kissed you that night at the tackiest of Long Island's attractions. It was not a gesture, nor a posturing obligation to be good to you or kind. I reserve my kindness for those who clearly want such strange behavior. Like you, I, too, am weary of human connection that, prior to the event, feels emotionally dangerous, leaving my true head vulnerable.

Nevertheless (a word I once promised myself never to use), and although not written, I have descended upon the very thoughts you have formed. I'm safe knowing we share this.
Love,
Robert

it was I who wanted a pleasure never to use I promised myself to use

About About Rapture

I think our emotions events in any factual sense what Freud a given to any literary pales under a nearly full a problem remembering sense I crash through squeeze backwards melded together on bed sheet at the beach as individually informed for the most part the luminous circle slide down the white muscles surf booms and the exhaustion sex so dependable and rarely squeeze a shoulder for a few not a gesture not a posturing as for compassion reserve for those who clearly want I'm pretty critical of my no obligation to be good to you it's better distracted by tasks Magnificent Adhesives tackiest of attractions the island camerados ideally the best friend many dream of M.E. its own history and path me grounded in reality drowned despair moist green not the dry I touch and can imagine smells sweat tastes sugar fancy discourse denial you might say never to use the delight my hand the drunken hunter's moon those clearly want preoccupation Robert hunting never beautiful serious, simple, stark sex to carry being good to carry me a world I once promised at least each other I believe I kissed recently the thrilling access wallowed in great pleasure from being the difference even scarier to notice leaving my true head for others' weaknesses of the

the spray for love from you it always comfort and security a
very sexy way I you on the other hand the hand that received
mine compassion lack you I too I have descended my insis-
tence I am enraptured weary wary of human connection
emotionally dangerous steps to want for myself I know
you know me immensely nevertheless not written real
safe knowing greenwood notice thrilling we share this
about

About the Authors

Freelance writer **Dimitri Apessos** keeps his stuff in New York, but lives on Amtrak, in an attempt to confuse evil spirits. It is not working. He is writing three novels, all of them queer replicas of the work of James Joyce (he has yet to read *Finnegan's Wake*). Dimitri lives vicariously through his e-mail address: TilApplesGrow@yahoo.com

Lawrence Ytzhak Braithwaite's work deals with people in desperate situations, struggling with shit, trying to survive, and taking charge of their own lives. His new novel *Ratz Are Nice* (Alyson Publications) is centered around Rudeboys and Skinheads in North America. His fiction has appeared in *Maka: Diasporic Juke* (SisterVision Press), *Holy Titclamps* and *RED ZONE: Victoria's Street People's Zine*. He has also appeared at Lollapalooza, the Mocambo Cafe, New Langton Arts Gallery, and Outwrite 1999. His first novel was *Wigger*.

M. Christian's work can be seen in *Best American Erotica, Friction, The Mammoth Book of Erotica, Men for All Seasons, Bar Stories, Uniform Sex, Quickies* 2 and more than one hundred other books and magazines. He is the editor of the anthologies *Eros Ex Machina, Midsummer Night's Dreams, Guilty Pleasures* and (with Simon Sheppard) *Rough Stuff: Tales of Gay Men, Sex and Power* (Alyson Publications). A collection of his short stories will be published by Alyson in 2000. He writes columns for www.scarletletters.com and www.bonetree.com. He thinks WAY too much about sex.

C. Bard Cole is a cartoonist and writer living in New York City. A longtime contributor to the zines *Holy Titclamps, Dirty,* and *Boy Trouble,* he has published six illustrated chapbooks and hosts the East Village queer reading series Readings A Go Go. His first collection of short stories, *Briefly Told Lives,* is forthcoming from St. Martin's Press in spring 2000. His fiction has also been seen in *Christopher Street, Men on Men 7, Flesh and the Word 4,* and the literary webzine Blithe House Quarterly.

Ferd Eggan is a gwm/pwa who works as the AIDS Coordinator of the City of Los Angeles. He has a long history of anti-racist and gay activism from the sixties to the present. He also directed the first feature-length porno movie in San Francisco in 1970 and has published many poems, articles and two books, *Your LIFE story by someone else* (Editorial El Coqui, 1988) and *Pornography* (Bench Press, 1990). He is single and available at ferdeggan@aol.com

Henry Flesh dropped out of Yale in the sixties and moved to Manhattan. Since then he has spent a great deal of time abroad, including sojourns in London, Morocco, and Crete. He currently lives in New York City's East Village, the setting of his first novel, *MASSAGE,* published by Akashic Books in 1999. His second novel, *MICHAEL,* about the end of the world, will be published by Akashic in the fall of 2000.

Luis Miguel Fuentes's stories, drawn from his life starting at age 13, appeared in the *NAMBLA Bulletin* between 1990 and 1998, and were published in 1999 in *Diary of a Lost Boy* (Wallace Hamilton Press). He was living in New York as of the end of 1999, but hoping to return to the Dominican Republic. For more of his work and his history, go to http://www.xs4all.nl/~johnie

Ishmael Houston-Jones is a writer, choreographer and performer living and making work in New York City. In addition to his own solo work, he has choreographed three evening length performance pieces in collaboration with the writer Dennis Cooper and one with visual artist Nayland Blake. Houston-Jones' own fiction, essays and performance texts have been anthologized in the books *Best American Gay Fiction 2; Footnotes: six choreographers inscribe the page; Conversations on Art and Performance; Caught in the Act; Out of Character;* and in the zines *FARM; Mirage; Contact Quarterly; Movement Research Journal* and *Porn Free.* He occasionally hires people and writes about them. His extremely lame web page can be found at http://hometown.aol.com/isaacsbro/myhomepage/index.html

Francisco Ibañez-Carrasco is a Chilean-Canadian freelance writer in Vancouver, British Columbia since 1986, He has written nonfiction for alternative magazines in Canada—*MIX, Border/Lines, FRONT, Alter Vox.* His short story "Hockey Night in Canada" was published in *Arts & Understanding* in 1997 and "Hurt Me, Amor Mio" in Arsenal Pulp Press's *Contra/Dictions* in 1998. Francisco leads a double life and has recently finished a Ph.D. on queer research methods, at Simon Fraser University.

Frontiers is **Michael Jensen's** first novel, and he's pleased to hear he can write a hot sex scene. Michael currently lives in Los Angeles with his partner, Brent Hartinger, and is at work on his next novel.

Aaron Lawrence has worked as an escort since May, 1995. When not entertaining clients, he is pursuing a career as a porn star as well as producing his own line of amateur tapes. A longtime exhibitionist, he has appeared in the September,

1998 issue of *Freshmen* and in *XXX Freshmen*. He can be reached at www.aaronlawrence.com. He lives with his lover in suburban New Jersey.

Shaun Levin is a South African living in London. He teaches creative writing and runs No Holes Barred, a gay men's erotica writing workshop. His work has appeared in *The Evergreen Chronicles, Mach, Queer View Mirror 1, Queer View Mirror 2* and in other publications—academic and otherwise—in England, the United States, Canada and Israel. His e-mail address is shaunlevin@yahoo.com

Douglas A. Martin is the author of two collections of poetry, *my gradual demise & honeysuckle* and *Servicing the Salamander,* as well as co-author of *the haiku year.* His first novel, *Outline of My Lover,* will be published early in 2000. He has completed a collection of short stories and begun a new novel.

By day, **Ian Philips** is the mild-mannered managing editor for Damron Company's series of lgbt travel guides. By night, he's in bed with a good, strong book. He's gathering this story, along with other favorites in *Best Gay Erotica 1999* and *Bitch Goddess,* into a collection called *See Dick Deconstruct.* He can be reached at iphilips@aol.com.

Andy Quan frequently passes through Vancouver, most recently on his way from England to Australia, where he was living at the end of 1999.

Dominic Santi is a former technical writer turned rogue whose flights of lascivious fancy are available in *Frictions 2 & 3, Best Bisexual Erotica 2000, Sex Toy Tales, Casting Couch Confessions,* and assorted other smutty anthologies and magazines. Santi, editor (along with mjc) of the electronic books *Y2Kinky* and *Strange Bedfellows*, is the section leader for Alternative Eros in CompuServe's erotica forum http://go.compuserve.com/eroticelit

This is **Simon Sheppard's** fourth appearance in the *Best Gay Erotica* series. His work also appears in the 2000 and 1997 editions of *The Best American Erotica,* and in numerous other anthologies. He's the co-editor, with M. Christian, of *Rough Stuff: Tales of Gay Men, Sex and Power* from Alyson Publications, and the author of the forthcoming *Hotter Than Hell and Other Stories* (Alyson, 2001). His syndicated column "Sex Talk" appears nationwide in the gay press. He lives in San Francisco, and hasn't been to Rome in years.

Don Shewey has published three books about theater and written articles for the *New York Times, the Village Voice, Esquire, Rolling Stone,* and other publications. His essays have been reprinted in such anthologies as *Contemporary Shakespeare Criticism* and *The Mammoth Book of Gay Erotica.* His 1991 "X-rated" interview with Madonna for the *Advocate* was syndicated around the world. He grew up in a trailer park on a dirt road in Waco, Texas, and currently lives in midtown Manhattan.

Matt Bernstein Sycamore is the editor of *Tricks and Treats: Sex Workers Write About Their Clients* (Haworth, February 2000). His writing has appeared in *Best American Gay Fiction 3, Obsessed, Flesh and the Word 4* and other publications. He is currently at work on three projects: *Dangerous Families: Queer Writing on Surviving Abuse; Resisting the Gay Mainstream,* an anthology of radical queer activist essays; and *Sketchtasy,* a collection of short stories. He lives in New York City, but might flee any time. He can be reached at tricksandtreats@hotmail.com

Karl von Uhl lives in rural central Iowa where no one can hear you scream. For more than three years he wrote the column "Vox Clamavis" for *Bear Magazine*. His fiction has appeared in *Bear* and *Powerplay* under the pseudonym Cord Odebolt, and he has a story in the forthcoming book *Rough Stuff*.

M.J.F. Williams is from Pennsylvania and Maryland, and attended college in Vermont. "Finding" is an excerpt from Matthew's first novel, recently completed and with the same title. He can be reached at mjfwilliams@yahoo.com. He would like to thank Kevin Koch for his invaluable assistance with the ollies.

Tom Woolley is the author of *Toilet* (MP&M, 1998). He lives in New York where he is currently working on his sophomore novel, *Portland*. He would like to thank Dan Seitler.

About the Editors

Richard Labonte is general manager of A Different Light Bookstores in West Hollywood, in New York, and in San Francisco, where he lives with his partner Asa and their pup Percy; Kirk Read, Richard's friend and Asa's little sister, completes the family. Richard helped found A Different Light twenty years ago, after a ten-year career as a reporter, editor and columnist for a daily newspaper in Ottawa, Ontario. He will someday retire to a two hundred acre farm he has owned communally since 1976 with several friends who met in college; there he will read all the books he's sold to bookstore customers but never had time to read himself. He is a very occasional reviewer for *Lambda Book Report,* and has been a columnist for several years with the *Feminist Bookstore News,* writing about gay men's books.

D. Travers Scott is author of the novel *Execution, Texas: 1987* and editor of *Strategic Sex: Why They Won't Keep it in the Bedroom,* a collection of writings on public sex. His writings on sex and culture have appeared in dozens of anthologies and periodicals, including *Gay Men at the Millennium, Best American Gay Fiction 2, Obsessed, Best Gay Erotica 1996 & 1997, Switch Hitters, PoMoSexuals, International Drummer, Steam, Women & Performance* and *The Mammoth Book of Gay Erotica.* His performance work has been featured in NPR's "This American Life" and *Harper's,* and presented solo and collaboratively in Brazil and locations throughout the United States. For more than two years he served as managing editor of *P-form,* an international performance art quarterly. He lives in Seattle: http://home.earthlink.net/~traversscott